FREENET

STEVE STANTON

ECW PRESS

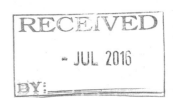

Published by ECW Press
665 Gerrard Street East
Toronto, Ontario M4M 1Y2
416-694-3348 / info@ecwpress.com

LIBRARY AND ARCHIVES CANADA
CATALOGUING IN PUBLICATION

Stanton, Steve, 1956–, author
Freenet / Steve Stanton.

Issued in print and electronic formats.
ISBN 978-1-77041-229-3 (pbk)
ISBN 978-1-77090-836-9 (pdf)
ISBN 978-1-77090-837-6 (epub)

I. Title.
PS8587.T3237F74 2016   C813'.54
C2015-907276-X   C2015-907277-8

Cover design: Rachel Ironstone
Interior Illustrations: Jean-Pierre Normand
Cover image: "Bennu's Journey — Early Earth" ©
NASA's Goddard Space Flight Center Conceptual
Image Lab. Use of this image does not constitute
endorsement by NASA of this work.
Editor: Chris Szego
Text design: Lynn Gammie

The publication of *Freenet* has been generously supported by the Canada Council for the Arts which
last year invested $153 million to bring the arts to Canadians throughout the country, and by the
Government of Canada through the Canada Book Fund. *Nous remercions le Conseil des arts du Canada
de son soutien. L'an dernier, le Conseil a investi 153 millions de dollars pour mettre de l'art dans la vie des
Canadiennes et des Canadiens de tout le pays. Ce livre est financé en partie par le gouvernement du Canada.*
We also acknowledge the Ontario Arts Council (OAC), an agency of the Government of Ontario,
which last year funded 1,709 individual artists and 1,078 organizations in 204 communities across
Ontario, for a total of $52.1 million, and the contribution of the Government of Ontario through the
Ontario Book Publishing Tax Credit and the Ontario Media Development Corporation.

PRINTED AND BOUND IN CANADA   PRINTING: FRIESENS   5   4   3   2   1

DEDICATED TO THE MEMORY OF MY FATHER,
AIR CANADA CAPTAIN DAVID E. STANTON 1931–2015,
FOR A LIFETIME OF INSPIRATION!

"THE STRENGTH OF OUR LIBERTY DEPENDS UPON THE CHAOS
AND CACOPHONY OF THE UNFETTERED SPEECH."

Federal Judge Stewart Dalzell (Philadelphia, 1996)

White wisps of vapour began to dance like ghosts on the nosecone of the shuttle as Simara carved her trajectory into the alien atmosphere. A mottled brown globe lay below, the desert planet of Bali, a horrible place by all accounts. But a worse fate lay behind.

Congratulations! You have been selected for a free boost to Cromeus Signa on the party cruise of a lifetime—toward understanding the organic multiplicity of human consciousness—the Governor has not published comment on water rationing measures effective yesterday—orbital microwave generators at maximum output—I just wish—

"Simara, you little tramp, get back here with that shuttle!" Her stepfather's voice broke through the V-net chatter on the emergency override, an angry, drunken voice raspy with phlegm. She could still see his leering face in her mind's eye, smell the stench of fermentation on his breath, barley mash and bad mushrooms. He had surprised her out of a deep sleep in her bunk with probing fingers between her thighs, a stinky fencepost pushing from his pants, cooing nonsense about his dead wife, the pervert. She had punched him on the chin and fled in her pyjamas to the shuttle.

"I've alerted Trade Station to take you into custody. If you put a damn scratch on the paint, I'll take it out of your share!"—*Minister of Finance calling for absolution of cybersoul proxies—the elegance of*

any scientific theory is no guarantee of practical utility—cold gamma
readings reaching record levels in the suburbs of New Jerusalem—

Simara wasn't heading for Trade Station or anywhere near the clutches of Transolar authority. She had been foolish to put off her escape this long, with her stepfather ogling her ass and rubbing against her at every opportunity. She should have jumped ship at the Babylon station and claimed her rights as a citizen when she had the chance two weeks ago. Now she would have to settle for the desert badlands of Bali. Never mind, the decision had been made.

::YOU ARE ENTERING A DEAD ZONE,:: mothership intoned in her mind. ::ELEVATE FIFTEEN DEGREES FOR A SAFE ORBIT.::

Too late for that. "Show me the landing targets," Simara said.

::NO DATA AVAILABLE.::

"Give me the manual coordinates."

::NO DATA AVAILABLE. DEAD ZONE IMMINENT.::

Turbine brakes whined with resistance as the air became solid in the mesosphere, and Simara could feel the grasp of gravity sucking her slender craft into the rabbit hole. She tipped the wings up to take some speed off her approach. Why was mothership giving her such a hard time? "Show me the mapview."—
he eats meat, the vile cretin—discrimination against omnidroids is
rampant today in all segments of society—frequent feelie users may
experience an irrevocable desynthesis of paradigms—

A holographic image of the planet appeared in Simara's virtual space, a spatter of green dots indicating human outposts. There were two Transolar mining colonies with airstrips for the ore transports, but she zapped them offscreen. Too dangerous for a runaway. Her stepfather would surely sound warning the moment he calculated her trajectory, any second now.

"You little bitch! You can't go down into that gravity pit. You'll be trapped in the dead zone forever. Get your sorry ass back here!"

—*makes you wonder about the whole purpose of empirical science—download took almost five seconds, and me standing there like a vacant—mathematical blueprint of the cosmos was evident before the beginning—*

Simara toggled to the emergency frequency to have the last word to her stepfather. "Go to high heaven, Randy," she said evenly, tasting bile in the back of her throat as she cut the mike. Her old life had ended; her innocence had been stolen away.

A brilliant flash snapped with a sizzle, and the lights and cameras went out on her instrument panel. Holy shit! She blinked her eyes against afterglow in the sudden darkness. "Mothership, what happened?"

Her virtual space was black, her brain cold and quiet. What the hell? She tapped the signal amp on her earlobe implant, trying to log back into the V-net, feeling nothing but vacuum in her brain, a gut-wrenching emptiness in her soul. Mothership was gone. How was that possible? She tried her omnidroid chats and couldn't get a pingback. Everything was offline.

Simara grabbed the manual flight-stick with both hands as panic clawed inside her abdomen. She pulled back on the braking flaps, trying to visualize her pilot capsule in the velvety black, calling up system specs from deep recesses of memory. There was supposed to be a panel in the floor to slide open for an outside view in case of emergency. She scrabbled under the keyboard to release the interlock and kicked at the carpet below her feet. A burst of brightness shot up around her as the portal slid open to a raging, crimson crescent rising over Bali. A blast of heat rose from the tiny window of diamond glass. She had done this only once in the simulator and had crashed the damn thing. Where was her backup telemetry? Where the hell was the V-net? "Mothership?"

The air began to heat up in her cloistered cabin, her nose-cone now burning red like a meteor heading to fiery Armageddon, shrieking like a haunted soul. Gravity had claimed her into a tight hellhole, and she was coming in way too fast for a controlled landing. Simara tightened the straps on her shoulder harness as her shuttlecraft bucked with turbulence, her fumbling fingers slippery with sweat. A pall of acrid smoke gathered like a heavy tapestry around her, the smell of burning wires and melting plastic. She was going to roast in her pyjamas and die on a crappy desert planet. Shit!

A flash of lightning exploded around her.

PART ONE: SIMARA

Simara woke flat on her back on a hard surface, panting for breath under a smothering weight of gravity. She reached for her hammock straps and flayed empty air. What the hell? Nausea and unfamiliarity gripped her as she peered at a craggy stone ceiling in musty, murky darkness. A cloying humidity filled her nostrils and throat, the smell of something mouldy and putrid. She gasped and sat up with alarm as an afterimage of trauma filled her mind—her escape shuttle screaming through stormy clouds, a lightning flash, an explosion, the dark face of doom. Her remembrance seemed splintered and sparse, broken fragments lacking in detail, and her memory backup was mysteriously offline. She tapped her earlobe amp to login to the V-net and got a dead blank. Mothership was gone and all her omnidroid chats were quiet. Even the newsfeed was down. Shit.

A handsome young man stared at her from under auburn ringlets, sitting cross-legged on the rocky floor beside her, barefoot, wearing strips of animal skin over muscular shoulders and a leather loincloth at his narrow waist. He smiled at her with peaceful good nature. "Hi," he said. "How are you feeling?"

Simara could not place his strange accent—not trader-space, for sure, probably a virgin grounder, a primitive cave dweller by the look of it. His words seemed slurred, his tone serene. His eyes were brown and beautiful. "Where am I?"

"Bali," he said, "second from the sun. I brought you in from the desert." He shook his head. "It's not safe out there."

A string of pin lights revealed a gloomy cavern enclosure. She was imprisoned in rock, trapped underground at the ugly bottom of the gravity well with no V-net signal. Simara patted her hips under the thin padding of a zippered sleeping bag. "Where are my clothes?"

The boy pointed behind with his thumb. "Soaking. You soiled yourself." He shrugged with complacence.

The air rumbled with thunder in the distance to match her rising temper at his indecency. "You wiped my bare ass?"

The boy pouted in consternation at her outburst. "Um, I guess so. I thought you might be dead."

Simara grimaced as more memories flooded her consciousness, the sexual assault from her stepfather, her fight and flight for freedom, the loss of mothership. She was alone now on an alien planet with no technology, a vagrant fugitive cut off from her friends and social network. A sickness welled inside her, a coiled spring that demanded immediate and commensurate release, and she hung her head as tears spilled onto her cheeks.

"I barely peeked," the boy said. "I didn't mean anything." He rose to his feet and took a few cautionary steps back. "I was just trying to help."

"No." She waved a hand to brush away his complaint. "My stepfather tried to rape me." She wiped her nose with a sniff. "Not the first time. His wife died a few months ago in a vacuum breach. The whole damn ship is a rattletrap." She sobbed again and resigned herself to a good cleansing cry.

The boy dropped his gaze. "I'm sorry. I saw your shuttle coming in fast and trailing smoke. Your cockpit blew out the top just before the crash. I followed your failsafe chute and found you unconscious two days ago. My name is Zen."

Simara blinked back sorrow and looked up at him in surprise. "Two days?"

"Yes. Are you sure you're okay? No broken bones or anything?"

She patted herself more carefully now, fearful of injury, checking for pain or inflammation, every movement a push against the heavy gravity. She was wearing socks and a bra and the signal amp on her earlobe, all she had left in the world. She tapped her ear, but the grid was still dead. Even her subconscious psychic connection was gone.

Thunder rumbled again, and the rock seemed to tremble. A cough rasped in her throat. "Do you have any water?"

Zen ducked through a rocky archway and returned with a ceramic cup. Her eyes slowly adjusted to the dim light. The cave walls were dry and the floor sandy, the low ceiling decorated with spiny creatures like sea urchins hanging upside down. Simara pointed. "What are those things?"

Zen glanced up. "Argonite clusters. Stone flowers, we call them. Iron impurities in this hill give them that pinkish hue."

Simara studied the strange rock garden on the cave ceiling. Perhaps some weird magnetism in the iron was scrambling the V-net bandwidth, blocking her signal. Zen wore no earbug, probably living without a brain implant in these primitive conditions, a digital virgin. How the hell did he communicate? "Don't you have the net?"

"A net? No, I use a spear for fishing. The carp in the deep caverns are blind, so they're not hard to catch."

"Not a fishnet. A communications network. You have no wristband, no eyescreen, no tablet?"

Zen nodded his understanding. "My father had a wristband, but it only worked in orbit on the dark side. All radio signals on Bali are scrambled by solar flares. We have computers in shielded installations underground where thermal energy is converted to electricity, but nothing on the surface. Even at night we can't get a stable connection through the geomagnetic storms."

Simara grimaced. She was net-dark and -deaf on a desert planet, and mothership was gone. She took a sip of water and spit it out with disgust. "It's salty!"

"You don't like salt?"

She handed the cup back and rubbed her tongue against her teeth. "Do you have anything else?"

"I have guava mead, but it's fermented."

She shrugged. "Please, anything to get this vile taste out of my mouth."

Zen bowed and ducked again into darkness. He returned balancing the brimming cup, and she sampled his new offering, an exotic mix of warm beer and fruit juice. "Don't you have refrigeration?"

Zen shook his head. "We're out in the badlands. This base is a minimum campout, just bare-bones. The lights are solar powered, but the voltage is low. Sorry."

"That's okay. This is good." She saluted him with the cup and took a long drink.

"So," Zen said as he resumed his seat beside her, "no broken bones?"

"I'm fine. Thanks for saving me. My name is Simara." She held out a hand in greeting, and he stared at her fingers in confusion. Didn't people shake hands on Bali? Was the boy some sort of fanatical recluse? He hesitated for an awkward moment and finally took her palm with a gentle caress. That was weird.

"We're an hour from the main community cave," he said. "There's a doctor there and cold drinks. We should get someone to check you over."

"I don't need a doctor. Just some food and a walk outside. I can't stay long in this coffin cave. I like to be high up in the air where I can see everything at a glance, preferably weightless in space. Gravity sucks, you know?" She offered a smile at the old trader joke, but it went unrequited.

Zen shook his head again. "You can't go outside during the day on Bali. The solar flares are too hot, and the rads will scramble your brain. Even at night you can't go out without a breather. Cactus spores will clog your lungs."

Simara frowned. What an awful situation. "Why do you live in such a horrid place?"

A hint of indignation clouded his features. "This is my quadrant," he said sternly. "I have native salvage and mineral rights on my heritage claim. I'm third-generation landed, which is rare, 'cause it's not a great place for humans to breed."

Oops. Simara spread her palms for peace. "I'm sorry, Zen.

I hate to be such an idiot, but my system is down and I don't know the first thing about Bali. We were just passing by to offload some merchandise at Trade Station."

Zen pressed his lips and nodded. "Hardly anyone comes to the surface. Bali is strictly a mining colony—volcanic minerals, gold, copper, zinc. The equatorial zone is a treasure-house of magma."

"Is that the rumble I keep hearing? Volcanoes?"

"No, that's dry lightning from the geomagnetic storms. We get it all the time here in the desert, and sometimes a bare sprinkle of rain, hardly enough to keep the lizards wet."

"I think I got hit by lightning on my way in. I saw a blue flash and my board went black. Autopilot must have failed. I thought I was going to die."

Zen's face was grim. "Those new escape pods have failsafe eject on the altimeter when the power is off, but it's a hard way to go. I think you pull about six-g in reverse to cancel your downward acceleration. You probably blacked out even before you hit the ground."

Simara stared with curiosity at this muscular caveboy. "You seem to know quite a bit about rocketry."

He raised broad shoulders at the compliment. "I've claimed a bit of salvage in my day. Not many shuttles get in past the lightning. Not many pilots survive."

A memory flashed back to the dead instruments on her shuttle dashboard, her helpless feeling of panic in the darkness. "I'm lucky you noticed me in the sky."

"You were like a paintbrush stroke across the heavens," Zen said as he moved his hand in a slow arc, "a shooting star from the desert god Kiva and sure sign of his destiny. He brought you here for a reason."

Simara boggled at the notion of patriarchal deity and tilted her head at him. How could he speak of providence to a woman who had just been sexually assaulted? Why would any god orchestrate an attempted rape? Weren't gods supposed to be loving and righteous? "I'm sure you don't mean that to condone domestic violence against women."

Zen winced with discomfort. "No, of course not. What your stepfather did was evil." He sighed a gentle whisper. "And I'm sorry about your stepmother. But Kiva brings good out of bad, and reconciliation between light and darkness."

Simara glanced away to calm her spirit. "That sounds wonderful, Zen," she said quietly, thinking him a harmless acolyte of some grounder folk religion. "Thank you."

"I know it sounds like superstition at first, but that's okay. Every onion has many layers."

Simara smiled. "You have onions in the deserts of Bali?"

He grinned at her and nodded. "They grow in terraced gardens on the windward side of the mountains."

"Anything else to go with them?" She held up her empty beer mug. "I'm famished."

Zen took her cup and rose to his feet, his brown legs rippling with strength as he towered over her in his leather loincloth. "Would you like to soak in a hot geyser while I make breakfast?"

She gaped. "Really?"

"Sure." He pointed to a crevice in the wall where a string of pin lights twined past a jumble of craggy boulders. "There's a grotto down the tunnel to the left. That's one of the reasons I picked this cave. Natural hot springs."

Simara wondered if her bad luck could finally be changing. A handsome grounder boy with a hot tub? It sounded too good to be true. "Well, that sounds wonderful, but I didn't bring a swimsuit."

Zen slapped his forehead in a pantomime of stupidity, then held up a finger and disappeared through the archway. He returned in a moment and handed forward a pair of raggy turquoise boxers, faded and frayed. Simara hesitated for an instant, but nudity seemed an unwise option in the company of a primeval caveboy dressed in a thong, so she tucked his boxers into her sleeping bag and wrestled them awkwardly up her legs, like a butterfly working in a tight chrysalis. She extricated herself with a bare modicum of confidence and tested her bra for decency with her fingers.

Zen crawled into the rocky crevice, and she followed him down a narrow corridor encrusted with glinting salt crystals that felt sharp and granular on her forearms and knees. A pungent, briny scent wafted up from the depths as they burrowed their way downward following a single strand of pin lights. A moist heat collected on her skin like dew. Finally the tunnel opened up into a huge cavern hung with stalactites and murky with fog. Simara rose gratefully to her feet and stretched aching limbs. A foamy pool bubbled with promise in the grotto, and Zen crouched to feel the water with his hand. "It's almost scalding today, so be careful."

"Thank you, I will." She took off her socks and dipped in a foot. "Whew, that's hot."

"You'll get used to it once you're in. I'll bring breakfast in a few minutes." Zen ducked back up the tunnel as she nestled slowly into the hot spring, inch by burning inch until she hit her belly. She reached with her toes for purchase, feeling a promise of buoyancy in the saltwater, and found a ledge on which she could crouch in up to her chin. Soon she was floating freely in weight-lessness—home again in her natural state, liberated from gravity in blissful relaxation. She revelled in abandonment to the heat as her face flushed with blood and pebbled with a cleansing perspir-ation. This was great. She had survived a crash in the badlands of Bali and ended up in a luxurious spa retreat!

Did she dare trust this native caveboy? He seemed nice enough at first glance, but could she ever feel safe with a man again? Her own stepfather had betrayed her. The drunken oaf had treated her with vile disrespect, called her a slut, a tight pussy. She was still shaken, still wary.

Zen returned with a wooden bowl and dangled his powerful legs in the water from a rock shelf. He plucked a morsel with his fingers to show by example and held the bowl out with invitation.

"What is it?" Simara asked as she pulled herself up beside him.

He shook his head. "It's a secret."

Simara pursed her lips in thought. Probably cactus and sand lizards, maybe bird or snake. Oh well, it should certainly be better than starving to death. She tasted a salty, chewy bite of meat. Not bad, not raw, so Zen must have cooking facilities of some sort. She tried another bite, a mushy, stir-fried vegetable, and together they settled into a steady rhythm of eating. Everything was too salty, but she didn't dare complain. "Great," she said as Zen watched her with open fascination. "Thank you."

She wondered if he was ogling her breasts through wet trans-parency—probably so, after untold weeks living alone in a cave in the wilderness with no V-net. Beer for breakfast and now wet lingerie for brunch! At least her pool-boy was handsome and pretended civility—she was thankful for that and damned grateful for everything else. Maybe it really was destiny, a change in her fortune from the grounder god of Bali, the Kiva spirit. By any measurement, it was totally better than a fiery crash in the barrens of the desert. She turned to Zen for eye contact. "So what are we doing today?"

He smiled with good-natured charm. "It's almost dusk. We can go outside safely now with breathers. I have a full charge on my buggy, enough to get us back before morning. We'll salvage your crash site."

"Will there be anything intact?"

"I made a quick inspection and camouflaged the wreckage after I got you safely home. The control capsule is mangled beyond repair, but there may be some working components. The angle of entry was oblique, and the sand dunes pillowed the impact. You can always find treasure at the end of a long furrow."

"Really? So that's how you make your living?"

"Oh, I do okay." His face was weathered and rugged, an outdoorsman with purpose in his eyes. "The scrap metal in the circuitry will be valuable, platinum and refined silver, maybe gold or rhodium. We're going to be rich, Simara. You're a skyfall princess from the stars!" He reached for a morsel of meat and placed it on his tongue as he relished the moment.

Simara tilted her shoulders back at Zen's strange notion. A princess? No way. Her skin might be pure from her years in space, but her soul had been bruised and blackened by sin. She carried a scar of betrayal deep inside, a wound raw with anger.

Simara shook her head and glanced away, pretending to study

the cave walls as she considered her situation. She had narrowly escaped death and been dragged underground by a scantily clad aboriginal in the desert. Now they were a team, about to be partners in business, and she had nowhere else to go. She slipped back into the hot spring and drifted with languor for a few more minutes. She could do worse.

"Time to get moving," Zen said. "Our window of opportunity beckons. You sure you're okay?"

"Much better. A little exercise might get the stiffness out of my bones. I'm not used to this heavy gravity."

Zen studied her for a moment, nodding. "Okay, let's go."

The breather turned out to be a full facemask with bug-eye goggles, a monstrosity that made her feel claustrophobic at the very sight. "You've got to be kidding," she said when Zen showed her.

"It's as light as foam," he said. "Here, try it on. Just breathe normally." He pulled the cowl over her head and tugged strands of her short black hair from beneath the flexible seal. The breather covered her eyes, ears, and nose, tight under her chin with a filter mesh over her mouth. She felt like she was tank-diving on a tether in space again, gambling with death on a maintenance detail outside the hull. Her pulse quickened with panic. She pressed a palm to her chest.

"That's good," Zen said. "Take your time. Settle yourself." He pulled on his own breather and looked like a stormtrooper in a bikini thong. Simara giggled.

He tipped his head to one side. "What's so funny?" His voice sounded machinelike, a strange, filtered sound vaguely derivative of humanity.

"Nothing." She stretched her neck from side to side, trying in vain for balance.

"Safety first," he said as he reached for a bucket of oily guck at his feet. "We need to lather up to go outside."

She shrank back. "What is that crap? It looks disgusting."

"It's sunscreen and pest control. All natural ingredients, safe for the environment. Turn around and I'll do your back. Hold your arms up."

She turned and felt his hands spreading hot oil on her body, kneading her flesh with gentle strength. He was very thorough. "Careful there, Johnny."

"You have to get every inch," he said.

"Even under my clothes?"

"Especially under your clothes. That's where the scorpions like best."

"Scorpions?"

"Here," he said as he offered the bucket. "Do the rest your-self." He took a handful and smeared it on his muscular chest. "Get my back for me, will you?" He rotated to offer his bronzed body to her ministrations. His beefy neck felt like a stone pillar, his burly shoulders like sculpted metal.

She finished him and turned attention to herself, thinking about crawly things on her thighs, between her toes, freaking right out as she spread stinky guck on her skin. She felt hot and sweaty in her bra and boxers with grounder gravity dragging her implac-ably down, her worst landfall ever. The breather smelled foul, and her dry lips tasted salty.

Zen handed her a small package on a leather string. "There's a pouch of water in here with nutrients and electrolytes, in case we get separated in an emergency. And a stick of dried protein."

"More snake meat?"

"Not exactly, but snake is good if you can get it."

"I was kidding," she said. Kill a snake and eat it? No, that was too weird. "Are you sure this is safe?"

"No, Simara, it's not safe. That's the whole point." A sigh of exasperation sounded through his breather mesh, and she resolved to curb her tongue from then on.

Zen's dune buggy was a stripped-down desert truck with a battery behind the passenger cage and extendable rear wheels. He unplugged a sturdy cable from an overhanging solar collector and keyed a silent motor to life. "Buckle up," he said as she climbed into the co-pilot seat beside him, and they set off toward the setting sun with barely a whisper.

Wind and sand flayed her exposed skin as they accelerated, and the air baked her sweaty body like an oven. Within minutes she was drenched with an unholy mix of sticky grime and oily guck, an abomination. No wonder the pests would not come near; she could barely stand it herself. Zen looked like a mythical sandman with the head of a gargoyle, a creature made of dust.

A menacing sun was veiled with red fog, and lightning flashed like craquelure from low clouds as thunder rumbled in waves over the dunes. The air was thick and oppressive, a tangible presence. The smell of sweat encircled her like a stifling aura, and the seal of her filter mask stuck against her face like a wet suction cup. Her bra chafed against her skin with every movement, and the elastic strap of her boxers felt like emery paper. She closed her eyes and stifled a groan, then opened them again in surprise, as they were suddenly airborne over the top of a ridge, her stomach floating freely.

"Whoa," Zen said as they landed and bounced on balloon tires, but he didn't slow down. The sun was setting fast toward a mountainous horizon, the setting eerily wondrous, electric pink and purplish. She could see why a primitive man might summon the notion of deity on this planet, the continuous flashes of lightning like fireworks from the desert god Kiva. The closer she looked, the more she could see: the forks of lightning had fingers like tree roots, multi-brachiate into weblike filaments—a curious artistry of fractal mathematics. In the distance she noticed two vehicles beside a mound of dirt, lights off and quietly waiting in the twilight. Zen raced up and parked close by. He jumped out to greet the eldest of three figures, and they touched their forearms together in a cross.

"Katzi," Zen said in greeting.

"Good job, kid," the man said. "Well hidden. You got the black box out?"

Zen nodded. "Old Joe's hole."

"I knew it. Choppers are swarming the trench already."

"Really?" They both turned to stare at Simara, their faces obscured by masks, their postures wary. Zen waved her closer. "Simara, this is Katzi, an old friend and partner. This is Simara, the pilot."

The elder man approached with his left elbow up and forearm at an angle, a tangle of black hair curling out from his breather. He had a mat of grey fur on his barrel chest and a heavy paunch hanging over his thong.

Simara matched his gesture to cross his arm in this strange battle greeting.

"Do you claim salvage?" he asked.

"Uh ..." Simara glanced at her rescuer and decided to go with the flow. "This is Zen's quadrant."

Katzi turned to Zen and bowed to seal the verbal contract, then swept an arm at the other two figures. "This is my crew, Keg and Sufi. Let's get to work." Keg, preparing a cutting torch with a portable tank on wheels, was a gaunt young man with bony limbs, his rugged skin crisscrossed with white scars. Sufi was a muscle-bound woman with a braid of hair down her back and a thick strap of leather squeezing her breasts. She wore brown gloves over big hands and a leather skirt over ample buttocks. They seemed like automatons in their breather masks, gargoyle worker drones.

The mound of dirt Simara had seen in the distance turned out to be camouflage netting over the twisted ruin of her escape shuttle, and Sufi tossed her a pair of gloves and began to peel back the covering. Simara jumped to her aid as Keg lit his cutting torch and tuned the flame. Katzi and Zen began to work on the buggy trucks, extending the back tires and folding down flatbed panels to hold the salvage. Everyone moved with determination and furtive haste, and Katzi repeatedly checked the horizon all round where the lightning flashed and rumbled. An angry sun turned orange like an enemy ember as it slid toward mountain peaks.

The cowl of the shuttle was fractured and crumpled, the control panel a wreck. Simara was lucky to have ejected before the impact. She was thankful to be alive, dripping with sweat in her shabby, borrowed boxers. She wanted to spit out a terrible taste in her mouth, but didn't dare waste the bodily fluid. She swallowed and gagged, and blinked out tears to keep her eyes in focus.

Miniature scorpions skittered like ants from under every component as they dismembered the vessel piece by piece and threw the wreckage in the buggies. Keg worked his torch with fluid expertise, cutting deftly with precision at key structural points, slicing and dicing in a shower of sparks like a manic demon. Katzi and Zen did the heavy lifting, and Sufi pulled full weight beside them, making Simara feel weak as she struggled just to keep upright against cruel grounder gravity.

"Break," Katzi finally shouted, and they all collapsed together in the shade of a loaded buggy. He offered bottles of water with snakelike straws, and they tucked them under their breathers and sucked for sustenance. "Are you somebody special, Simara?" he asked after they had rested a moment.

She turned to study him. "What do you mean?"

He shrugged. "Choppers are tracking your black box already. Freelance hirelings, no markings. We don't usually get much attention out here in the desert. Even the insurance companies don't bother with scrap metal down the gravity well. Why are you so valuable?"

"I'm nobody," she said. "Just trader trash." Her stepfather would be glad to be rid of a daughter he had never loved, though the missing shuttle would set him back a fistful of creds and serve him right.

"You're wearing a skullrider," Katzi said.

"What?"

He tapped the side of his breather. "You hear voices from the air."

"It's just wi-fi," she said, "but the grid is out because of the magnetic storm."

Katzi nodded. "Bali is a dead zone. There's no chance of radar or surveillance. But you've got brain implants. That must be worth something."

Simara reached to rub scars at her hairline. Zen must have done a thorough investigation while she was out cold. Barely peeked, huh? She shrugged. "Everyone carries a trinket on the trader circuit these days—it's just good business, nothing special. Advertisers pay for the surgery to secure market share." She touched her earlobe amplifier. "I've had this one as long as I can remember." A rare octahedral array was buried in her brain, but even so, no one was going to hunt her down for a few bucks' worth of scrap metal in her head.

Katzi turned to examine the wreckage, tapping a finger on his knee. "Any payload in the shuttle? Drugs? Contraband? Weapons of insurrection?"

She shook her head. "I don't think so. Nothing that I know about." Could her stepfather have stashed something in the escape pod, that bastard? Something easily jettisoned in an emergency, biohazards or meta-mindscapes? Could he be involved in something illegal?

Katzi bobbed his breather. "Then what we have here is a mystery, Simara." He rose to his feet and turned to address the crew. "We won't leave anything behind this trip, kids, not a scrap of evidence. Don't even pee in the sand. Let's go."

They all jumped back to full activity, though Simara was dragging behind in the heat, her skin coarse with oily grit, bleeding at her waistband. A blazing orange crescent burned on the horizon behind a veil of red smog, and a webwork of lightning flashed brighter under low purple clouds in the distance. An evening breeze stirred the dust like small spouts of steam rising from the roasting sand. Surely hell could be no worse, but Simara was glad to be alive.

They checked behind every bulwark for packages of powder, combed the wreckage for secret compartments or hidden weapons. Simara wondered what devious activity her stepfather might be embroiled in, the pervert. No evidence was exposed to the waning light as the sun mercifully hid its face below craggy hills—no mysterious vials of biological menace, no laser cannons or restricted armaments. Darkness fell suddenly as Simara stumbled back and forth loading wreckage on Sufi's truck. She lost her orientation momentarily as she lurched forward through deep purple haze and bumped into the burly girl with an exclamation of pain. Simara fell back and landed flat on her spine.

"Watch yourself, wench," Sufi growled.

Gravity claimed Simara like a magnet as she lay prostrate in the searing sand. She pushed a glove to find purchase and rolled onto her side, barely able to move.

Sufi kicked sand at her. "Get up before you burn that parchment skin."

"I can't see," Simara said.

"Turn on your night vision." Sufi crouched down and switched on a battery pack at the bridge of her nose. "That better?"

A viewscreen came to life inside Simara's goggles, a caricature of the desert landscape in red and green. Areas of light became brilliant with eerie luminescence, and the sand glowed red with retained heat like an electrical element. She turned her head to view the strange virtual horizon where dark mountains disappeared into burning clouds. A demonic ghoul stood before her with the head of a gargoyle and a fiendish, phosphorescent body. A helicopter sounded in the distance with a beating whine of turbines.

"Kiva!" Sufi exclaimed, and kicked another sting of sand at Simara on the ground. "Help me cover the truck. Quickly!"

The urgency in her tone propelled Simara to her feet. She staggered to the dune buggy with her arms outstretched into a cartoon world. They unrolled a tarp behind the seats to cover the pile of mangled components in back, as the men scrambled to do the same at the other trucks, shouting instructions and cursing the gods. Sufi pulled Simara under cover as a brilliant spotlight beam approached like a mythical cyclops.

"Keep quiet," she said. "Don't move."

Panic rose in Simara's throat as the helicopter drew close. The noise seemed amplified by the hours of quiet, a horror of charging armies. Simara felt like a trapped animal cowering under a tarp with a devil at her side, the viewscreen in front of her a mad chimera of reds and greens, the oxygen in her mask sucked dry. Overcome with fear and the certainty of destruction, she scrabbled at the clasps behind her head to get a fresh breath of air, some respite from torment, but Sufi cuffed her hand.

"Don't touch your breather, fool," she hissed as the helicopter roared above them.

Simara gasped with anguish and sucked for life. The gargoyle woman smelled rank with sweat and pesticide, a bug-eyed demon. A click of data transmission sounded in the back of Simara's brain, a whisper of home from a nearby wi-fi node. She heard a sputter of disconnected voices emerge from static as her system began to boot up—*life of the party*—*across quadrant seventy-seven*—*blue coyote*. She clenched her brain against the incoming signal, hoping to prevent a ping bounce back to the transmitter. *No data in, no data out, please, mothership, don't let me betray my new friends.* The helicopter charged by and disappeared in the distance as she and Sufi lay panting in their oven, cooking under their cowls. They waited a few minutes for the return of sure doom, but the desert stayed silent until Keg snapped his torch alight with a flint.

"Let's tidy up and get out of here, kids," Katzi said, and Simara groaned against gravity as she crawled out and clambered to her feet.

Keg carved up the last few fragments of the shuttle and lashed his fuel cylinder in the passenger seat of his buggy, his sunken chest blackened with smoke and charred hair, as the crew piled on the last remnants of salvage and tied down the treasure. They packed up their gear and raked the sand, then climbed into their loaded trucks and sped off in different directions with barely a word of goodbye, a hard day fought and rich with bounty.

"Buckle up," Zen said as she vibrated with exhaustion in the seat beside him. They ran without lights in the darkness, and Simara wondered about nocturnal carnivores. Did they have dinosaurs on this forbidden planet? Giant snakes? She squinted her eyes into the night-vision viewscreen in search of hungry raptors or an angry cartoon T-rex. She brushed a scorpion off her knee as a helicopter sounded in the distance behind them.

"They're widening the search," Zen said, his voice serene with fatigue. "Who are you, Simara?"

"I'm nobody, Zen. Just an orphan trader girl with no family and no home."

"You can stay with me."

Simara studied him as he drove through this garish landscape. He looked like a masked villain in his breather, a grim and angry robot at the wheel with lightning sparking and cracking in the background in a web of green evil. She closed her eyes and tried to imagine the hot geyser where they had shared a tranquil breakfast, his statuesque body, pretty face, and refreshingly courteous manner. She struggled against exhaustion to find some hope in her hellish new world.

Two

Simara's stepfather came to her again in her bed, smelling of jar gin and hallucinogens, his pupils crazed pinpoints, his leering face contorted with lust. He fondled her nubile breasts and pulled at her panties, speaking to his dead wife, murmuring obscenities. He stuffed a rag of blanket in her mouth to stifle her screams and pressed her hips with his torso. Simara struggled for breath, choking on dirty cotton as consciousness began to slip away into a dark haze. No! Never! A surrender to coma would leave him free to violate her. She knew what her stepmother had endured—no spaceship had ever been built for privacy!

She forced her eyes open to her stepfather's lecherous face— such an ugly man, grizzled and unshaven, his touch like greasy sandpaper. He grinned at her as his hand pried between her thighs. *My little slut. You like that, don't you?*

No! Never! Simara curled a fist and reached back, summoning a last remnant of energy out of encroaching darkness. She braced her neck for purchase and let fly a murderous blow to his face, felt a sure connection with pulp, a perfect pain on her knuckles. A wave of euphoria engulfed her, an ecstasy of retribution, as he cried out and released her. She felt purified by catharsis as blood streamed from his eyes and broken nose, as his face melted away like wax and disappeared to hell and sure damnation. She drifted content in her bunk, finally at peace and alone ...

And woke to the pain of gravity in her bones, every joint and sinew in her body shrieking with complaint as she reached for her hammock straps and flailed at emptiness. She cried out in confusion. Where was she?

A single eye stared down at her from twilight. A string of pin lights on a grotesque ceiling cast meagre shadows in the cave. A brown face framed with auburn ringlets came into focus. "You okay?" Zen asked.

Simara groaned as recent memory constructed a shaky edifice of reality around her. Zen's left eye was swollen shut below an ugly purple bruise. "What happened to your face?"

"Oh." He reached up to touch his cheek gingerly below the wound. "I must have bumped something in the night. Or maybe a spider bite. I'll be fine."

"I had a bad dream." She must have punched him in the face. She was almost sure of it.

"That's okay. You're safe now."

Simara patted her hips to find a pair of turquoise boxers caked with blood and dirt. Her skin felt grimy with oil and pest repellent. She tested her brain for clues, but could not seem to remember things clearly without the digital support of the V-net. Her inner space was black and quiet. Where the hell was mothership? "Did you carry me up here?"

"Yeah, pretty much. You were dizzy with exhaustion."

"I'm so sorry."

"That's okay. We got the job done just in time. The choppers have been screaming overhead all day."

Simara turned away to spit grit. She wiped at her tongue with the back of her hand. "Sorry," she said again. "I must look like an evil witch. I feel ugly and broken."

Zen studied her with a single squinting eye. "Please don't say that. You're a beautiful girl and a good worker. Do you want to freshen up in the geyser while I cook breakfast?"

Simara blinked at him in surprise—a beautiful girl? Why was he being so nice to her? "Yes, thank you." A moan escaped her lips as she pushed herself to her knees in this unbearable gravity—Bali was a huge planet, a monster of mass! Every muscle in her body was cramped and sore from all the hard work in the desert. She felt like a rusty toy pulled from a garbage heap, stiff with corrosion. "How can you live with this oppressive gravity?"

Zen stood back to give her plenty of room. "I never really think about it."

Of course not! She was being an idiot again as usual, trader trash at landfall, scum of the station. Simara vowed to keep her damn mouth shut. She stood and bumped her neck on a bony stalactite. "Oww, shit."

Zen took a few more steps back for safety. He pointed to a crevice in the rock. "Down here to the grotto. Mind your head."

The hot spring felt glorious when she finally managed to crawl down the tunnel to reach it, and she groaned with near-orgasmic pleasure as she settled her rebellious body underwater. Finally, she was weightless again, home to her natural state. Gravity *so* sucked!

She floated blissful and wiped away grime and bad karma with salty bubbles. She let it all go, her failures, her suffering, her stain of betrayal. From here she would build herself up again from scratch, create a new persona that she could live with. She was not a cheap whore, no matter what her stepfather had said. She was a worthy being.

Zen had called her a princess.

She unhooked her bra and wafted it underwater to get grit out of the seams. She had welts under her breasts where the skin had rubbed raw, and another ugly red patch circling her waist. The saltwater was a balm to her damaged body, inside and out, and in time she felt cleansed and renewed, ready to face this difficult new world.

Her pool-boy arrived to serve her a floating bowl of scrambled eggs minced with green and red vegetable cubes, and she didn't have the heart to query him for the source. Dino eggs and chopped cactus? Lizard embryos? She didn't want to know. It tasted fabulous.

"We're going into town tonight," Zen said, "to the main community cave. It's the Vishan festival, a celebration of the last day of winter."

Simara gaped. "You mean Bali gets even hotter than this?"

"A little bit," Zen said—an understatement, judging by his frown.

Oops, she was supposed to be watching her tongue. "Sounds great."

"I'll buy you some clothes," he said.

"Lovely, thanks." So she wouldn't have to parade around in public in her underwear anymore. That was a step in the right direction. Simara finished her breakfast and clasped on her bra, careful not to expose herself above the water surface—not that

Zen hadn't got both eyes full already. She had little worth hiding when compared to Sufi's bulging body, but Simara still felt an innate sense of modesty. She was thin, like most space-wasted traders, but she could fill a cocktail dress when the rare occasion arose at landfall.

Funny how easily she had grown accustomed to seeing Zen nearly naked all the time, handsome and muscular, with his V-shaped back and little-boy butt. She never would have dreamed . . . well, okay, maybe just a few times, but she didn't find him provocative or sexually enticing. His bronzed physique was just part of the exotic alien landscape. Everything was so weird already.

She groaned at the sight of her breather and the bucket of guck by the exit corridor. "Not that crap again!"

"Safety first," Zen said as he smeared oil across his chest. "Scorpions never sleep."

"Oh, mothership," she complained. Her breather stank of sweat and halitosis.

"Turn around and I'll get your back."

She sighed and slumped her shoulders as he began to work guava gunk into her skin with deft consideration. He took time to rub the back of her neck and massage her stiff and swollen muscles. What a blessing. She relaxed with sensuality for a few moments, content with his diligent ministrations, and when he stopped she felt an ache of loneliness, a disconnection. She turned to test his eyes and saw a fleeting glimpse of embarrassment, a boy with his hands in the cookie jar. He smiled, but she felt certain that he had betrayed some basic innocence, an unsullied nature. She wondered if he might be a virgin. A man of his age?

They finished gearing up and made their way to the dune

buggy parked under camouflage. The heat was stifling, and the geomagnetic storm continued to crackle and boom with dry lightning and thunder. They unloaded piles of junk and selected the most valuable components to take to market. The solar batteries had a full charge.

They sped off toward the setting sun and were quickly coated with desert grit again, another evening in Gehenna. The wind scoured Simara's fragile skin like sandpaper, and wounds opened anew at her waist. The elastic band of her boxers felt like a wood rasp. She eased them down to her hips and longed to bundle them in her fist and toss them to the dunes forever. Everything was so unbearably hot, the air dry and searing. She closed her eyes and forced her thoughts back to the gentle saltwater of her geyser bath, floating in a blissful womb of weightlessness—mind over mayhem in a dreamy attempt to find respite.

In time they bumped to a halt, and Simara woke from delirium. "Are we there?"

"No, just a quick stop." Zen jumped out and made his way to the back of the buggy.

Simara scanned the horizon for signs of life. They were in an area of rolling foothills at the base of a mountain ridge. The sand was dotted with cactus spires and scraggly brush, hardly a comfortable rest area, the only shade provided by a small pyramid of loose stones. She climbed out to join Zen as he pulled a boulder from the buggy. "What are we doing?"

"There's a pilot buried under that marker." He pointed with his chin to the pile of rocks. "He made me promise not to forget him, to bury him deep so the lizards would not have their fill." Zen grunted as he hefted the boulder and strode toward the funeral pyre. He placed it carefully near the bottom and took a few steps back.

Simara walked up beside him as he stood in vigil. "You rescued someone else before me?"

"His name was Cary, the only Earthman I've ever met. He came across the universe through the Macpherson Doorway to ply the trade routes of Signa, only to end up crashing here on Bali in my quadrant. He had two broken legs and blood in his urine, but he might have made it to town with a breather. That's why I keep a spare now."

Simara's hand flung up to her chin to touch the base of her breather. "The cactus got him?"

Zen nodded. "It doesn't take long. The spores germinate almost immediately in any moist spot." He turned his gargoyle face toward her with an unspoken implication: So keep your mask on and quit complaining!

She felt like an ingrate. From here on, she would be thankful for every stinky sniff of filtered air.

"He seemed like a nice guy," Zen said. "Gave me salvage rights without a care. I thought I could save him."

"I'm sure you did your best for him."

"Every time I drive past, I add another stone to the tomb. It's the least I can do for a good man."

"It's a wonderful gesture," she said, wishing she could offer some solace in the face of death. She might be desert dust herself if Cary from old Earth had not paved the way for her, provided a spare breather and a chance for life.

A whisker of movement caught Zen's attention, and he stabbed out a protective arm in front of her. "Get in the buggy."

She followed his gaze and saw a giant lizard creeping closer, an armoured creature with a ridge of spines down its back and a long tongue slipping past jagged teeth, tasting them.

"Never turn your eyes from a sand lizard," Zen told her. "Step slowly backward." He patted his hand toward the vehicle. "No sudden movements to trigger the attack reflex."

Simara moved cautiously as Zen began to circle the lizard in the opposite direction. He kept the goggle gaze of his breather fixed on the lizard and began a lilting chant. "Kiokilala, kiokilala."

The sand lizard swivelled its head to follow Zen as Simara reached the buggy and jumped aboard. She scrabbled under the console for tools or an emergency kit. "Do you have any weapons in here?"

"Kiokilala, kiokilala." Zen widened his circle with each revolution around the desert creature. The lizard licked the air and turned to follow his movements, crouched and ready to pounce, ready to attack at any provocation, hungry for dinner. The monster smelled fetid, and dragged a huge bag of testicles at the base of its tail—a male dinosaur, an evolutionary pinnacle of aggression.

Zen moved with stealthy precision. "Kiokilala, kiokilala."

The sand lizard stiffened and glanced around in apparent confusion. He held his armoured nose up and sniffed the air, breaking eye contact with his prey, and Zen took the opportunity to quickly bound for the buggy. He leaped into the driver's seat, and they sped away with wheels churning a cloud of dust.

Simara held her hand to her palpitating chest as they made their escape. "What did you do back there?"

"They have an acute directional sense. If they get confused, they have to stop and reorient to landmarks. The trick is to get them dizzy, in a sense."

"Where did you learn that?"

Zen shrugged at the wheel as they raced onward. "I dunno. It's common lore."

Simara studied her companion anew: self-deprecating charm, a man of hidden talents. She struggled to stifle the rushing adrenalin in her blood, the urge to bolt and run. The grit on her skin and welts at her waist had lost all priority, her bodily discomfort of little consequence with a buried corpse and a hungry dinosaur in her wake.

A helicopter carved the evening sky above them with the beat of a thousand wings, and they looked up in unison. Simara tensed. "Are they following us?"

Zen peered forward to navigate the rough hills ahead, banking and twisting past craggy boulders. "I doubt it. There'll be lots of traffic for the festival. We're just another bug on the map. For safety's sake, we'll keep the crash confidential at the party. You're just a trader making a social stop, a visiting tourist for Vishan. I'll handle our finances discreetly. Is that okay with you?"

"Are we in serious danger?"

"I was hoping you might tell me that," he said, "when you're ready."

"Holy mothership, do you think I'm keeping secrets from you?"

"Everything about you is a mystery to me."

"Ask me anything."

"Who's mothership? Is that who's chasing us?"

"No. I told you. I ran away from my stepfather when he tried to rape me. He hasn't got the resources to stage a manhunt like this. Mothership is just a construct of convenience, the ghost in the data. She's an omniscient hive-mind."

"A voice from your skullrider? Like a conscience?"

"Okay, I guess so. Look, normally I work in a sea of data on the V-net, like swimming in a river of numbers. I'm cut off here, and I can't live like this. I need your help to get back."

Zen nodded. "It's a sure deal, partner. We've got all the treasure we need in the back of the buggy. Stick with me."

Well, she hardly had any choice. Simara tried to remember fresh air on a planet far away, a cool breeze on the ocean beach of New Jerusalem where windblown palms fanned the sky. She felt something skitter up her leg, and slapped at a scorpion on her thigh, a big one. Mothership, she hated bugs! A purple mountain loomed ahead and disappeared into dark clouds above. "We're not going up that cliff, are we?"

"No, we'll go in a low tunnel close to the eastern showers," Zen said. "It's kind of a back door to the city. We can't make a grand entrance until I get you some clothes. You're an adult petite, right?"

"With a size six sandal. Can't I pick my own outfit?"

"The clans of Bali are colour coded. Visitors wear white during Vishan. There's not a lot of fashion selection south of Trade Station, as they say."

"Ahh, I see. Well, something loose but flattering would be great. I don't have armadillo skin like you."

Zen barked in his breather, possibly a laugh, and in a few minutes had parked his buggy in the night shade beside a dozen others. He plugged in a charging cable and signalled for her to follow him through a tight crevice in the granite wall. A musty breath of cool air wafted up from below as they edged their way down a sandy incline. A flexible tube on the ceiling lit the way with bright fluorescence.

"The city is powered by geothermal turbines," he said. "The air is filtered and climate controlled, and there's light in every public tunnel. I'll leave you in the women's showers while I market our merchandise. You can fill a tub and soak for a while."

"Let me help you unload the truck first."

"No, you've done enough. I'll grab a friend while you get freshened up. You'll need your strength. The opening party goes all night the first day of Vishan."

Simara looked past him down the tunnel—a widening pathway ahead, a narrow opening behind. She felt a wave of anxiety at the thought of leaving Zen.

"Look," he said, stepping closer to speak in hushed tones. "I know you have a thing about nudity, but it's perfectly okay in the company of other women. Just don't touch anyone."

"Of course not." She did not have a *thing* about nudity, no more so than any normal person. He had obviously misinterpreted her nervousness.

"Okay, I'll meet you in an hour with a white tunic and shorts, adult petite. I got it." He tapped the side of his breather to indicate his perfect memory.

"Size six sandal," she repeated.

"Right," he said as they continued down the tunnel together.

The air grew noticeably cooler as they progressed, and they reached an area where stairs had been hewn out of the rock, worn in the middle from years of use. At an intersection of corridors, they came across a woman making a turn ahead.

"Trish," Zen yelled, and she stopped and tilted long dark hair at the sound. She wore a bright yellow shirt with a red crescent on the left breast and matching satin shorts with red trim.

Zen pulled off his breather as they approached. "Trish, can you help my friend to the showers?"

"Zen!" she gushed with recognition and flashed perfect teeth. "I haven't seen you in a lizard's life. How have you been?"

"Good," he said. "I'm working out in the badlands."

"So I heard. And this is . . . ?"

"Simara. She's a pilot."

Simara struggled to unhook the clasps of her breather and gasped as she finally got it off. She choked on the moist air and spit harboured bile from her palate. Her mouth felt like a tinderbox.

"Lovely," Trish said as she surveyed Simara's strange bra and ragged turquoise boxers.

"She lost her clothes," Zen said.

Trish smirked with friendly amusement. "How convenient."

"I'm just going to pick up a few things for her. Can you take her to the showers and stow her gear?"

"With pleasure," Trish said, her chirpy voice melodious. "I'm intrigued. Does anyone else know?"

"Oh," Zen said, "no." He wagged his palm. "We're not . . . we're just . . . you know, working."

"Right," Trish said as she studied Simara, "alone in the badlands."

Zen turned toward Simara, swinging his breather in hand. "You okay, then? One hour?"

"Great," she said with false confidence. "You sure you don't need my help?"

"I got this," he said as he turned to dash off.

Trish helped her store her breather and clothes in a plastic locker, led her to the showers, and pulled down a towel from a clothesline, dampish but clean. She seemed anxious to help and boisterous with energy. The shower ran hot and cold with firm pressure, and Simara toyed with the taps to find a tepid balance. She brushed off oily gunk under a refreshing blast of saltwater, and found and filled a small bathtub in an open area of communal bathing. Trish returned with a small plastic vial and held it out with invitation. "Are you allergic to rosaline?"

"I don't know," Simara said. "What is it?"

"Perfume soap. I can't imagine what you've been through. Were you in a fight?"

Simara glanced down at the open welts on her skin with a sigh of humiliation. "No," she said. "Just working."

"It's none of my business, I'm sure," Trish offered with condolence. "They say it's hell in the badlands."

Simara took the perfume and squeezed a dollop onto her palm. She sniffed it and was pleasantly surprised by the fragrance, a mix of cinnamon and rose petals. She turned on the tap and squeezed out another dollop for an instant bubble bath.

"It's made from a selection of local flowers with natural healing properties," Trish said, trying to mingle hope with the pity in her eyes. "I've actually got to be running along, now that you're settled. I'm supposed to be decorating an ice carving for the gala."

Ice? Simara could not remember the last time she had touched frozen water. "Sounds wonderful," she said. "Thanks for the perfume."

"Enjoy. It's been a pleasure meeting you. See you later at the dance?"

"Oh," Simara said with doubt, "I don't know."

"C'mon, everyone parties at Vishan. It's the biggest event of the year." Trish splayed her fingers and puffed up her chest to indicate her golden costume with a bright red crescent. "Let us show you our famous local hospitality!"

Simara did her best to summon a social smile. "Okay."

A few older women showered and dressed after Trish dashed away, but none gave Simara more than a passing glance as she soaked quietly in her tub and counted her blessings one by one. She had escaped being eaten by a lizard just hours previous, and now was bathing in perfumed splendour. She had been chased by helicopters across a deadly desert and now was safe underground in the security of a crowd, preparing for a gala celebration. Simara began to feel almost human again after a time, but her welts remained raw despite the healing balm, and her brain was still crippled without access to the V-net.

A young girl with a blue tunic and shorts approached with a small bundle. "Are you Simara?"

She sat up with a splash. So much for anonymity. "Yes?"

"A man from Star Clan asked me to give you this package." She thrust it forward.

"Thank you," Simara said as she accepted the bundle of clothing. "That's a lovely shade of blue in your outfit."

"Sky Clan," the girl said with a hint of perplexity. She was prepubescent, preteen, and had already noticed the welts on Simara's skin.

Ahh, a ubiquitous blue in a colour-coded culture, not much

to compliment. "Yes, but it matches your eyes so well," Simara said in quick recovery, and the girl smiled as she ducked away.

Her new clothes were nothing fancy—short white pants, a plain tunic, and white sandals. Zen hadn't bothered with undergarments, which was probably just as well. The last thing she needed was constriction brushing against open wounds. The fabric was a soft twine, tightly knit and thankfully opaque. Simara dried herself off and dressed quickly, then hung her towel on the line and rushed to meet Zen in the hallway. He wore a green robe that hung to the floor with a bold silver star emblazoned on the chest.

"Wow, you look great," he said.

She eyed him askance. "Why are you wearing an evening gown?"

"It's not a gown. It's a ceremonial cassock."

Simara looked down at her bare arms and legs. "Why am I in skimpy pants with half my ass hanging out while you look like a monk?"

"The men dress up for Vishan out of respect for Kiva," he said and held palms up in helplessness to tradition. "Don't you like it?"

Simara touched two fingers to her brow. "I'm sorry. I guess I'm just nervous. Did everything go okay with business?"

"Perfect." He winked. "But don't tell anyone about our newfound riches, or all my distant relatives will want loans. Don't worry. You'll be fine. Enjoy the food and wine. Have some fun. Just try not to touch anyone."

"Of course," she said. That much should go without saying.

Zen sniffed at her. "What is that smell? Is that you?"

"It's rosaline. It's perfume soap. Do you like it?"

He bent closer to savour the scent, breathed deep near her

ear. "Mmm," he said, "wonderful." He peered into her eyes, grinning with enthusiasm.

Simara felt a tickle of pleasure at his consideration. Zen was a native prince and built like a stud horse, probably a wonderful lover. Mothership, what was she thinking?

She brushed self-consciously at damp curls on her forehead. "It's a nice change from the smell of pesticide."

He nodded with approval. "Sure is. The party's upstairs. Follow me."

More steps led up to a natural tunnel of rock, the gnarly walls irregular and ribboned with dark striations. The flexible tube on the ceiling gave faithful light, branching at intersections and feeding electricity throughout the cavern complex. After a few minutes, the tunnel opened up into a grotto hung with white icicles, a wondrous, sparkling masterpiece of nature. "Wow!" Simara said as she stopped to survey the spectacle. Her voice echoed in a tinny reverberation, and she turned her head to follow the noise. A mirror of water stood on the ground off to the left, showing the ceiling in a perfect reflection. No breeze stirred the stillness, no ripple marred the surface. "It's amazing."

"This is Secret Lake, one of the ancient caverns," Zen said with a dozen echoes off the icicles. "It's been here for millennia."

Simara squinted up at the ceiling in the meagre light. "Is it frozen?"

"No, that's crystal calcite. It's made from minerals that have seeped down through the mountain. You can see they're still dripping. That means they're still alive and growing, but it takes centuries. We'll never notice any change in our lifetimes. If you look through a single calcite crystal, you see a double image. It's weird. We used to play here as children, and swim in the cool water."

"Those are stalactites?"

"Right," Zen said, nodding, "very good. The ones growing up from the floor are called stalagmites, and they *might* join together someday into a column, like that one over there." He pointed to a white stone cylinder that ran from floor to ceiling. "The bigger ones are called pillars. You'll see some upstairs in the grand ballroom. C'mon."

Simara stooped over the lake to check her reflection in the looking glass. She combed her fingers through a tangle of loose black curls in a pitiful attempt to primp for the party. Her space-wasted cheeks were hollow under high cheekbones, her eyes dark under thick lashes—she had a plain face with a pointed chin, hardly worth a second glance in a crowd, but today her mouth looked cadaverous, and she longed for a smudge of lipstick to add a touch of colour. Her new collared tunic looked smart and dressy, punched out with youthful vigour even without a bra. At least she had that much going for her. She rubbed her rough lips with a fingertip.

"Don't worry, you look great," Zen called back from across the cavern, and his voice echoed in a lingering chant as she turned to follow. ". . . you look great . . . you look great."

"Geologists think the ballroom was once a volcano that was buried in a flood," he said as they walked. The tunnel walls in this area seemed to be coated with antique white porcelain, the ceiling pebbly and convoluted like underwater coral, the air damp and cool, every surface shiny with condensation. "Millions of years later it was pushed up into this mountain range by tectonic action, and the softer sediments were washed away to hollow out the interior. Then the calcite started to coat the walls and collect into pillars. The cave was discovered by the early colonists and became one of the first underground cities. The corporate mining camps come and go as they scrape away the surface of Bali, but our native community is carved into the bedrock of the world." Zen beamed with pride for his culture and heritage, his striding gait regal and purposeful.

Simara heard a steady pulse-beat of drums in the distance, then a bustle of voices and a hum of music as they approached the festival. The tunnel widened into a vestibule where a handful of men chatted together and passed a smouldering stick of weed. One man in a matching green cassock stepped forward as they approached. "Sneaking in the back door, Zen?" he asked as he raised an elbow in greeting.

"Rising up from the underground, brother," Zen replied as he crossed his arm in passing.

The man chuckled and nodded as he returned to his friends in a cloud of pungent smoke.

As they entered the ballroom into a milling crowd, Simara was overcome by sparkling brilliance and loud music. She shaded her eyes and blinked with surprise. The cavern was immense, stretching up above as far as she could view, the walls glassy with white calcite, glowing with strange phosphorescence, huge columns and rock-falls, mounds of flowstone decorated with colourful clan banners. A band raised a cacophony on a raised stage to her left, a ring of drummers surrounded by musicians with stringed instruments and horns. The harmony seemed discordant, the easy beat pervasive, a slow, chugging pace that prompted her body to move in time.

Merchant tables stretched along the wall to her right, filled with all manner of jewellery, scarves, tapestries, tunics, and beaded curtains. A lavish buffet occupied the centre of the ballroom in a giant U-shape pointing away from her to a kitchen area where a steady stream of servers balanced platters on their shoulders to replenish the supply from the interior. The rich scent of tamil seed competed with a host of strange spices to permeate the air with freshness.

"What do you think?" Zen shouted with a swaying palm.

"It's breathtaking," she said, amazed that such an extravagant expanse could be found underground.

"What?"

"Beautiful!"

"Yeah." He nodded and smiled. "Worth the trip, huh?"

"I shall never doubt you again," she said. Six clan colours made up the mingling crowd: blue, green, yellow, orange, purple, and an ochreous red. Not many visitors dressed in white. The men all wore ceremonial cassocks, except for a few young boys in short pants, and the women were all bare-legged except for a few elders with their waists wrapped in saris. No infants were visible in the crowd, no babes in arms, and only two toddlers in the boisterous mix.

A familiar face framed with long dark hair popped into focus in her line of vision—Trish from the showers was pointing in their direction and speaking to a tall blonde woman in a satiny purple outfit and a shorter woman dressed in green. The group had clearly been waiting for them near the back door, the shortest route from the showers, a trio of girls already exchanging juicy gossip. Trish grinned and waved.

"Zen, darling, over here," the blonde shouted.

Darling? Simara quickly turned to Zen to gauge his reaction. His face softened with pleasure, but turned pensive as his brain chugged ions. He glanced at Simara with fleeting guilt and back to the woman waving frantically. "Uh," he said, "I'll introduce you."

The signs were obvious. His former girlfriend had been alerted to his presence, primed with some tawdry tale about a scantily clad stranger in the showers, a usurper. Simara followed Zen with determination, skipping to keep up beside him as he strode forward.

"Jula!" he shouted as they approached the trio. "You're looking fabulous. This is Simara," he said with a wafting hand. "Simara, this is Jula, and Marjum." He pointed to the shorter woman with black hair, tawny skin, and a critical stare. "And you already know our friend Trish."

Simara studied the three girls for social cues, but their mixed expressions seemed incongruous. Without the V-net she was blind and helpless on this world, hampered by paucity of experience with no background information. In her natural state, she would have known everything about the trio at the moment of first contact. Facial recognition screening would have given her instantaneous data. Pictures from infancy onward would have spilled into her mind, scholastic files, chat records, spending habits, all their intimate proclivities. She would have known the girls better than they knew themselves. Instead she was trapped in a two-dimensional tableau like a wooden theatre backdrop, trying to interpret a cheap semblance of reality from visual and verbal signals alone. How did people live like this?

"A pleasure to greet you all," Simara said as she stepped boldly forward with her arm outstretched to offer them each a hearty handshake in turn. The three girls shrank back in unison and wiped palms on their upper thighs, their faces dour with distaste, and Simara frowned with consternation.

Zen reached to touch her shoulder and pull her arm gently down. "She's just kidding," he said to the girls with a grin of regret. "Simara's visiting from offplanet."

Jula quickly fluttered her fingers up to dismiss any worry. She offered her elbow out to cross forearms with Zen, then turned to Simara with a supercilious smile. "So you're a trader?"

"Yes," Simara said, wondering what sordid prattle had poisoned her arrival.

"How long are you staying?"

"I'm not sure." She glanced at Zen.

"You must find it terribly hot in the desert," Jula said, and the other girls murmured the consensus, terribly hot.

"It's quite lovely here in the city," Simara said, but the trio clammed up at that, not wanting to offer any hint of invitation. They pasted false smiles on cardboard faces and flitted their eyes.

Zen steered her away on the pretence of fetching drinks, and Simara stopped to confront him. "What the hell just happened back there?"

"You can't offer your hand in public like that," he whispered. "Hands are for sex."

She furrowed her brow in disbelief. "What?"

"They thought you wanted to have group sex."

Simara felt her face boil with a flush of blood. Oh, mothership, what kind of stupid custom was that? Had she really just invited three women to a lesbian orgy? "Are you kidding me?" she asked with irritation. "Your culture has sex with their hands? Have you never heard of coitus?"

Zen grimaced and frowned. "Don't be a pervert, Simara. We're not breeders. Babies don't survive on Bali."

Simara paused to study him. She quickly reran events in her mind since her landfall. The salvage crew had crossed forearms in close quarters, no high fives, no back slapping. She glanced around the cavern at the couples talking and laughing. No one held hands, no one fondled or embraced. How could she have failed to notice something so obvious? "But you touched me," she said.

"I thought you might be dead," he said crisply, and stepped away toward a nearby table piled with food.

She followed on his heels as he took a plate and began to select items with his fingers. "What about eating? You have to use your hands to eat, don't you?"

"Please don't make a scene," he hissed. "This is hard enough already."

Simara picked up a ceramic plate and struggled for composure. "Sorry," she murmured. "Help me, please, Zen. I don't want to make a fool of myself." She followed his example carefully as they moved down the buffet table, taking only what food he had on his plate, feeling like a total outcast.

"Traditionally, the right hand is used for eating and sex," he whispered, "and the left reserved for activities related to toiletry. But a few decades ago there was a movement against discrimination, so left-handed people are now free to express themselves in public. If you're right-handed, you should stick with the rule, or people will talk. It's a big thing to share food with someone. A communal plate is generally reserved for religious observance."

Again Simara tested memories now growing potent with meaning. Zen had shared a breakfast with her at his hot-spring bachelor pad, their first meal together. He had massaged her back with pest repellent. Apparently, they had been intimate without her knowledge. Heavens, they were practically married—he had wiped her bare ass with both hands while she was unconscious and near death!

Zen gripped her plate to steady her trembling hand. His brown eyes sought her own and held them like searchlights. "It's okay, Simara. You're doing great. Don't worry about stupid social rules. You're a skyfall princess." He had soft eyes, trustworthy eyes, and his face was stern with understanding. She bit her lower lip and nodded.

"C'mon, let's find a table and get some honey mead," he said. "The dancing will begin soon."

She followed mutely and sat with thankfulness, feeling weary. Dancing in this gravity? What a cumbersome fate. She longed for a geyser bath and weightlessness as she nibbled at food of mysterious origin. Zen fetched her a mug of frothy mead, and she reached for it absentmindedly with her left hand while she ate. But stopped and quickly dropped her arm. She finished her right-hand bite and took the drink in due time with civility. Zen chuckled quietly, his face impish: *That wasn't so bad, was it?*

She downed half the mead with a burp of satisfaction and slammed her mug on the table. Damn them all anyway. Zen grinned and followed her example, sloshing beer onto his plate in the process.

He returned in a few minutes with two more mugs of strong ale and a plate of fluffy pastries. He tipped a few onto her plate with sugary fingers, sharing food and relishing the impropriety. What a funny man. Spotlights blinked on and off in the central courtyard as buffet tables were moved aside to clear space. Musicians began to assemble on a terraced balcony up above where a patriarch in a purple cassock grandly announced the traditional Vishan dance about to begin at the stroke of midnight. Simara felt new gravity in her seat as Zen turned to her with query in her eyes. She shook her head. No way.

Jula coalesced out of the crowd as if on signal, a blonde beauty in purple satin. "Happy Vishan," she proclaimed with a boisterous slur. "It's our dance, darling."

"Happy Vishan," Zen said, "but I'll take a break this year. I've been away so long, I'm not sure I remember the steps. Thanks, anyway."

Jula smiled with dedicated grace, had probably expected as much under the circumstances. "Perhaps later," Jula said with an awkward bow, and glanced at Simara with a tight lip and undisguised malevolence in her eyes: *Happy Vishan, bitch.*

Simara sipped her mead and turned to Zen after she was out of earshot. "Was that a big deal?"

"Naw, don't worry," he said with a finger flip. "We broke it off long ago."

Drummers began a slow and stately rhythm as mixed couples assembled back to back in the clearing. A loud gong sounded, a deep vibration that seemed crystalline in origin, and Simara turned her attention to the musicians on the terrace. The gong rang again, stately and magnificent, and she realized with surprise that the sound emanated from a huge stalactite hanging from the ceiling. One of the musicians was pulling a chain to strike a trip-hammer against the calcite crystal! Five repetitions, six, and on the seventh gong an orchestra began playing as the dancers took two steps forward and turned to face their partners with a single arm raised to full extension, waving back and forth in time to the chorus like a fanning palm branch.

A symphony of gongs began a complex melody as the musicians pulled cords with both hands to strike stalactites high above, each crystal exquisitely tuned to a single note on the diatonic scale. The couples on the dance floor whirled in unison and ended up facing away again, beckoning to the distance with a sultry invitation to incoming spring. The barefoot dancers wore anklets with tiny bells, and their synchronous movements added a jingling accompaniment to the crystal chorus from above.

"It's a prayer for crop fertility," Zen said close to her ear. "The beginning of the rainy season."

"You have rain in the desert?"

He shrugged. "Sometimes. Mostly just mist from the clouds on the western face of the mountains. Kiva provides everything we need, but never enough to store up in complacency."

The stalactites began to resonate and hum with increased amplitude as the musicians continued to hammer the gong notes, and the entire amphitheatre seemed to embrace the sound, to join in the symphony of celebration. Simara felt it in her bones and blood, a sound of angels playing celestial carillons on heavenly shores. Louder and louder the vibrations magnified until the whole mountain seemed to sing with praise.

The Vishan dancers cavorted like ballerinas in synchrony, a choreograph designed for supple spines and flexible tendons. The couples stayed connected with their partners in symbolic monogamy even when they spun apart in wild pinwheels of motion. In times of chorus they returned again and again with cascades of furious desire, but halted each time just before the moment of embrace, building a tension of sensuality from the lack of bodily contact. The women flayed their arms wide in artful submission with their breasts punched up and faces tilted skyward while the men wagged chins over the bounty with arms locked behind their backs in ritualistic chastity, the erotic symbolism made all the more provocative by the absence of touch, a raw sexuality held in abeyance behind a thin veil of imagination.

Chimes began to sound on the outskirts of the room as another line of dancers began to form with metal bells in hand. They swayed gently in time to the music, following the same rhythm and timbre as the main dancers in the courtyard, but their stylized movements were much simpler, and their melody a repetitive tune. They appeared to be a younger crowd, unattached to partners, their dance less sensual but still restricted by form. Children with baskets began to circle the periphery distributing wristlet bells to the audience, and soon everyone had a trinket to add to the noise. Simara accepted a bell and slipped it over her right hand, following Zen's example. The bell jingled each time she raised her cup to her lips.

The pace began to accelerate as the musicians continued to hammer the stalactites, and the symphony reached a frenetic pace as the ballerinas pranced to the quickening beat. Simara's body began to pulse with the rising tempo—she could feel the vibration of the mountain in her teeth, an impossible ecstasy of resonance. "I'm almost ready to explode," she shouted into Zen's ear.

He grinned and nodded as he watched the cavorting crowd. "It takes real stamina to get this far," he said in admiration of the dancers. "We're getting near the end." He turned to face Simara and bent toward her. "Everything falls silent at the last gong." He cut the air with a slanted palm. "No sound, okay? Only Kiva may speak at the pinnacle of Vishan. You'll see."

Simara returned to her drink. Everyone was having fun in a pandemonium of movement and gonging chimes. The pastries were cloying with sweet icing and the ale flowed freely. Children laughed and played with tinkling timbrels.

As the performance reached a crescendo of exuberance, the crowd stood to applaud the dancers now sweating with exertion as they stood waving their arms to the ceiling in pulsating reverence. A final harmonic cadence sounded like a crystal thunderclap as the musicians hammered a closing gong note. Everyone froze to listen with expectance. Young and old closed their eyes in unison and bowed their heads in worship as the mountain reverberated and the calcite crystal sang alone.

Simara strained to hear the voice of Kiva in the afterglow of majesty as the vibrations echoed down every tunnel and into every heart. The transcendent harmony lingered for many moments, and every smile turned beatific at the sound. As the magic mountain cried out divine, everyone knew without a doubt that spring had begun and the future would be better than the past. The desert god Kiva provided enough for all to share and none to prosper. A hum of holiness settled and drifted to a lingering silence.

Applause followed in a rising thunder as the dancers bowed with humility and thanksgiving, and a fresh cornucopia of food emerged from the kitchens along with full trays of mulled ale. Simara gained directions to the lavatory while she still had good wits, and she slid through the bustling crowd like an eel in oil.

On her return, she noticed Jula and her two cohorts talking at a table near the back, giggling and tipsy. She approached with sure dignity, emboldened with the first blush of intoxication. "I'm not really a pervert," she told them point-blank.

"Oh, it's fine, dear," Jula said with a slur as she stood and waved Simara closer, careful not to touch. "Come and sit with us. You can be our famous friend from the stars." Her breath was hot and beery, her smile radiant.

"And you know what they say," Marjum piped up with a wink, "one hand in the darkness is as good as another." The girls all laughed uproariously at this. Apparently an all-female environment allowed for much more social leeway, or perhaps it was the alcohol talking.

"I wouldn't know," Simara said, trying to be frosty without raising a shield. "I'm sorry if I gave the wrong impression earlier."

"She's just teasing," Trish said. "We all know Zen is a glad hand."

"And a *sturdy* performer," Marjum added with a leer. A chorus of sniggers offered knowing corroboration.

Simara glanced furtively at nearby tables, wondering who might be within earshot. "I wouldn't know," she said again to set the record straight. Could all these girls have had sexual experience with Zen, a small community coming of age together, playing masturbation games with no hope of procreation? How could a culture survive such an evolutionary dead end?

"Oh, sure," Jula said and rolled her eyes with doubt. "Don't be too *hard* on the girl." Another round of drunken hilarity made Simara blush with consternation.

"I have to get back," she said in dismissal. "Happy Vishan." Simara shook her head with regret as the girls laughed behind her back

By the time she returned to Zen, he had hooked up with Katzi on business, the older man's paunch covered by a matching green robe with silver star, his hair a greasy black tangle. They stood cheek to cheek talking quietly in each other's ear, and a wad of cash disappeared into the folds of Zen's robe as they exchanged nods of satisfaction.

Simara stepped close and jabbed Zen in the ribs. "Can we go home now?"

He smiled. "No, we can't go. It's Vishan. You remember Katzi?" He tipped his elbow out subtly in signal.

"Yes, certainly. You look fine tonight, sir." She offered her forearm out in greeting, and he crossed it dutifully.

"Not as lovely as you, I must say," he said with a bow. "You look much prettier with clothes on."

Simara blinked at him in surprise. What the hell kind of thing was that to say to a girl half his age? She looked down self-consciously at her skimpy white shorts and glanced at her partner. Zen quivered one eye at her to indicate that all was well, so she turned and pasted on a smile for the elder man. "Thanks. Zen picked it out."

"An eye for detail, that boy," Katzi said. "Pleasure doing business with you both." *Drop by anytime. Feel free to crash in my quadrant.* Simara's imagination was running wild. She had probably had too much to drink.

"You have a hard-working crew," she said.

Katzi grinned with delight as though that might be the highest compliment possible on any planet. "I'll give them your accolades."

"Please do," she said. It was hardly a lie. They were all a bunch of freaky worker drones. "But tell me, where does the salvage go? There's no one building shuttles on this planet. I don't see any signs nearby of industry or technology."

Katzi nodded. "The geomagnetic storms hold us back here on the surface. Computers are unreliable and communication is sparse. Insurance companies pick up the tab for most of our work, and the mining corps are always looking for strategic metals. Our salvage is worth twenty times as much up the gravity well. All we get is the crumbs from the table." He spread his hands as though indicating the obvious. "We're all just dead weight down here. I keep telling Zen, he should get offplanet while he's young and strong. The sky is his true heritage. His father was a famous politician who boosted to Trade Station every year for meetings. All Zen needs is a good partner with a head for business. There's a grand universe out there waiting for a couple of brave kids."

Simara smiled. "Are you trying to get rid of me? I've only just arrived."

"No, you take your time. Enjoy your success. Vishan is the season to be thankful." He swept an arm in grandeur at the festive crowd, then leaned forward conspiratorially. "But keep your head down and your money in your belt."

"Wise advice always," she replied. So there was a shady side to the salvage business, as she'd expected. Insurance companies and mining corps were not known for friendly dealings even in broad daylight.

Zen stood content, and Katzi seemed in no hurry, so Simara turned to watch a group of musicians setting up for after-hours entertainment with stringed instruments and a squeeze box. How much longer could this go on? She could feel gravity sucking at her again, dragging her implacably down. Her vision went fuzzy as waves of nausea made her stomach lurch upward, bloated with frothy mead. She almost reached out to steady herself on Zen's shoulder, but resisted the urge—no public groping in front of this crowd! Boisterous voices sounded too loud around her, and she imagined Jula and her gang whooping it up at her expense. Her own skin felt rough and abrasive against her flesh. Even her hair ached. Finally she could stand it no longer. "Zen, I've got to rest. Is there a hot spring nearby? This gravity is killing me."

He turned with a look of concern and scrutinized her face as she wavered unsteadily. "Come with me. I'll find you a place to lie down."

She relinquished herself to his care, barely able to focus her attention as he led her through the crowd under a waterfall of flowstone to a tunnel opening on the wall. Steps led down into darkness, but a glimpse of light appeared in the distance as they descended. They travelled down a length of tunnel and turned into a large cave hewn from the bedrock, the walls creviced with chisel marks and decorated with tapestries. "Luaz?" Zen shouted. "Are you in?"

"Zen, is that you? Bless Kiva!" An older woman strode into the cave wiping her hands on a cooking apron. She embraced him with an open show of affection that made Simara tense with alarm. A lover? A pervert? She felt disconcerted with anxiety at these strange people with their mixed messages. The woman turned to study her with inquisitiveness, her grey hair pulled tight behind her ears in a braid.

Zen reached an arm behind the woman's back and held the other palm up for an introduction. "Simara, this is my mother, Luaz. Mom, this is Simara. I found her in the desert."

Simara almost fell back in surprise. His mother? Zen was taking her home to the family so soon? What the hell? She looked from Zen's warm brown eyes back to his mother's face, Luaz's eyebrows now wide with wonder, her smile a tight line. "Hi," Simara said. No hand out in greeting this time, no elbow up. She dared not move a muscle for fear of interpersonal insult.

"She's feeling ill," Zen said. "Can she rest here for a while?"

"Of course," Luaz said with a nod of welcome. She pointed with both palms toward an opening in the cave wall. "Come this way. Are you sick with the cactus?"

"No, I don't think so. Just the gravity."

"Gravity?" Luaz glanced at her son and back. "Oh, of course. You're from the sky."

"She crashed in the desert," Zen said. "We're keeping it a secret for now. Just for safety, okay?"

"Of course," Luaz said again, invincible with experience. "You run along back to the party. Don't worry about a thing."

"Thanks, Mom. You're looking great."

"You, too," she said, "except for the black eye." She tipped her head at him in query.

"It's nothing. Just a spider bite. The best from Kiva." He turned and hurried away before she could follow up on the interrogation.

Luaz stood quiet for a moment, then turned to Simara with

a motherly smile and an open arm pointing with invitation. She led her down a gentle decline to a small cave where a hammock hung from corner to corner, draped with a tasselled tapestry and adorned with pillows. A wooden chest of drawers rested against one wall, a strange anachronism, probably an expensive heirloom. Simara had yet to see a tree growing anywhere on this hellish planet.

Luaz settled her in a gently rocking bed and covered her with a sheet of linen. "Are you partnered with Zen?"

Simara stiffened with growing confusion. "No, I . . . I'm not sure what you mean."

"I see," Luaz said with a worried face and wary smile. "Has my son harmed you in any way? Have you been in a fight?"

Simara sat up and almost fell out of the hammock. "No, certainly not. He has been nothing but a gentleman." The room swayed around her, and she stifled a stomach spasm with a fist on her abdomen.

"There, there," Luaz said as she pantomimed a push back down, careful not to touch. "Rest easy. All will be well. I'll leave you in peace and check back later." She stood and rolled a tapestry down over the doorway as she ducked underneath.

One single filament of light hung from a wall bracket near the pebbled ceiling of the cave where stalactites had been broken off to leave flat stumps of rock. A crude painting hung on one wall, the brush strokes childlike in simplicity, a fertile landscape with lush vegetation under a haloed moon, an image of paradise from a book perhaps. This was probably Zen's room as a child. His personal effects were probably still in the chest of drawers. Dizzy with sickness and too much ale, Simara felt like she was infringing on Zen's privacy, invading his past. Awkward circumstance had thrust her into his life, and now into his family. She had embarrassed herself in front of his former lovers. What must they all be thinking about her, the strange alien girl from the stars?

THREE

Her stepfather came to her in a dream again, the same midnight horror, his slavering face stinking of alcohol and rough with stubble. His fingers groped her, pinching between her legs. *Give me some tight pussy, you cheap slut.* He pressed his body upon her, his penis a dead weight. *You dirty girl, you like that don't you?* She screamed and lashed out against him. She punched him in the face and kicked him in the scrotum. "No!" she shouted. "Get off me, you drunken bastard!"

They fell in a tangle as the hammock tilted upside down. Simara grunted with pain as her arm and shoulder hit against solid rock.

"What in Kiva's name?" Zen said as he stood and staggered back against the wall. He brushed at a wall switch to turn on the single filament of light, a bare candle in the darkness. His eyes were red and bleary from too much mead, his stance wavery and uncertain. "What are you doing in my bed?"

Simara looked up and rubbed at her elbow. Her arm had gone numb and fuzzy with pain. God damn it all.

Luaz flung back the tapestry as she barrelled into the

bedchamber. She surveyed the scene in an instant and froze for an explanation, her eyes wide with astonishment. Simara burst into tears, her stepfather's face still leering in her mind's eye, a poison of violation roiling inside her.

"I . . ." Zen began and stopped, clearly drunk and disoriented. He seemed to be pondering some great paradox as he rubbed a fresh bruise on his chin.

Simara picked herself up and hobbled past them for the cave mouth, desperate to escape.

"Wait, just a minute," Luaz said behind her, but Simara dared not turn back for a confrontation. She ran blindly up the tunnel and followed the sound of music in the distance, wandering from corridor to corridor until she found her way back to the crystal ballroom. The crowd had thinned for the afterparty, but a trio blowing brass horns accompanied a string band now, and a circle of onlookers gyrated to a jazzy tune. The style of dance had changed markedly from the formal rituals of tradition to a wild freeform of movement, the dancers younger, some with drinks in hand. Incredibly, the buffet table was stocked with fresh pastries, and Simara gorged on fruity concoctions dusted with icing sugar until she felt strength return. She took a cup of guava mead and sipped her drink as she searched for a secluded corner to hide from the riot of colour and noise.

A young man caught her attention from across the room, and she turned away too late. He began to push toward her through the crowd, a blond boy dressed in a bright yellow robe with a red crescent emblazoned on the chest. He strolled up to her with lazy confidence and smiled. "Can I serve you anything?"

Simara sipped her drink. "No, thank you."

He nodded, nonchalant. "Great party. Happy Vishan. I'm Justin."

"Simara."

"You're looking well."

"You also," she said with caution, wondering about every nuance of communication and trying to play it safe. "I'm just visiting."

"I can see that," the boy said as he plucked at his robe.

Of course, her white tunic marked her as a tourist. Everything was colour coded in this crazy place. She smiled with wan resignation.

"I'm from the clan of the moon lizard," Justin said.

"That sounds like a frightening creature. Do they eat humans?"

He laughed with a pleasant lilt. "No, they're quite small. About the size of a cave ferret."

"Hmm," she said, wondering how big a cave ferret might be and whether that was a new cause for worry.

"Where are you staying?"

She thumbed absently over her shoulder. "With a friend. He's busy at the moment."

"Would you like a guided tour of the caverns while you wait? See the wonders wrought by Kiva?"

Simara splayed her fingers at the magnificence of the ball-room. "It's all phantasmagorical to a space rat like me."

"You're from the stars?"

"Not exactly. You can't actually land on a star."

"Ahh," he said. "Wow."

She shook her head with self-effacement. "It's not all that great."

"So, what about the tour? I know all the local sights."

"Sure, I guess. Someplace quiet would be nice." She followed his elbow of invitation into a new branch of tunnels lit by the ubiquitous glow tube overhead. The upper mountain was riddled with a labyrinthine maze carved naturally by water and smooth to the touch. The cavern ceilings were hung with all manner of exotic stalactites, some like icicles, others flat like tapestries.

"First stop is the drapery room," Justin said. "It took a million years to make these designs." He waved a hand up grandly. "These giant sheets formed from seepage through fractures in the bedrock. Some are so thin you can see through them."

"Amazing." They did indeed look like hanging cloth in elaborate folds, white and shiny like porcelain. Simara reached up to touch a wet edge. "They're still growing," she said as she rubbed liquid between her fingers. Down at her feet, the rock was mounded with a convoluted texture that reminded her of brain tissue.

"Just over a centimetre every hundred years," Justin said with a nod of sure wisdom. He poked her elbow to get her attention. "Next up is Kivakulia, the Apparition of God."

Simara dragged her eyes away to follow Justin up another tunnel. They climbed a steep incline and grappled loose gravel with their hands to steady themselves. A damp odour reminded her of the smell of clouds and rain. A reddish glow emanated from the top of the hill and grew brighter as they approached.

"This is the most holy place in the mountain, Kivakulia. The early explorers knew they had found God when they came upon this formation." A huge, glowing angel stood before them, stretching from floor to ceiling, flared out and flattened in the middle. The column emitted light in the red-orange end of the spectrum, seemingly by magic in the darkness. A fence with an iron railing had been erected in a hexagon around it.

"No way," Simara said in awe. "It must be a trick."

"Imagine creeping through these tunnels in the days before Bali had electricity," Justin said, "exploring in the darkness with your headlamp beam or flashlight in hand, and seeing the Apparition of God for the first time. That must have been something."

"Why does it glow? Is it hot?"

"No, it's fluorescent calcite," he said, "activated by impurities like manganese. The invisible short-wavelength radiation is absorbed by the crystals and remitted as a longer wavelength that we can see. It's also slightly phosphorescent, which means it will continue to glow after the light source is removed."

"It's not magic?"

"No, but it was thought to be a supernatural manifestation for many years. You can see why."

"That is totally awesome!"

"Kivakulia," he said with pride.

"Can I touch it?"

He frowned. "No, the oil from your fingers might harm these delicate crystals. But there's more. The lover's room is just down this tunnel to the left. It's a cavern filled with standing stones growing up from the floor."

Simara followed him farther into the fantastical maze, marvelling at each new texture of marbled calcite—gourds and clumsy ribbons, fountains and stubby fingers. For untold millennia before the arrival of humans, the seeping waters had toiled over these artful creations, drip by steady drip. Could it really be just an accident, a chance variation of rainwater and underground streams? Or was this Kiva's declaration of glory?

"Watch your head here," Justin said as he stood by a narrow crevice. He pushed the back of her neck to guide her forward past a craggy overhang. She stooped and felt a brush of rock at her hair.

The tunnel opened up into a dimly lit grotto of wonder. Huge marble statues rose erect from the ground like a white army at attention, their heads blunt and rounded, glistening with life. Corresponding stalactites hung dripping high above in darkness, and a few had reached their partners to form pearly columns of calcite. "You can touch freely in the lover's room," Justin said. Simara stepped forward to the nearest formation and stroked cool calcite, smooth as glass and hard as iron. She envisioned primitive explorers surrounded by these standing stones, praising the wondrous works of Kiva. Murmured voices sounded in the distance, and as her eyes adjusted to the meagre light, Simara noticed couples sequestered in distant shadows.

"About fifty centuries ago, there was a drought in the water supply here," Justin said behind her. "You can see that the stalagmites were narrowed for awhile and then renewed."

Simara peered up at the huge columns anew and noticed the bulbous tips on each one. Oh, mothership, each one looked like a penis at attention! "Wow, that's definitely an army of phallic symbols."

Justin chuckled knowingly with invitation. "That's why the lovers meet here."

Simara felt a flush of insurgent fear as she turned to him. Sure enough, he had pulled up his yellow robe and held it above his naked hips as he leaned with casual ease against a marble column.

The white stalagmite between his thighs stood upright with promise. *Can you give me a hand, good friend?*

With a gesture of pure instinct, Simara hauled back and sucker-punched Justin with a vicious roundhouse blow straight to the cheekbone. He cried out and fell to the ground with his nose in his palms as blood began to drip between his fingers. He rolled and cried like a wounded animal as Simara curled her bruised fist in her abdomen, wondering what the hell had just happened. She felt like a dirty girl again, violated anew. "Cover yourself up, you pervert," she said as she kicked his naked thigh, and Justin groaned and scrabbled at his gown with bloody hands.

A crowd of lovers quickly surrounded them and sent for aid, and the local constabulary arrived within minutes to take Simara into custody. An hour later she was in jail, stuck behind iron bars in an austere cave just big enough to recline, cold and shivering under a scrap of rotting canvas—from the heights of majesty to the depths of desolation in one act of thoughtless violence. God damn, what a mess. She had assaulted two men in less than two hours, and there was no use crying about it now. This was the absolute end. She could fall no further from here, and mothership would never find her in this underground prison. A calm and vacuous dread of depression surrounded her like an impenetrable curtain. She surely deserved a cruel fate, and a just punishment awaited her.

A magistrate official guarded her from his desk across the cavern, where he sat creaking in a leather office chair while he scanned a digital reader. Simara felt the weight of a towering mountain of calcite above her, ready to fall and crush her like a bug. She buried her face in a mouldy blanket and drifted in fitful sleep. She tossed and turned on the rocky surface and felt worse with every awakening. Out of habit, she tapped her earlobe when she woke and got a dead blank from the V-net each time—no audio, no vidi. Mothership had forsaken her.

A buzzing drone sounded in her ears, a permanent headache of fatigue. She stirred to a familiar voice and struggled against a dull heaviness of slumber. She pressed her cheek against iron bars to see Luaz arguing with the magistrate and gesticulating with animation. "I demand the right of substitution for my clan," Luaz said.

The official shook his head. "She's not of your clan. She's an offworlder and must pay the specified ransom."

"She's staying in my cave. She's partnered with my son."

The man wiped at his brow, testing deep furrows. "Damn you, woman. Do you think I want to spend all Vishan in this office?"

"I demand the right of substitution for my clan as decreed in the Charter of Privilege," Luaz repeated, her chin defiant.

The magistrate reached into his desk drawer and slammed a key card on the table. "Do it yourself," he snarled. "I wash my hands of your insolence."

Luaz picked up the card and strode to Simara's cramped prison cave. She swiped the lock mechanism and swung the bars open. "Get out," she said fiercely.

Simara squirmed forward and slid out of captivity, stumbling to her knees under the weight of gravity. She straightened aching muscles and watched in horror as Luaz crawled into the tiny crypt and pulled the iron door closed with a clang. "No," Simara croaked.

Luaz blinked at her, resolute, a stubborn old woman.

Simara held out an open palm. "Give me the key."

Luaz shuffled her body into the cave as far as she could go and glared back, her face a stern white mask. Behind them, the magistrate spoke into a communications device in his cupped hand, his voice a whisper of aggravation.

Simara sighed with confusion. "What are you doing, Luaz?"

"I have the legal right to take your place."

"You don't even know me. I'm a terrible person."

Luaz shook her head. "You may think so now, but I've seen the hand of Kiva. Obedience is my privilege of consecration."

Oh crap, that sounded like religious jargon—no point in trying to argue. Simara settled cross-legged on the rock in front of the cold iron cage and stared up into eyes glinting with holy light from the dark recess. Surely the woman would listen to reason. "Do you have a partner? Someone I can contact?"

"His name was Valda, a good man to the core, a wonderful father. He died two years ago from a quick cancer."

"Zen's father?"

"Zen's heart followed him to the grave on that final night. His soul turned black and vacant with despair, and he fled alone into the wilderness to grovel in his ruin. I lost my two loves in a single stroke of fate. My life was wiped away, scrubbed clean to the bedrock. How could I start again at this age?" The light from her eyes went dark as she ducked her head. "Zen's few visits on the days of ceremony were those of a ghost, a boy devoid of hope, a stranger in the skin of a man."

"I'm sorry," Simara said.

"Not your fault." Luaz waved a hand. "The rads take us all in time—the great plagues of Bali." A pause lingered between them, an emptiness longing to be filled. "When I saw Zen return with you for Vishan, my son had come back from the dead. He has spark in his eyes again, and life in his heart. Whatever you did to him was a blessing from Kiva. Whatever they do to me now will never matter, now that I have seen his true face again."

A stalactite dripped steadily in the distance for many minutes as Simara examined her feelings for Zen. He was an attractive and sensitive man, a comfortable friend, but did she love him? Could she live her entire life with him? Mothership, they had only just met. She could not imagine being intimate with him, sharing his body.

Hunger began to gnaw inside her. She wondered if she might be allowed to bring food for Luaz, who surely must be in grave discomfort by now at her age, but realized with a start that she was completely lost underground. She couldn't wander the tunnels on her own in search of a kitchen pantry and risk getting trapped in a sinkhole or killed in a fall. She was still at the mercy of her captors, trapped in a maze of rock on an alien planet. She folded her arms and settled her back against cold prison bars. "How did you birth a baby here, Luaz? Zen said it was impossible."

"The rads on Bali ruin all delicate DNA, but Trade Station stays in protected orbit on the dark side from Signa, shadowed from danger. Valda was a governor in those days, so we were able to travel to the station for fertility enhancement. Zen was conceived by genetic cleansing and lived his first year in a controlled biosphere."

"It must have been terribly expensive for you."

"We were rich in those days," Luaz said. "We took too much for granted."

"You raised a fine boy."

"Yes, that much is true," she said wistfully. "The early days were the best, the days when Zen was in school, before the turmoils of adolescence. The teenage years seemed so fraught with meaning, every nuance of life blown out of proportion. Was it the same for you?"

Simara shook her head, unable to empathize. "I don't think so. I lived a solitary life in space, conjoined with machine intelligence." Her guardian mothership was her only real friend, but this elder woman would have little understanding of digital consciousness or the psychic realms of the freenet. In simple grounder terms, Simara had spent most of her waking life as a V-net avatar, a phantom in the machine. "My stepfather went through a series of wives, so I had surrogate parents of sorts and a good relationship with the latest one. She died a few months ago in a vacuum breach."

"Oh, I'm sorry to hear such tragedy," Luaz said in sympathy.

"That's all right. We've both had our share of pain."

"There will always be pain," Luaz said. "That's the one constant of life. We must remember the joy and dwell on it anew every day."

Simara lapsed into silence as she considered the wise and gentle counsel of the elder. Her own memories were filled with bad images and emotional trauma, leering faces and foul language. Where was her happiness? Where was her reward?

Finally Zen and Justin arrived in the prison house and approached the magistrate's table with contrition. Zen looked bleary-eyed with a hangover, his chin speckled with downy stubble. Justin's face was puffy and bruised, his parrot-nose red and swollen. The magistrate spoke in hushed anger to the boys as they exchanged courtroom evidence outside Simara's earshot. He looked over at her periodically with petulance, and finally summoned her with a growl. She hobbled over and stood with her head bowed, afraid to speak, feeling a doom of impending punishment. The boys had matching purple welts under their left eyes and Justin's nostrils were stuffed with cotton. Of course she should have noticed his romantic signals. He had touched the back of her neck on the way to the lover's cavern—that was probably the height of foreplay on this horrible planet!

The magistrate scrutinized her from under bushy brows. "You are a dangerous woman."

Simara struggled to swallow against a constriction of panic. Should she agree or disagree? Admit guilt or decline responsibility? She was bereft of social custom in this place.

"We don't allow physical violence on Bali," the official continued. "Life is too short and precious."

"I understand and agree, sir," she said, and raised her voice a notch for the benefit of Luaz in her cage. "Life is precious above all."

"Serious charges have been brought against your account, and you have surely disgraced your clan." He nodded with determination toward the cell where Luaz lay imprisoned in her stead.

Simara bowed her head, afraid to speak and trembling with fear before judicial authority.

"The law is clear in matters of romantic entanglement," he said, "and I want to make your situation plain before you enter your petition."

"Thank you, sir. My ignorance of your statutes is no justifiable excuse."

The magistrate's face seemed to soften a notch at her expression of humility. That was good. Maybe she was on the right track. "I may have sampled some strangely mixed drinks while visiting your festival for the first time," she said. Was she laying it on too thick? Trying too hard? Surely intoxication was a common problem during Vishan.

The magistrate frowned. "You would do well to show some care in the future."

Simara felt a surge of promise in her knotted abdomen. Did she have a future, some chance of penance? Could she dare hope for a simple slap on the wrist?

"Your clan mother has offered atonement for you and will suffer penalty in your place," the magistrate continued, louder so that Luaz would not miss a word with her ear to the bars of her cage. "The Charter of Privilege grants her this legal right and is of no small judicial consequence." Was that a hint of displeasure at potential paperwork, some legal jargon? Simara could sense an opening before her, an escape route through the choking haze of rules, but could not grasp it clearly, and could only stand downcast in confusion.

"However . . ." The magistrate cleared his throat to signal the importance of his upcoming declaration, as only a judge can do. "If it can be shown that the accused was partnered to another person in a situation of domestic violence," he said, "then onus would fall on the male interloper to honour that commitment, and he would have no justified argument against any . . . self-protective gesture."

"I did not know the girl was partnered," Justin spoke up. "She gave no such indication and wore no scarf!"

The magistrate raised a palm. "The facts are clear, and let the truth guide us henceforth." He turned deliberately toward Simara. "Unprovoked aggression does not go unpunished on Bali. Do you certify for the court that you are partnered with Zen Valda of Star Clan, son of Luaz who has redeemed your honour?"

Simara's jaw dropped into a downshaft. Partnered? As in *married*? What the hell? So that was the bottom line of patriarchal law on Bali. The dice were loaded, the table rigged. She turned to Zen wide-eyed with surprise. What a crazy ride they had been on together in such a short time, like twin stars rotating in gravitational frenzy! First a handsome rescuer in the twilight, then a cute pool-boy sharing her breakfast beside a hot-spring geyser, Zen had turned out to be a hard-working and hard-drinking businessman. Now he was a man of heritage, son of the politician Valda, firstborn of Luaz, her redeemer suffering silently in her stead, paying the penalty for her sin. How could this be? She scrutinized Zen's bruised and bleary face, searching for a signal, some portent from Kiva. Could this man be her partner, her potential soulmate destined to her by this convoluted trail? Did he care for her as much as she cared for him? Did he love her? His eyes were brown and beautiful, and his face was healing quickly. His honest smile emboldened her to speak with clarity from the heart. "Yes, sir, I do."

The magistrate quirked a smile to indicate she was on a delicate track to freedom, and turned to her husband with a nod. Zen sidled closer and took hold of her sweaty palm, causing her to stiffen with shell-shock at his public touch.

"Simara and Zen of Star Clan, do you press charges of violation against Justin of Moon Lizard Clan?"

Carefully, Simara studied the magistrate's graven face. A serious condemnation was clearly at stake, some crime of passion, likely with dire consequences. She turned to Justin to gauge his reaction. The blond boy looked as if he might pee his pants in consternation, but he dared not offer another outburst of complaint. His eyes pleaded for pity. A charge of violation? He had exposed himself in public in a moment of drunken romance, but he was hardly an adulterer. Would the other side of the interpersonal coin leave Simara open to slander as a slutty housewife inviting obscene advances, a shameful wench pandering to youngsters? What a sordid business.

"Certainly not," Simara said. "It was an accident, a mistake, a crude clash of social customs after a long night of festivity." She caught the eyes of the magistrate with a steely stare. "This young man deserves no blame on his record, and Luaz must go free." On this she would stand her ground and stake her reputation, and damn their stupid rules!

The magistrate tightened his lips in deliberation for a moment and cast a glare at each person in turn to confirm his final authority. "So it shall be, and greater care will be taken by all. This matter is hereby absolved. Get your women out of here, Zen."

Justin turned and fled quickly with downcast eyes as Zen helped Luaz from her prison perch. Simara stilled her pulsing heart as the magistrate tidied his desk with a smile of satisfaction at a job well done and a conundrum avoided. He probably had family waiting for a private Vishan celebration at home.

Luaz came close and placed a palm on Simara's shoulder in

motherly love. "Whatever you do," she said, "go with the grace of Kiva always." Her flagrant touch was a signal of celebration mixed with sadness, a welcome to the family mingled with recognition of divergent paths ahead, the last goodbye so soon.

"Of course," Simara said. "Thank you for everything, and bless you."

Zen seemed sullen and thoughtful, probably still suffering a hangover, and they followed Luaz home in silence, trudging in single file down narrow corridors of hewn rock while Simara battled with her imagination. What must Zen be thinking, forced into a marriage of convenience with a strange alien girl? What behaviour might he expect from her? To serve and obey in some traditionalist fantasy? To cook his meals and keep his cave clean? And what about sex, or what passed for pseudo-sex in this backwater world? Simara was certainly not practised in the art of erotic massage.

Back in their private quarters, Zen took off his ceremonial cassock and folded it in a drawer for safekeeping. He dug his money belt out of hiding and strapped it on under his leather loincloth. "We should probably go," he said.

Simara put on an airy smile with a show of good nature. "Yes, I think I've caused enough trouble for one Vishan."

Zen winced and nodded. "You don't need to apologize."

"I wasn't going to."

Zen studied her with a hint of perplexity. "So we're good, then?"

Simara shrugged. "I'm ready to leave. Do you need to say goodbye to anyone?"

"I didn't go back to her."

"What?"

"Jula," he said. "I didn't see her while you slept."

So he was still thinking about his ex-girlfriend, and on his ersatz wedding day no less. Simara frowned. Wait a minute, did he suspect she had sought out Justin to gain revenge for some imagined slight? Simara squinted at him. Had they stumbled together into some complicated interpersonal morass? "Zen," she said with as much sincerity as she could muster, "it was a simple accident with Justin. I didn't think anything bad about you or Jula." She cast her hands down at her hips. "My brain doesn't function without digital support. I really am as stupid as I appear on this planet."

He grinned at her theatrics. "Don't say that. You're the smartest girl I've ever known. You have mysterious wisdom."

"Well, let's get out of here before I break some new religious observance. I can hardly wait to get home to our hot tub." She splayed a palm for him to lead, and followed his beautiful butt with thanksgiving as he ducked under the door tapestry in an escape to freedom. They gathered their breathers from lockers near the entrance showers and slapped on guck from a cauldron of pesticide near the tunnel opening. The buggy had a full solar charge, and the late-day sun baked the desert like a griddle. DNA-blasting rads rained down on them, spectral messengers of infertility, and Simara could imagine her cells shrieking and popping as they bounded across the sand. Cosmic rays, gamma rays—Bali was whipped daily by solar flares and too close to the sun for civilization. She could never live here as a colonist in these primitive conditions, cut off from the V-net and separated from mothership. She was only half human in this place—less than half. Digital life was her true existence, not this torture in the body, this tedium of flesh.

Sand gathered in her tunic and shorts and chafed her blistering skin raw with every movement as she sucked hot air in her breather. Her mythical sandman was at the wheel again, his skin caked and fissured with dry mud. A garish striation of pink cloud blocked the sun as it waned to the west, a brief shadow of respite. A trio of sand lizards loped across the dunes, pacing their path for a few minutes before falling behind such difficult prey. They passed the monument where Cary the pilot lay resting at peace in a foreign and dangerous land.

In time they arrived at their bunker and parked the buggy under an overhang of camouflage. Simara stretched aching legs to touch ground again and steadied herself on shifting sand. Zen plugged in his solar charger and joined her at the entrance to their nest. He blocked her path with an arm and bent to one knee to investigate the rock. He rose and surveyed the horizon. "Someone's been here," he said.

A chill of electricity stiffened Simara's spine, an urge to fight or flee. An intruder in their home? "How do you know?"

Zen pointed. "Spiderwebs are broken. I feed the star spiders here to keep a healthy colony. By now the entrance should be covered with a spoked wheel of webs."

Simara peered into the tunnel darkness. "Could they still be inside?"

"We can't chance it. Only an offworlder would be out during Vishan. Or a bounty hunter. We'll have to go."

Simara whirled to squint into the blistering desert. "Go where?"

Zen shrugged. "Find some shelter. Build a new campsite."

"Are you kidding me? Spend a night with the scorpions?"

"Keep your voice down," Zen said as he turned back toward the dune buggy. "It's you they're looking for."

A reverie of shock took hold of her for a moment, a vacancy of momentum. She stood staring into the badlands of Bali, wondering what the hell was going on. Her stepfather did not have the resources to hire a bounty hunter on an alien planet. Who else would care enough to track her down?

"Simara," Zen said as he eased his electric buggy quietly close, "get in."

She climbed aboard and scrabbled for her buckle, back on the road to nowhere. "I honestly don't know anything, Zen," she said as they sped away. "My stepfather was paid an allowance for me from a sponsor. It wasn't much. I always assumed it was just some welfare subsidy from the government. I have my work online where I live in a virtual world. No one cares about me."

"I care about you," Zen said. "I'll keep you safe."

"We can't cower in caves the rest of our lives."

"I know the terrain, the secret places. We can keep moving."

Simara shook her head. "I can't stay on Bali. I don't belong here."

"Okay, then, we'll head for the spaceport." Zen looked up to check the raging sun on the horizon. "Due west. We can get a fresh battery at Katzi's hideout and be there by morning."

Simara turned to study her benefactor. "Do we have enough cash from the salvage for a boost?"

Zen nodded his breather. "Enough for a first-class ticket to Cromeus."

"Oh, mothership, really?" A surge of delight swept up from her abdomen in a victory dance, but caught on a corner of her heart at the thought of leaving him behind. "Come with me," she blurted.

The mythical sandman paused in slow deliberation as they bounded across the dunes. His hands went white on the wheel as he grappled with possibilities. "This is my heritage. I could never leave Bali."

"Yes, you can and you will," Simara said, taking his hesitation to heart. "You weren't born on this planet. Your mother told me the truth. You were conceived in space in a genetic scrubber just like me. We're not beings of gravity. We were born weightless, floating free. We're both just visitors on this ghetto world, just passing through town in a cloud of stardust. We'll buy two tickets to Babylon and work our passage to Cromeus on the trader route."

"I don't know," he said. "I haven't priced it out."

"You could sell the buggy to Katzi and cut him a deal for the unsold merchandise."

"What would we do on an alien world? How would we eat?"

"Not a problem at all," Simara said. "We'll build a trading business together. I'll claim my adult stipend to get some scratch money, and sponsor you as my landed husband. You're valuable to the system, Zen, like salvage treasure. The government knows you'll be an active consumer someday—that's all that matters, moving goods and services from planet to planet. We'll be set up as a team. It's not hard to be successful when no one else is trying."

Zen hung his head, but seemed to be warming to the idea. "You can make it happen?"

"Oh yeah," she said with confidence, taking his assent for granted now. "I know the celestial mechanics like the back of my hand. Babylon is on a fast elliptic approaching opposition with Bali this month. That's why I'm here. Sure, you can boost to Cromeus in a couple of weeks if you accelerate all the way to the midpoint, but you can't make any money blowing antimatter out your ass like that. Smart traders tag a free ride orbiting Babylon and take their time, then boost across to Cromeus just before the long apogee into darkness. No trader worth his trash spends winter on Babylon. Trust me, this is my natural world."

The mythical sandman turned to face her as the buggy coasted. "Are you sure you want me to come along? I won't be much good up there." The mesh on his breather gave his voice a mechanical edge, but the undertone of meaning was clear. He wanted to know the truth about their relationship. He wanted some confirmation, some reason to leave everything he had ever known for a girl he had just met. What did he expect from her? Love, sex, a bonding of souls? This was not a simple business decision for him. He wanted more, but Simara had nothing to offer, nothing that she could understand. She was an empty husk without mothership, barely functional at all without the V-net, but she could not bear to lose him now.

She reached to place her palm on his naked shoulder. "I'm sure, Zen. I don't have much, perhaps nothing at all, but everything I have is yours, I promise."

PART TWO: ZEN

FOUR

Zen studied the booster rocket from across the tarmac as he parked his buggy under a solar collector at the spaceport. Emblazoned with the Transolar logo, a red shield with horns of fire, the rocket looked like a giant arrowhead with shiny wings atop a slender silver shaft, a projectile to pierce the heavens of Kiva. He had seen a launch only once, as a child on an outing with his father, and the memory seemed distant now—a rumble of thunder that quaked the ground under his sandals, a white, spouting flame of condensed energy and angry clouds of smoke. Valda had travelled regularly in space to argue politics on Trade Station along with his elected peers, an annual pilgrimage to fight for native recompense and civil rights for miners. His father had died a bitter man in the end with dreams unfulfilled, his constituents still living in slavery to the Transolar monopoly and surviving on subsistence income. The huge corporation owned a slice of every business deal and controlled all facets of society from behind a nebulous curtain of intrigue. Transolar was the only link to the human populace on Cromeus and Babylon, the sole source of space technology and the only hope for any escape from Bali.

Zen plugged his cable into the solar collector and buried the keys under a wheel for Katzi to find later, his final payment and last goodbye to his old partner. A new life in the starry heavens awaited with the girl of his dreams—an exotic skyfall princess whom he had seen naked but had yet to touch in sexual glory. Simara needed time to heal. He knew enough about that, having fled into the desert for his own time of spiritual replenishment after the death of his father. All wounds congeal over time, and old scars become less sensitive to touch. Zen grabbed a bundle of clothing from the backseat as Simara stretched her legs beside the buggy. She was beautiful even in her breather, lithe and strong, a good worker. He pulled a purple sari from the pack and draped it around her shoulders.

"Remember to cover your hair when you get through the showers," he said. "And fold a swath of material across your nose and mouth like I showed you. You're Loki, a veiled mystic."

"Don't act so nervous," she said. "We're supposed to be on our honeymoon."

He scanned the parking lot for webcam surveillance. They were probably on camera even now. "Okay, just keep your head down and follow my lead."

Simara slanted a sneer in sarcasm. "I know the plan—three steps behind, a subservient bride. No problem, I got it."

Zen sighed as he struggled with anxiety. Would the bounty hunters be watching the spaceport? Would they dare to interfere with an untouchable Loki girl? In their breathers they were still anonymous, but on the other side of decontamination they would be exposed and vulnerable. Anything could happen, and an emergency getaway would be difficult.

They walked single file to the airlock and cycled through to a locker area where they stowed their breathers. Stick-figure signs pointed women to the left and men to the right, and Zen watched Simara saunter away into a corridor buzzing with fluorescence before turning to run his own gauntlet of UV irradiation, foaming germicidal showers, and infrared dryers. Safe and sterile on the other side, his skin tingly with poison, he took a drab cellulose tunic and shorts from a fabricator and pulled them on over his money belt.

Swathed in her purple sari, Simara stepped up quietly behind him as he made his way to the ticket counter. Zen paid her little heed, confident now in his chauvinistic role.

"Two boosts to Babylon," he told the attendant, an older man with grey hair at his temples wearing a pressed-linen uniform. A red Transolar insignia on his breast pocket shone like a beacon of authority.

The man looked up, deadpan with boredom. "Palm on the pad, please."

"We're not registered," Zen said as he placed a stack of plastic bills on the counter. "I'll have to pay cash."

The attendant tipped his head and studied him with wary eyes. "Do you have ID?"

"No, I'm Zen of Valda, Star Clan."

"Governor Valda?" The man smiled with recognition at the name. "I haven't seen him in a dragon's age. How is he?"

"My father's dead. Almost two years now."

"Oh . . ." The attendant winced. "Sorry to hear. I can see his features in your face, now that you mention it." He peered past Zen's shoulder at Simara. "And this is . . ."

"My wife, Kishandra. With a K. She's Loki."

"Ahh." The man nodded. "And what's your business on Babylon?" He fingered the cash on the counter. "Did you win the lottery or something?"

"We're taking a honeymoon trip. The money was a wedding gift."

"A honeymoon on Babylon?" The man chuckled. "That's a new one—not exactly a romantic destination."

"It was as far as we could get on limited funds," Zen said with a hopeful smile. "We've never been offplanet. I can pay extra for your trouble."

The attendant swiped away the cash and began tapping a keyboard down below the counter. "Governor Valda was a good man," he said. "Zen of Valda and Kishandra of . . ."

"Pinion."

Two boarding passes spat up out of a slot. "Are you stowing any luggage or gear?"

Zen took the passes with trembling fingers. "No, we're travelling light. Keeping expense to a minimum."

The attendant returned a few bills to the counter along with a receipt slip. "You're all set to boost to Trade Station on Gate Five in about two hours. It's the only launch today. You'll connect there with *Infinity's Choice* and register for bunk selection to Babylon. Everything's on schedule, but keep an eye on the board for any updates. Happy Vishan." He smiled and looked past Zen for a token nod of religious observance to Simara. "Blessings, my lady. Pray for me."

Zen turned away with solemn dignity as Simara dutifully bowed in response. They shuffled slowly to a waiting area and picked up two bottles of carbonated water from a vending machine—past the first hurdle now and one step closer to freedom. The surrounding desert flatlands were visible through tall windows with no signs of trouble or plumes of dust from armoured vehicles. Simara slouched into a corner seat and feigned sleep behind her veil while Zen sat watching a public viewscreen—a recruitment vidi for the Transolar Security Guard, the vast corporate army that maintained authority throughout the solar system. The music was upbeat with blasts of trumpet horns and thumping drums as a deep male voice lured young men and women to sign up and see the universe: "Join the future with Transolar Security! Keeping the peace on three worlds without firing a weapon!" A promotional vidi followed about gold mining on Babylon where an apparent treasure trove of volcanic deposits lay hidden, and lucrative careers were available. Miners in orange coveralls worked without breathers, even above ground, but the craggy landscape looked forbidding and cold with white caps of snow on distant mountains.

Simara stirred after an hour to visit the restroom and find a food dispenser. She returned in a few minutes and tossed a slender tube into Zen's lap.

"What's this?" he asked as he eyed the fiery-horned Transolar shield on top.

Simara tore the end of her own tube with her teeth. "This is goop. They serve it on every Transolar station. And almost everywhere else, for that matter."

"Goop?"

"It's factory protein laced with nutrients. All you really need." She squeezed a glop of grey paste onto her tongue and masticated.

Zen followed her example and tasted unfamiliar spices, perhaps a hint of pepper.

"Pretty bland, I know," Simara said, "but it's free and ubiquitous, so get used to it." She sucked her tube empty and tucked the roll of plastic into a pocket in her shorts. "Low in sodium, low in sugar, but filled with every trace vitamin necessary for a healthy body."

Zen rubbed his tongue over his teeth and gums, trying to decide if he liked the stuff. "Do they have any other flavours?"

"No, goop is goop, but nobody starves. Specialty products in space are for people with money to burn, but that's not us at the moment. And really, solid food is not all that healthy."

Zen nodded with controlled doubt. Only water to drink and grey goop to eat? No wonder spacers were so thin. He glanced over at three passengers ambling nearby—executives with their noses buried in data tablets as they took their seats. They didn't look dangerous. "You'd better cover back up. Just a few more minutes until boarding."

Simara pulled her veil across her face with mock obedience. "Yes, husband." The mischief in her eyes made him feel better, as though their charade was an elaborate game and she knew all the rules. She was close to home and gaining confidence.

Their boarding call came over the intercom, and the small group of travellers rose and began to gather belongings. Zen's stomach roiled with unease, and he burped a taste of goop. He hoped the strange food would stay down during his first experience of rocket flight. The acceleration of thrust he understood from his early days racing buggies across the dunes, but flying was new to him and foreign. Humans were not made to fly—only dino-birds with leathery wings and pilots who crashed and died in the desert. Zen swiped two boarding passes at the launch portal and led his veiled wife down a narrow walkway into the rocket. They climbed ladders up a central tunnel to their double payload slot and crawled into cramped launch beds facing upward. The windowless compartment had no room to manoeuvre and barely room to breathe, the next row of passengers overhead reclining in similar slots like corpses in stacked coffins. Mass was a liability in this place and every centimetre expensive. The stale air reeked of polyvinyl chloride and chemical solvents, but Simara seemed not to notice the smell. Perhaps it was the natural scent of space and a reminder of home—hot circuitry and warming ceramic shielding. Viewscreens came to life inches from their faces and relayed a long and laborious series of safety procedures as Zen struggled to compose his nervousness, all sense of adventure having dissipated to dread.

A five-second countdown sounded during a rumble of pre-ignition, and Zen braced himself for violence. Thrusters exploded below him like an erupting volcano, and Simara reached to grasp his hand as gravity began to claw his bones back toward Bali amid a grinding torrent of noise. All he could think about was sex at her touch as a thunder of rockets pushed him skyward. She was a lovely girl, and he was blessed by Kiva to have and hold her so close—she was the most exhilarating person he had ever met! His cheeks flattened into his face as he clenched his jaw against brutal acceleration, travelling faster and harder than he had ever imagined. One full minute passed before a jolt shook the craft as the rocket booster disengaged, then another thrust of acceleration pressed him back into his couch as the shuttle engines ignited briefly for a trajectory correction.

Suddenly they were weightless and floating free from the clutches of gravity. With a bubble of buoyancy in his stomach, Zen looked over to see Simara convulsing in her bunk as though charged with electric shock, her eyeballs moving frenetically under closed lids and her lips quivering with half-formed speech. What in Kiva's name?

"Are you okay?" he asked, but she continued to twitch and shake in silence, her face pasty white with panic. Was she having an epileptic seizure? A brain hemorrhage? Was she dying before his eyes?

"Kishandra?" He wondered if he should dare call out for help and draw attention to her plight. Perhaps this was just a side effect of her skullrider implant, some strange digital delirium. She might be getting a wi-fi signal now that they were above the geomagnetic storms of Bali. Maybe she would snap out of it in time, if only he was patient. But what if she needed immediate medical aid in this state of crisis? What if she suffered permanent damage because of his neglect? He felt helpless, paralyzed with indecision. "Simara, can you hear me?"

"It's okay, Zen. I'm getting good bandwidth. Give me a minute to catch up on things." She kept her eyes closed as her face contorted through dozens of expressions in rapid-fire sequence. Tears slid onto her cheeks as she rode a roller coaster of emotional drama inside her mind, her body bucking with tension as the muscles in her arms and legs contracted in response to secret imaginings.

Zen exhaled with relief, cursing Kiva under his breath. He should never have said her real name out loud where it might be monitored and recorded. Simara should have warned him. How was he supposed to know anything about crazy skullrider culture? He watched her quake and convulse for a while, and finally could take it no longer. "Kishandra, wake up and tell me what's going on!"

She blinked her eyes open and smeared the weightless beads of tears pebbled on her cheeks. "Everything has changed, Zen. Our situation is much more complicated now."

"What?"

"You may be in danger from legal authorities."

"What sort of danger?"

"I can't say. The less you know, the better."

"That's never true. I need to know."

Simara closed her eyes as though ready to return to her wi-fi catatonia, but Zen grabbed her hand and fondled her palm in the most intimate manner he knew, trying to draw her back. "We're bonded in partnership. You have to tell me."

She turned to face him. "Two of my friends have been killed in an accident. Everything has changed, but I can't tell you the details without compromising your plausible deniability. Bali is the only place you'll be safe."

He continued to caress her hand in sensual union, intense in his care for her, though he had absolutely no idea what she was talking about. Plausible deniability? A serious accident? "I'm so sorry for your loss. But it's okay to share with me. I love you."

Simara frowned and pulled her hand away. "No, you can't love me."

"Why not? We're supposed to be married."

She shook her head. "I'm not a lovable person. I'm not like you, or any normal human. I have special brain enhancements known as 'omnidroid.' That's my job on the net. I fix things and streamline rootkit systems for mothership. There's just so much automated surveillance data coming in all the time, it tends to pile up in convoluted folds like dirty laundry. Information degrades into unmanageable garbage without the omnidroids keeping it straight." She held up a finger. "Just a sec," she said as her eyes rolled up under closing lids.

"So you organize things in an imaginary world?"

Simara's body shivered with a pulse of galvanic electricity. She blinked and smiled with grim forbearance. "Your naïveté is truly refreshing, Zen, but the real world is not that of the physical senses and the vagaries of consciousness. The true essence of humanity is contained within the data generated by behaviour as recorded digitally in the virtual domain. That's why my work in cryptologic management is so vitally important, both historically and prophetically. I get a kick out of it, really. There's a hardwire in my pleasure centre that reacts to order, so I feel satisfaction when I see numbers in neat rows or names in alphabetical sequence, that sort of thing. I have an octahedral array of surgical implants that allow for data evolution through several transmission nodes, building complex algorithms into architectural subsystems for mothership. Most of it is subconscious."

Zen studied his marriage partner, speechless in wonder as her eyes rolled up for another mysterious connection in virtual space. An omnidroid with skullrider technology in her pleasure centre? How could he compete with that? Simara seemed like a different person, aloof and devoid of emotion like a robot, a machine of vast intellect. How could things change so quickly?

"You can't give up on me because of some secret message from your virtual world. This is real. You and me. Right here, right now."

"I'm not giving up on you. I'm trying to protect you. Wouldn't you withhold information from Luaz to keep her from danger?"

"I don't think so."

"Your own mother? Someone you care about more than anything? Wouldn't you want to save her from harm?"

"Luaz went to jail for you. That's what family does."

Simara tilted her head as though surprised by an innovative thought. Perhaps he had finally gotten through to her. He decided to press the point. "A few minutes ago we were partners on a honeymoon trip to Babylon. You can't change that in a blink of an eye."

Simara sighed. "It pains me to think of losing you, Zen—you're so beautiful and have such a genuine spirit—but I've always prepared for that eventuality in my heart and mind. You're the only person ever to take a personal interest in me, sorry to say, but from the first moment I saw you, I could not let myself believe in love. It's too dangerous to be that vulnerable. You must understand—it's just so obvious. Love can only hurt."

"But we're legally married. We've been joined by Kiva."

Simara shook her head sadly. "Our marriage is a civil sham forced on us by circumstance and not worthy of any constraint. We both know that."

"Kiva works in mysterious ways. It's not up to us to question his methods." Zen braced himself with determination. "Give me a chance to prove myself, no strings attached. We're still on track, and nothing has changed between us. We have a good plan, *Kishandra*, and we should stick with it." He arched his eyebrows and gave her the boyish grin that had worked so well for him over the years, the one the ladies always loved, giving it his best effort now that it truly mattered. "I'll protect you."

Simara smiled with amusement as she dropped her eyes, and in that moment Zen saw that he had lost her. He noticed a softening in her stance, a relinquishment of purpose as her identity shifted. "Very well, husband," she said with smug assurance as she reached for the purple sari at her neck. She draped it overtop her head and wrapped the Loki veil across her nose. "Whatever you say." Her actions spoke louder than epic poetry. She was playing a façade, hiding behind a double veil of secrecy. She would not give him her heart, just a stage version of her splintered persona—like a computer taking a preferred route of maximum efficiency, the best strategy for the situation.

Jula had been like that as well, a woman with multiple characters, a personality for every occasion. In public she portrayed a social charade, snide and showy, at family events she affected genuine concern and empathy, but only when she was alone with him and naked in his hands did he feel connected to the foundational archive of her personality. The vulva was the secret gateway to the heart of a woman, and Zen was a dedicated master at tactile manipulation. At the height of a cyclic orgasm, gazing into the eyes of his lover as his hands worked a magic massage, Zen knew he had access to the true soul of a woman in a shared revelation of intimacy—something he might never experience with Simara, hidden to him in her kaleidoscopic virtual reality. He had won the argument, but lost the reason behind it. He had lost the girl.

Zen felt a wave of dizziness and hopelessness, a cosmic disorientation like a sand lizard spinning in shifting dunes trying to reorient to familiar landmarks. A burst of deceleration rocked them in their couches, and Zen realized that his body had adjusted to a standing position in his mind, falling back to common ground-er training. Though weightless, he now felt that he was propped upright, and as he glanced around he could see nothing to cancel that perception. A small exit sign above the closed hatch at his feet pointed left along the now horizontal floor. A tremor shook the craft as they docked with Trade Station, and lights flashed green as the portal below slid open with a hum of hydraulics. An inter-com relayed a series of instructions for disembarking, and he swal-lowed a few times to clear the pressure in his ears as air exchangers pumped in an oily smell mixed with a stench of disinfectant.

Simara tucked the trailing ends of her sari under her arms as they floated down out of their passenger slot into the central tunnel of the shuttle. Pressing back buoyant nausea, Zen gripped handrails to propel himself after her toward a flashing exit sign. The area was cramped, and every edge was rounded to prevent snags or injury, every handle recessed and every conduit inlaid. A few spots on the wall were scraped bare of paint and a few corners were burnished with wear, the craft showing age but not disrepair, the fiery Transolar insignias bright and clean.

Outside the shuttle door, they squirmed down a short orifice into a wider antechamber where uniformed clerks redirected pas-sengers into launch gates for connecting flights to Babylon and Cromeus. A male Security officer in a blue Transolar uniform pulled Simara out of line and locked her wrists in a nylon hand-cuff as another guard approached Zen with a grim expression of authority. What was this? Bounty hunters? Zen craned for view as Simara cast him a backward glance filled with dismay, but he had lost purchase for the moment and could only twist and flail for a surface to reorient his weightless body.

"Zen Valda of Star Clan?" the guard said as he offered an elbow.

Zen steadied himself against the man, thankful for something solid as his stomach roiled in free flight. He swivelled quickly to catch a glimpse of Simara as she was led away through a small tunnel above. Who were these people, corporate hirelings?

"Sir," the man said, "can you please confirm your identity?"

"I'm Zen of Star Clan," he said and pointed after Simara. "I'm travelling with my wife."

"We'll follow her this way," the guard said as he propelled them both upward into the open tunnel. He seemed to move without effort, redirecting his momentum with simple kicks and pushes here and there, always in motion, never far from any surface, but rarely touching anything around him. Zen was glad for the guidance and clung to his elbow for navigation.

"Simara Ying has been taken into custody," the guard said. "We're going to ask you a few questions under oath. Would you like to have a lawyer present?"

"What?" Zen said, squinting and clenching his brows in confusion. "No, a lawyer won't be necessary. I've done nothing wrong. What's the big problem?"

The Security officer pulled them into a bare vestibule and closed a portal below their feet. "She's under arrest for the murder of her stepfather, Randy Ying." The man studied Zen's face with professional detachment. "She led us on a merry chase through the badlands of Bali, I must say." Again the guard paused to study Zen's reaction. Every nuance was going on record now, every expression of horror and amazement as Zen's mind cartwheeled through possibilities.

Zen pressed his fingers to his forehead as he struggled to process the terrible news. What in Kiva's name? Murder? That was not a word to bandy about lightly. Could Simara have killed her stepfather in her struggle to escape sexual assault? She was certainly capable of violence with her wicked right fist, and he still had the black eye to prove it. She had admitted to fighting in self-defence. Had she kept the real truth hidden? Murder? Had Zen harboured a fugitive all this time and abetted a criminal act? Did he carry second-hand guilt? He gulped stale, oily air and turned to the Security officer. "I think a lawyer might be a good idea."

The guard bobbed his head once as though the obvious could be arranged with ease. "Wait here," he said as he kicked off toward an open portal up above. "It might take a few minutes to summon a representative."

Zen examined his surroundings with care, checking for cameras or surveillance equipment. The grey vestibule was a claustrophobic section of hexagonal conduit less than a man's height in diameter with a bench seat ringing the circumference at the midpoint and two access gates fore and aft. The upper doorway was not closed, but it might as well have been, for Zen had nowhere to hide from the constabulary on Trade Station and no escape from Transolar authority. He spent a few moments studying the circular bench seat, trying to decide which surface to rest upon. Both sides were covered with a spongy texture that might pass for austere padding. No landmarks on the walls indicated up or down, and Zen tried both directions with little comfort in the absence of gravity. He kept a hand on recessed grips in the wall at all times, fearful of flying free and flailing for purchase. Without a handhold, he could fall forever in this terrible place.

He felt a vacuum of purpose that he remembered from two years ago—the day his father shocked the family with news of his impending death from cancer. Valda had delivered the verdict without emotion to his wife and only son in the caves of Keokapul, his eyes dark with bitter foreboding. His tests had come in, and the results were not good—an acute leukemia that would take his life in matter of days, his own lifeblood turned sour and poisonous within him. Zen remembered the woeful absence in his heart at the death of his father, the sense that Kiva had failed him and life was no longer worth the ponderous effort. Stifled by depression, he could not summon anger or denial, nor trouble himself with the stages of grief. He felt only emptiness, an all-encompassing disconsolation. First his father taken to the grave, and now his bride would be plucked from his grasp, his skyfall princess shipped off to a prison colony on a planet far away.

An elderly man dove into the vestibule from above and quickly reoriented to match Zen's chosen equilibrium. He floated downward with fingertip brushes along the wall, his thick grey hair marbled with dark streaks and his face craggy around lively eyes. He wore long pants of plain cellulose and the collared shirt of a corporate professional. "My name is Genoa Blackpoll," he said in the lustrous baritone of a man accustomed to public speaking. "I knew your father and mourned his loss."

Zen ducked his chin and kept silent, feeling lost and alone like a vagabond child, wondering whom he could trust in this nightmare. His father had never mentioned a compatriot by that name.

The man settled close and faced him on the bench opposite, barely a metre away. "I'll be your public representative for a meeting with the prosecuting attorney and his empath in a few minutes."

"I have money," Zen said as he held up his boarding passes, "and two prepaid tickets to Babylon."

Genoa Blackpoll took the tickets and pressed grim lips with a nod. "Don't worry about the cost. My expenses will be reimbursed by corporate authority without prejudice to your case. I'll have these tickets refunded to your account until current matters are cleared up. This private meeting is confidential, but your upcoming interview will be under oath and recorded as court evidence. An empath will be present, a woman with biogen augmentation, a technical specialist with expertise in reading nonverbal gestures—galvanic response, muscle tone, subconscious cues. The chance of successfully portraying any falsehood will be minimal. Do you understand?"

Zen cringed at the belaboured officiousness of his tone. "I've done nothing wrong."

Genoa smiled and nodded with dutiful patience as though addressing a student. "The evidence indicates that you were travelling with Simara Ying and purchased a booster ticket for her under an assumed name. Is that correct?"

"Yes."

"Do you also wish to claim that you are partnered in marriage with the woman?"

Zen studied the man's solemn face for a moment and wondered about a winding trail of consequence. "I owe her that much."

"You owe her? How long have you known her?"

"Just a few days. She crashed in my quadrant."

Genoa frowned. "The evidence indicates that you helped her

conceal a stolen shuttlecraft from an extensive search. You could be open to a charge of wilful collusion in harbouring a fugitive during a murder investigation. In legal parlance that is known as accessory after the fact, a very serious charge."

Zen grimaced with panic. "Did she really do it?"

The public representative spread his hands and pressed thin lips below a stubbly hint of grey moustache. He had a skullrider scar on his right temple below a receding hairline. "That won't be for me to decide. The cargo ship *Legacy's Hope*, registered to Randy Ying and Vanessa Edwards, was found abandoned with the cameras destroyed and the airlock open. There were signs of a struggle and traces of his blood found in Simara Ying's quarters."

Zen nodded. "They had a fight and Simara fled for her own safety. Her stepmother died a few months previous in a vacuum breach."

"Yes, that much has been entered into record." Genoa raised an eyebrow in query and waited a few moments in silence. His eyes were black holes of night, his dilated pupils wide chasms. "If you have nothing else to add, we might as well get started." He tapped a pad on his earlobe, and two people entered the tunnel from above and floated down headfirst toward them. They reoriented in concise space with practised elegance to sit opposite Zen as Genoa slid around the wall against his thigh.

"I'm Detective Alil," said a young man with shaggy hair and dark bangs. He laid a palm toward his female compatriot, a teenager with tawny skin and a bristle of black hair. "This is Nakistra Gulong, our registered empath." The girl's face remained staid, her unwavering gaze intent, her mind a mystery of bioengineered enhancement. She carried no data pad or recording device, but

Detective Alil continued without pause. "This preliminary interview is simply to gain information related to the homicide investigation in progress. Do you submit to oath, Zen Valda of Star Clan, planet Bali?" The man had an unusual offworld accent, his words only partially formed and hurried in expression.

Zen shrugged. "I have nothing to hide."

The detective offered a reedy, businesslike smile. "Say 'I do' for the record, please."

"I do."

"Fine. Now, Zen, can you present any evidence of your formal relationship to Simara Ying?"

Zen pouted for a moment and darted his eyes at the recording empath, wondering if she could read his mind with the magic of science in her brain. He felt exposed like a blind cavefish in a glass aquarium, surrounded by skullriders with a host of invisible witnesses talking about him behind his back, analyzing his every gulping breath. "Magistrate Loring of the community cave Keokapul has entered our partnership statement into record."

"And this is a relationship known as *common proximity* in your parlance, not the result of a civil ceremony, correct?"

"Yes."

"You also have entered into a business partnership with Simara Ying to dispose of the debris from her shuttlecraft for financial gain, correct?"

"She crashed in my quadrant and granted salvage rights. We used the proceeds to pay for boost tickets."

"Yes, very good. And what became of the flight recorder from the vessel?"

Zen glanced at his representative. These people knew

everything already. What hope did he have? "I dumped the black box in Old Joe's hole in the deep trench along Zogan Ridge."

"And this was done to avoid detection?"

Zen huffed a sigh. "We take the GPS beacons out of skyfalls to keep pirates from stealing our treasure."

"Was this action taken at the behest of Simara Ying?"

"No, she was still unconscious. She almost died."

The detective glanced at his empath, but the biogen never wavered from her steady gaze. She was an automaton to duty, a robot with eyes to pierce the soul of man.

"Do you believe that Simara killed Randy Ying?"

"No," Zen said hastily. "But if she did, he must have deserved it."

"Hearsay evidence," Genoa Blackpoll interjected. "My client has no firsthand knowledge of any events prior to Simara Ying's crash in the desert."

"Granted," the detective said. "I think we're done here. Move to adjourn?"

Zen whirled to face his representative and spun off his perch into weightless space. "Where's Simara? I need to see her."

Genoa Blackpoll reached to steady him as he careened into the empath opposite. "She's being held in solitary confinement pending a court appearance on Cromeus. She's a proven flight risk and is not allowed visitors." He pulled Zen back to his seat.

"Take me with her," Zen said. "I'm guilty. I admit it."

"Strike from the record," Genoa said to Detective Alil. "No charges have been laid against my client."

Zen turned to the empath. "But you know I'm guilty. Tell them."

Genoa tugged his arm. "Ms. Gulong does not allow herself the distraction of speech while she works."

"All omnidroids are intimately available on the V-net," said Detective Alil. "You can communicate with Simara at any time." He shook his head with finality. "The Crown does not require the presence of Zen Valda for court on Cromeus. Move to adjourn?"

"Granted," Genoa said with a tight grip on Zen's arm to hold him steady. "End of session. My client is released into my care."

Zen felt a fresh wave of helplessness smother him like a dark blanket, sucking the last dregs of energy from his weary body.

Detective Alil smiled at empath Gulong. "Closed. Thank you for your excellent work, Nakistra." He turned back to Genoa and extended an arm. "A pleasure to meet you again, Governor Blackpoll." After a quick handshake, he offered an elbow up to Zen in respect to Bali culture, but Zen felt too sick to move. His wife was gone, whisked away to jail on their honeymoon, their escape plans crumbled to confetti.

Detective Alil sucked his lower lip with regret and dropped his elbow to follow Nakistra Gulong up and away through the upper portal. Genoa Blackpoll slid effortlessly around the bench to face Zen and made no move to leave.

"I've got to go after her," Zen said.

Genoa nodded grimly. "Are you sure that's what she wants?"

Zen shook his head sadly. "No, I can't be sure of anything."

"Your resources are limited," Genoa said. "You could cash out your tickets for a shuttle drop to Bali and return a rich man. Or you could trade them for a ticket to Cromeus and risk your future on this *trader* girl." The tone in his voice said that a trader girl was a base and untrustworthy creature. "You might never get back home. Either way, I will help you out of respect for your father. We served together for our constituents and culture, and Valda died before his time."

Zen scrutinized Governor Blackpoll with a critical eye. His beady eyes were framed with crinkles of age and experience, his forehead ridged into a permanent frown, the sure mark of political wisdom. He cellulose dress uniform had creased edges fresh from a fabricator. "Why would a fancy bureaucrat on Trade Station take time from his busy schedule for a meeting with a wandering peasant? Are you working for Transolar?"

Genoa pursed his lips and nodded at Zen's cynical insight. "I volunteered for the job because of my familiarity with your case, and I don't mind billing the corporate bastards every fair chance I get." He grinned as though he might gain credence from Zen for the common grounder sentiment. "My authority comes from Bali, and my ultimate duty lies with its citizens."

"And your advice to a wayward youth from the badlands?"

Genoa's face relaxed into the dour stare of a man hardened by years of toil in political trenches. "I knew your father," he repeated. "You have a worthy heritage, and your mother, Luaz, must surely miss your presence. This *trader* girl . . ." He let the disdain in his voice linger. ". . . is beyond my understanding. An omnidroid is more machine than human, a multiplicity of virtual experience not to be trifled with. My advice is to go home and count your blessings."

Zen scowled. "And if I choose not to retreat like a cactus turtle with a bump on the nose? If I choose to protect the girl I love and chase her to the end of the universe?"

Genoa chuckled and clasped his hands in his lap as his eyes

crinkled again with animation. "Then your father would be proud of your blind courage at least, may the saints of Kiva sustain us all."

"You'll help me contact Simara?"

He grinned. "Shouldn't be too much trouble, if you don't mind trading privacy for freedom. Omnidroids are omnipresent. Plug up to the V-net and you're away." He tapped his earlobe with a finger. "But you'll have to get wired to join with her. She lives in a different world."

Zen shivered at the thought of joining the skullriders in their digital nirvana. He remembered watching Simara's body convulse in connection to the nexus. Is that what it would take to follow her? Did he owe her that sacrifice to keep his reckless promise of protection? "Will I need brain surgery?"

Governor Blackpoll rubbed at his chin in deliberation. "Well, that would be optimal, and there are plenty of corporate sponsors who will fund the operation for market share. But, you know, an implant changes things, alters the brain chemistry, even if you don't choose an augmentation. The quick alternative is a simple earbug and eyescreen. It's non-invasive—just a cochlear implant and contact lens with an exterior wi-fi amp." He turned his head and pointed at a tiny light blinking on his earring pad. "You'll be able to hear Simara's voice and see her face, but you won't have any tactile or imaginative sense. You'll get no feelie from her, no background of emotion."

"That's okay. Let's do it, just the minimum to get online."

Genoa nodded. "It's probably for the best. A full-blown connection to an omnidroid stays with you forever." He rolled his eyes up under closing lids to peer inside his skullrider forehead. A hint of a smile flirted at the corners of his mouth, and his lips moved in pre-formed speech similar to the lip twitches Simara had shown while working. He opened his eyes. "Your appointment is tomorrow. Get a good sleep. I've sent for a pill to make sure you're well rested."

That was it? So quick! Life was a whirlwind up here. Meetings were fast and business almost instantaneous. "Where will I stay? Are there any vacant apartments on Trade Station?"

"No, you'll sleep right here." Genoa floated upward and palmed a sensor pad that Zen had taken for decoration. A launch couch with sensor-studded armrests and comfy padding tipped down out of the wall on whirring hydraulics, as lights dimmed for evening repose. "You'll have to buckle up in a room this big."

Zen tipped his head back at the strange notion. "Big?"

"This is a double," Genoa said with a sly smile. He tapped another sensor and an opaque hologram filled the area at bench height where Zen's legs disappeared into a grey partition dividing the meeting space.

"Whoa," Zen said as he launched up out of the hologram and floated free. The acoustics of the room had altered to a quieter tone to deaden his exclamation. He windmilled for a moment in panic until he hit the wall, then lurched to latch thankfully against the Transolar launch couch. He pulled himself up and buckled in. So this was home for now.

"Your appointment tomorrow is at A5:15 on Level 4, medical clinic #259, with Nurse Stavos." He began tapping a keypad on the armrest. "I'll program that into your couch for you."

Zen watched Governor Blackpoll with chagrin. "Is it day or night now? I've lost track of time."

"Trade Station stays in perpetual shadow in synchronous

orbit around Bali to avoid the solar flares from Signa, so there is no day or night here. We divide time into three duty shifts designated ABC, seven hours to a working cycle, 60 minutes to an hour. It's C2:52 now, so your appointment is in nine hours and twenty-three minutes."

"How will I find the clinic?"

"You can access a map at any doorway by pressing here." At his touch, a schematic pattern became visible near the doorframe showing a complicated grid with trails branching off the main shafts like follicles on slender stems. Each hair in the labyrinthine maze had numbered bumps that Zen took to be hexagonal housing quarters similar to his own. There appeared to be no open areas or main thoroughfares, and *space* was a misnomer because there was none to spare!

"We're here on the docks at Level 1," Genoa said as he pointed, "so you'll move outward three levels to the clinic."

"Got it," Zen said as he calculated his route and noted the time C2:52 displayed in the lower right-hand corner. "Clinic 259 on Level 4 at A5:15."

"Very good. Blessings for your evening, then," Genoa said in typical Bali custom. He swung around the doorframe with ease and floated away.

A few minutes later, a green light blinked above the open portal, and a young boy poked his head in. "Package for Zen Valda?"

"Sure." Zen launched himself upward and crashed awkwardly against the doorframe as the courier eyed him with curiosity. Zen pressed his palm on the proffered sensor pad and was rewarded with a red flash and bad beep of negation. He felt like a peon from a primitive planet, an unregistered vagabond, but the delivery boy shrugged with disinterest and tapped in some sort of bypass code as he glided away. Zen opened the package to find tubes of grey goop and pouches of water, his breakfast, lunch, and dinner. His stomach ached at the thought of such minimalist fare, and he longed for the crystal caverns of his youth and a spicy, snake-meat stew. He found a blue sleeping pill in a blister pack and swallowed it with welcome relief, wishing he had a mug of honey mead to wash it down and calm his rattled nerves. There was no chance he could sleep without chemical aid in his state of trauma, trapped and alone in this foreign world. He had gambled with fate and lost everything.

Zen decided to double the calculated allowance for travel time to his appointment, thinking he would probably get lost along the way. He hugged the wall of the tunnel, crawling carefully from handhold to crevice, fearful of falling. According to his study of the schematic, he was moving up, but he struggled to hold that view without the solid anchor of gravity below his feet. He could just as easily be travelling down or sideways, and his stomach seemed to gyrate in all directions at once.

A man dressed in standard cellulose approached from ahead and drifted headfirst by him with his hands in constant motion and fingertips tapping the wall. "B'well," he said as he passed. "B'well," another man repeated as he squeezed by Zen from behind, touching his leg and shoulder on the way. Spacers flew by with natural ease—"B'well. B'well."—always in motion, never pushing, never pulling, and they thought nothing of fondling each other with open palms in passing to maintain equilibrium and preserve momentum.

Zen tried with halting success to mimic their fluid motion in weightless space, hopeful that an edge was always near in the constant confinement of the tunnels, fearful of floating free into helplessness. He was a slave to momentum in this place and couldn't manage a full stop without crashing into something, preferably inanimate.

With aching muscles and two purple bruises on his right arm, he arrived on Level 4 and found his appointed destination with 259 printed both above and inverted below the open portal. He ducked his head in. "Am I too early?"

A woman in a white uniform turned to him with wide eyes below a fashionably shaggy mop of blonde hair tufted with blue highlights. "Welcome, Zen Valda. I'm Nurse Stavos." She touched an identification patch that featured a prominent red cross. "Come in. I'll be ready for you in just a moment."

"B'well," Zen said as he floated down toward her, targeting the single launch couch that hung against the wall. The clinic was barely a closet with no room for error.

"May you be well also, sir," she said with careful enunciation as she reached for a floating pouch of instruments. "You're scheduled for a virgin cochlear installation without modifications and your chart shows right-handed preference. Is that correct?"

"Yes." Zen twisted in the air to avoid a collision with her hip. She was unusually buxom for a spacer and presented an attractive hourglass target. "Oops, sorry."

The woman took hold of his arm and deftly turned him so that he fell into the couch without injury or transfer of momentum. She studied him with interest, tapping the closet walls periodically with her fingertips to maintain equilibrium. "You've never connected to the V-net?"

"No. Is that bad?"

"Most installations are done in early childhood when neuro-plasticity is optimal in the brain. Do you have any experience whatsoever with virtual media?"

"Not really. I'm from Bali."

"Yes, I see that on your chart." She didn't hold a chart, but she wore a skullrider amp on her left ear and probably had his life story on fast-forward.

"I'm a bit nervous about the whole thing." The clinic was much smaller than he had expected, just another blister off the tunnel, and the woman was much more beautiful than he had imagined. Her creamy skin had likely never seen the sun, and her azure eyes reminded him of Jula back home. Her lips were painted a bright ruby colour to match the red cross on her breast.

"Yes, I see that also. Don't worry. I'll be here for you through-out your transition to guide you every step of the way. There will be no real danger at any time." She raised a small tube and twisted out a tiny brush. "I'll just dab this analgesic on your earlobe to pre-pare the site for implant. You don't mind if I touch you during the procedure, do you? I know your culture has certain *sensitivities*." She paused to assess him. "So, is it okay?"

Zen shrugged. "Sure."

She steadied herself by carefully resting a palm on his shoulder and hovered close in front of him as she brushed cool liquid on his right earlobe. Her flowery perfume mingled with the sharp, medicinal smell of the analgesic, and her large breasts punched out at him from behind thin cellulose, her mature body untainted by gravity. Zen swallowed with discomfort at her touch and peered nervously past her at an anatomical chart on the wall showing skinless musculature.

An intimate hand on the shoulder meant nothing here, and the woman had not strayed from a professional demeanour, but his hormones seemed not to recognize the innocence of her gesture. He began to perspire. "What was your first name again?"

The nurse slid her medicine stick back in its bottle and rummaged in her pouch as Zen's ear tingled and went numb. She turned to him with a small electronic device gripped in a pair of needle-nose pliers. "I didn't say, but it's Nancy." She flashed perfect teeth and bent to begin working on him, probing deep inside his aural canal. "It's a traditional name from Earth. Sounds a bit archaic, I know, but my parents still love the old feelies from home, nostalgia for the lost world, you know? They're first-gen colonists from before the embargo, very staid and conservative."

"I think your name sounds wonderful."

"Well, thank you. It's kind of you to say so." She made a cracking sound near his ear, and a pop followed like a burst of air. "There you go." Nurse Nancy straightened and smiled. "Your earbug installation is complete."

"So quick?" *So quick?*

She dabbed a tissue on his earlobe and showed him a spot of blood. "Your DNA is being sequenced, and your voice is being digitized."

"What do you mean?" *What do you mean?*

"Now open your eyes wide. Stay completely still for a second." She leaned forward with a pointing finger and touched a contact lens onto his right eye. "Welcome to the grid, Zen Valda. I always love this part."

"What's that noise?" *What's that noise?*

"We're running an initial biofeedback loop to set up your

voice register. The next thing we need is a primary fingerprint."
She held up a forefinger. "This will be the index finger on your
right hand. Place it on your sensor pad in the most comfortable
manner like this." She touched the skullrider amp on her earlobe,
and waited for Zen to follow her example. He felt a flat metal disc
on his ear and reached around behind with his thumb to feel the
stud that had been punched through his skin.

"This is your login identity for all credit and debit trans-
actions on the V-net," she said. "The subtle variations in your
other fingerprints and thumbs will give you nine more sign-ons to
program for peripherals. Remember that your right hand will be
most comfortable for your basic needs."

Zen held up his hands and studied his spread fingers.
"Really?" *Really?*

"Your next most important login will be for Help mode.
Normally we use the opposite pinkie finger for this, which is bit
awkward at first, but after a while you won't need Help, so you
don't want to tie up your main fingers. You've no doubt heard the
expression 'spinning with his pinkie in his ear'?"

"No, I don't think so." *No, I don't think so.*

Nurse Nancy tilted her head at him. "Starry heavens, you
really are a virgin. Okay, just put your left-hand pinkie finger on
the sensor like this and say 'Help Login.'"

"Help Login." *Help Login.*

"Your inception will be gradated to a widening sphere over the
next few hours. First you will connect just to your immediate vicin-
ity, and then you'll widen out from there." ::DO YOU HEAR ME?::

Her voice sounded inside his head, deep and lustrous. "Yes."
Yes.

"Good." Nurse Nancy scrolled her eyes up into her forehead as her lids closed like shutters. ::THIS WILL BE CHANNEL 1. DO YOU SEE THE INDICATOR?::

Zen glanced around the room. "No." *No.*

::THAT'S OKAY. YOU'LL SEE IT WHEN YOUR BRAIN ADJUSTS. DON'T WORRY ABOUT THE DETAILS FOR NOW. YOU'LL DISCOVER THINGS BY IMMERSION AND ADVENTURE. WELCOME TO THE V-NET.::

"This is weird." *This is weird.*

Nurse Nancy opened her eyes and tucked her pliers back in her pouch. "Congratulations, Zen Valda. Your DNA documentation has been successfully uploaded and installation creds have been downloaded to your account."

"That's it?" No echo now, no explanation.

Nurse Nancy seemed smug. "Would you like to join me for dinner? A grounder like you must find grey goop quickly tedious."

"Um, I guess so," Zen said, "if we're done."

Nancy ducked her chin. "Actually, I'm required to monitor you for the next twelve hours to check for side effects during your transition. I'm still on the payroll, but it's more fun to socialize at the same time. No harm, no foul?" ::IT'S OKAY. I'M HERE TO HELP YOU.::

Zen shrugged in helpless fascination. "Sure."

Nurse Nancy tapped the wall and swung a provocative hip swathed in white cellulose. "Follow me, good sir."

Zen blinked at a ghost in his peripheral vision, an image of his own face as seen and transmitted by Nancy Stavos. She seemed to be acting a bit flirty now that business was out of the way. Or maybe not. Perhaps it was just his imagination. He wasn't sure what was normal in this strange place. Zen kicked off after her heels as she floated away down the hall, conscious now of just how slow and clumsy he must appear. He felt an urgent need to put on a show for this beautiful woman, to impress her somehow as she drifted ahead of him and widened the gap.

::Hurry up, slowpoke.::

"Is this thing on all the time?" he yelled up to her. Other sounds became apparent in his background of experience. A male voice, two male voices—*question the aerodynamics of his presentation*—*following a predetermined migratory pattern across the desert*—and then something that was clearly an advertising jingle—*an apple a day keeps the doctor away.*

Nancy Stavos dragged her palms along the wall to give up her momentum and turned to face him as he clambered haltingly down to her. She smiled. "Are you climbing or falling?"

Zen peered back at the tunnel behind, trying to orient himself to the schematic map in his memory. Strange ghosts clogged up the edges of his vision, camera views from distant places, stray optical data transmitted to his prosthetic lens. "Falling, I guess."

::You are such a precious specimen.:: Nancy pointed to her earlobe. "You'll learn to filter out extraneous material as you get acclimated. The more data you view, the more creds you build up, and you earn bonus points for user-generated material. Soak it up for now. Have fun. C'mon, I'll teach you how to fly." She reached for his hand and held it tight. "Just relax, honey. I'll drive."

::You trust me, don't you?::

"Sure," Zen said, feeling a sweaty rush of sexual energy at her touch. Was she coming on strong to him, or was he misreading her signals? Had he gone completely crazy?

"Put your arm around my waist," she said. "Go ahead. I don't bite. Okay, now keep your arms tucked in and just get the passive feel of it with me." Nancy kicked off a conduit and flew them recklessly forward toward the next bulkhead as Zen stiffened his body and stifled an urge to squirm away from the oncoming collision. With the tips of her fingers, Nancy caressed the walls, plucking up momentum like treasure and subtly spiralling their trajectory, slowly spinning them away from danger. She had no up or down, no restrictions of perception, and the pulse of life in her writhing body made Zen throb with desire, his hormones raging out of control now.

He craned his neck to keep a forward view and tried to study the mechanics of their movement to calm his nerves—anything to distract him from this gorgeous woman in his arms! He analyzed target trajectories and tried to envision course corrections as a series of overlapping scenes crowded his view. Was he picking up signals from surveillance cameras, or was this actual human vision transmitted from contact lenses like his own? "What are all these images? Who are these people?"

"Never mind them for now. Focus on the moment. Don't be so stiff." Nancy slid an arm around his waist. "Loosen up a bit. Embrace the chaos. Let's try it tandem. Use your right-hand fingers, and I'll use my left. Be subtle. Relax. Push, don't drag."

Together they veered down the tunnel, overcompensating from side to side but keeping a relatively steady pace, and voices sounded in Zen's earbug as they passed closed portals along the way—*crackdown on illegal fermentation poisoning our delicately balanced biosphere—you can't do better than the logical invincibility of robotic hardware for a clean experiment—*

"This is a good speed," Nancy said and pointed ahead. "Remember that people come out of these doors. Collisions happen all the time. You'll see a green light flash around a portal in use, but you may get only a few seconds' warning. Keep close to the wall in case you have to drag. Oncoming traffic stays on your left, and pass only on the left or up, okay?"

Images continued to play across his field of vision, blocking his sight with bewildering perceptions from elsewhere, some of them fabricated like anime advertisements. Zen grunted and clenched his teeth against dizziness as he tried to squint past holographic ghosts for an unobstructed view—*any variant description of quasi-finite schemes must satisfy Zariski's original main theorem for birational morphisms*—

"Okay," Nancy said, "let's practise slowing down. On the count of three we'll drag our palms. One, two, three."

Zen stabbed out his hand and clutched at the next conduit, which caused them to swing like monkeys on a tree branch and spin into a backward somersault. He let go with a yell and flailed his arm in a frantic circle as his stomach muscles clenched with vertigo.

::DON'T PANIC! HOLD ON TO ME!::

Nancy Stavos pushed, curled, kicked, and danced in Zen's grappling arm as they spun together in a whirlwind embrace. Zen dragged his elbows and knees with every stray contact in hope of stability as they slowly gave up their momentum to friction and ground to a halt. Nancy laughed. "You are a crazy stuntman. And so strong! God!"

Zen punched out a wheezing exhalation and gasped an inward breath—*opportunity for sacrificial expiation presents a poignant intellectual conundrum*—Holy Kiva! This was too much for him! He buried his forehead in his palms. "I can't stand all this noise in my head. And all these mysterious vidis playing at random. I think I'm going insane!"

Nancy bent forward and kissed him on the cheek. "I'm right here, Zen. Everything else is an illusion. Focus on me. We're almost there. My apartment is just around the corner. Do you like apple? It's the latest rage."

Zen lowered his hands to study her pretty smile and sensitive eyes as he struggled to calm himself. "Uh, sure." He felt too embarrassed to admit any further scarcity of knowledge. What was apple?

Nurse Nancy thrust up her shoulder as she turned. "C'mon."

Minutes later they entered her home cubicle, what Genoa Blackpoll had dubbed a "double." The walls were draped with purple tapestries that billowed gently to the vacuum suction of air vents. A standard launch couch hung down from the wall draped with a woven blanket of cross-hatched design, and pink pillows on tethers floated like party balloons. A blast of freshness wafted in his nose, the same scent she carried with her always, but more concentrated here. She imbued this place with her femininity.

"Do you like it?"

The space was crowded with strange, ghostlike images and panoramic vistas from distant lands—*protests against a suspected omnidroid data monopoly continued on the streets of New Jerusalem today*—He blinked away impossibilities as he darted his gaze around the room in search of respite. "Sure."

"You can probably tell I belong to the Way." Exuberance shone in her face like a religious ecstasy.

"The way?"

"The Way," she said. "The natural Way, you know?"

The puzzlement in her eyes indicated that he obviously did not know, but Zen simply shrugged, weary now of being an idiot. "Sure." He ducked out of the path of a charging man in a spandex exercise outfit.

Nurse Stavos frowned and touched his arm. "It's okay, Zen. They're not physical. Don't get lost in virtuality. Rise above it. You can do this." She led him gently to the couch and landed him like a beached cavefish. "Have a seat and relax."

Zen closed his eyes, but a kaleidoscope of drama continued to parade across his eyescreen—*weak version of the first immersion theorem of differential topology is due to the transversality of two-dimensional manifolds intersecting generically in zero-dimensional space*—and he clutched his head and pulled at his hair, his brain a battlefield of noise and strange visions. "I can't process all this information! Turn it off!"

Nurse Nancy bent close to study him with clinical care. "Don't give up on me, Zen. You can get through this. Soon it will all be optional, just passing fancies."

"I can't tell what's real. I've got to get away." He flinched as a dark object fell across his field of vision like a meteor. He gazed past her at fleeting images and swung his eyes around the room in search of stability—*bringing the future to life with enough bandwidth for all your peripherals*—

Nancy took his hand and warmed it between gentle palms. "Stay with me, honey. We can work it out together. That's why I'm here. You'll get the hang of the net once your brain starts to filter out the sidebars. You know what they say: 'Tune it, tone it, and claim it.' That's the beauty of the V-net. Everyone creates their own reality, customized to individual perceptions and internalized assumptions, with advertising tailored to specific desires. You open your own windows and set your own parameters. C'mon, try to concentrate on my face for a minute. I'm all you need for now. Can you see me clearly?"

Her bright blue eyes filled his view and dispelled phantoms from the periphery. Her plump cheeks came into focus, her narrow nose and delicate chin. She pursed painted lips and blew him a dramatic kiss with a noisy smack. "Be here now," she said. "Smell my neck. I'm trying a new aroma this week—*Fantasius Trinity*. Do you like it?"

Zen poked his nostrils forward and inhaled. "Nice." He had noticed her enticing fragrance all along, but now it seemed overwhelming, a heavy, flowery musk. All his sensations were heightened, his awareness intensified, his skin tingly like an itch that needed a good scratch, and in his preoccupation with this emergent sensorium, the boisterous background noise seemed to dissipate for a moment into a purr of soft static. "Thanks, I think I'm starting to feel better."

"Good." Nancy pressed out a slow and calming sigh. "We'll continue with this line of therapy." She pulled out a tray from the wall beside his head and selected a foil-wrapped cube. "Here, try this." She cracked the seal with a pink fingernail and offered it forward.

Zen took the cube and sniffed—something fruity, somewhat acidic. He began to peel back the foil covering. "What is it?"

"Apple." Nurse Nancy smiled with expectancy. "The natural Way promotes bodily health and homeopathic balance. We embrace physical and social systems in defiance of ubiquitous digital life. That's our creed. And taste is the most transcendent of all natural senses."

Zen popped the food in his mouth and tested it with his tongue—cool and mushy, tart and tangy. "Wow!"

Nancy thrust her palms out like an excited youngster. "I know, right?"

Zen bobbed his head as he chewed. "That's very unusual."

"Try to be mindful of the experience of taste. Focus your attention with me, okay?" She poked through her tray and selected another morsel, cracked the seal. "This one is good, and very expensive. Tangerine."

"That's a citrus," Zen said.

Nancy nodded. "It grows on trees. Have you ever seen a tree?"

"Yeah, sure," Zen said as he sampled the new taste, thankful finally for the opportunity to show some expertise. "They have hard trunks, leafy branches. Trees are awesome."

Nancy studied him happily. ::YOU ARE SUCH A MUSCULAR HUNK.::

Zen frowned as he saw a clear image of himself in the mirror of her mind's eye. His brown skin and bulky shoulders seemed foreign in this place.

Nancy ducked her gaze to her tray as though caught in an impropriety. "Sorry, that wasn't very professional. I know you must fight gravity all the time. I have great respect for your native culture."

"No, that's fine." Zen waved an arm in dismissal. "I'm thankful for your help. You're an exhilarating woman. What else do you have?"

"Oh, I have everything," she said as she peered through her collection. "The indulgence of taste brings us back to our true animal nature. Humans are creatures of flesh, wonderful miracles of biological complexity. We're not just data on the wings of light. We have a natural heritage of sensuality."

Zen tasted cubes of curried chicken and smoked salmon alternated by raspberry candies and mango fruit, with Nurse Nancy hovering weightless above his lap, feeding him ceremonially by hand and telling stories of gastronomical delight. Finally he held up a halt sign to show his limit.

"Well, I have been talking your earbug off, and you're so shy. Tell me something about food on Bali. What's the best-kept secret of culinary delight? What do you serve to impress the ladies?"

Zen thought for a moment. "Well, you take the skin off a chicken, and cook it separately with oil and spices—terrion, tamil, and ginseng, whatever you have in supply. Then you drape it back over the roasted carcass when you serve. It's like a flavoured parchment."

Nancy scrunched up her nose with incredulity. "Really? Skin soaked in animal fat?"

"Yeah, natural grease and fat. It's supposed to be an aphrodisiac."

"Wow, that's peculiar. I love it! Tell me about religion on Bali. I've heard wondrous things. Is it true that cults arose from stranded colonists eating hallucinogenic mushrooms in the deep caves?"

"Uh, no, that would be a variant sect for sure. Bali is a big planet with lots of different outposts, but all denominations serve the desert god Kiva."

"Do they still use mushrooms as a sacrament?"

"Some shamans do, I suppose, on rare occasions. The fungus is generally smoked among the darker segments of society—not officially recognized. Kiva is not a god of ceremonies and performance. He lives in the hearts of his people and brings seasons of refreshment."

"That just blows my mind. I love it. Do you cavort around fires burning free oxygen?"

Zen chuckled. "Most people have geothermal power nowadays, but we still have campfires during winter festivals when it's cold at night. Children sit in a circle around the flames and sing songs of lore. The adults stay up and party till dawn with dancing and music."

"Oh, my God, you're everything we dream about in the Way!" Nancy eyes were wide beacons of awe. "You tower upright on dry land with open sky above your head, the king of all creatures. Have you ever caught a live animal and killed it for food?"

"I have," Zen said, "but it's not as nice as you imagine."

"Amazing," Nancy Stavos gushed. "Try this one last thing for dessert." She selected a dark bean from her tray and crushed it between her teeth. She bent forward as she chewed and placed her lips on his in a slurpy kiss. Her tongue probed in his mouth and swirled a wondrous taste inside him, a pungent mix like peppermint and cinnamon, acrid and insistent on his tastebuds. Her perverse sensuality overwhelmed Zen like a tidal wave of eroticism, and time seemed to stretch as she lingered with shocking intimacy, swirling a minty blessing on his palate. Finally she released him and smacked her lips with relish.

Zen gasped and sucked a breath. "What is it?"

"Juva ben," she said. "It's a recreational antipsychotic. You'll need it to sleep the first night. Don't worry. I'll help you along. Would you like a drink?"

His tongue tingled with spice, swollen with exotic chemicals, and he swallowed with difficulty. "Do you have honey mead?"

Nancy laughed. "No, nothing fermented. Just allkool, white or dark."

"White would be fine."

"Anything to mix? I have cherry, lime, lemon, um . . ." She thumbed through a selection of tiny pouches. ". . . sunrise, pear, margarita . . ."

"Lemon would be great." His voice sounded far away and foreign, buzzy with a change in atmospheric pressure. "That was weird."

"I know, right?" She tore open a pouch with her teeth and dumped it into a plastic bottle of clear liquid, shook it like a maraca. "Open up." She was brushing weight on his thighs now, hovering sideways above him with a prominent red cross bulging out toward his face. She squirted lemon liquor on his tongue, succulent and sweet, and his throat burned pleasantly with alcohol as he swallowed.

"A little sedation will take the edge off the juva ben," Nancy said. "You had me worried for a while there, but I think you're over the hump. Stay in this moment. You're doing great." She tipped the remaining allkool into her mouth, tossed the empty container in the open drawer, and began to unbutton her uniform. She pulled off thin cellulose and floated her shirt away. No bra, and why bother with no gravity to drag her down? "I'm so glad they chose me to monitor your transition. I really like you."

A sudden flurry of peripheral images framed his view of her, and a babble of noise erupted in his ear—*two immersions of one manifold are regularly homotopic if and only if they have the same total curvature—proof that any ratio better than a constant can never be achieved by a polynominal time algorithm—*

"Don't go back, Zen. I'm here for you. Focus your attention." Nancy took his hands and placed his palms against her nipples. Her skin felt warm and soft, but his body seemed to be moving down a vortex at great speed, a flashback of recent momentum in the tunnels, a rush of strange sensation. He felt dizzy and sweaty with exuberance, and his vision seemed to zoom in and out of focus, his depth of perception on a yo-yo string. All he could trust for sure were the luscious globes of flesh in his face. He kneaded them with delicacy.

"That's good," Nancy murmured as she wiggled against his thighs. "This is natural reality. Concentrate on the tactile sensation. I know you Bali boys are good with your hands."

—elegant body of work sure to manifest in your midbrain—

"You're pretty good yourself," he said with a dry slur. His voice seemed to come from great distance, across desert dunes of shifting sands and improbable horizons.

After a few moments of tenderness, Nancy kicked off her sandals and slid out of her pants with gymnastic efficiency, fluid and graceful, poised and comfortable in her weightless world. Her naked body was shorn bare like polished calcite crystal that had never seen the sun, a statue of loveliness from a wet dream far away. She rested her palms on Zen's shoulders and bent to kiss him again, her mouth rich with juva ben and her teasing tongue delightful. Her lips moved from his mouth to his cheek to his ear and moaned with pleasure as his hands found soft purchase between her legs and began the performance magic he knew so well from home. He fondled the gateway to her soul with a gentle massage, and the sound of her murmurs lingered in a blur of psychedelic sensation, rising and falling like a kite sailing in the wind, up and away, up and away.

"I am so horny," she said and thrust her hips against his busy fingers. "I think I'm going to climax." She shuddered with a spasm of quiet release and went limp in his embrace. "Wow, everything they say about Bali boys is true!"

They closed their eyes and drifted together, and the gentle sound of Nancy's breathing was like a rustling tree branch in the wind on the terraced gardens of Keokapul.

—*the multilayer feedforward architecture gives neural networks the potential to be universal approximators among continuous functions on compact subsets of Rn under mild assumptions of activation function*—A kaleidoscope of data began to play in Zen's mind, a prismatic unfolding of a mechanical flower with leaves like blades of broken glass. He studied the mental image with a strange detachment, passive in blissful observation and finally unafraid of the V-net. It seemed that he could watch without perplexity, and choose where to place his attention among the myriad channels of inquiry. He could see a vast library of information, a mountain of evidence, the complete summary of human collective experience and the final, timeless obliteration of self.

Nancy snorted back to wakefulness. "Oh, I zoned out, sorry." She shook her head and brushed shaggy blonde hair back from her forehead. "That was wonderful, Zen. What can I do for you? I mean, is it my turn?"

*—this method of reducing high-order derivatives to combinatorics is used extensively in quantum field theory to reduce arbitrary products of creation and annihilation operators to mathematically manageable sums—*Zen blinked away V-net visions to focus on her pretty face, her cheeks rosy with enthusiasm and her azure eyes bright with promise. "Well, that's the way we do it back home on Bali."

Nurse Nancy floated up from his lap and reached to tug at his waistband. Zen shifted to help her as she pulled off his cellulose pants, and he flexed blood into his penis for presentation. "Wow," she said, "that is something! Is that what gravity does? And so wild and unshaven." She flicked her eyes to his face. "I mean, it's great, you know. So *natural*." The stress in her voice sounded hoarse with desire, and Zen felt mutual emergence of passion as she hovered above him with a gaze of adoration. She seemed like a primeval woman, iconic in beauty, and time seemed to slow to a lazy, graceful river of abandon. "Let me show you how we do it where I come from," she said as slid her buxom body down onto him.

SIX

Bubbly fog filled Zen's brain when he woke. A gnawing hunger coiled in his stomach like a vile and guilty serpent as he struggled to piece together remembrance out of a hazy landscape of drunken bliss. He peered over the armrest of his launch couch to see Nurse Nancy's bare foot dangling from a couch facing opposite on the mirror side of the double room. He listened to the gentle purr of her sleeping respiration. So that much was true.

Panic welled in his chest as his situation came into stark focus—by all the saints of Kiva! What had he done? What would Simara think? How could he face her after sleeping with another woman? He was supposed to be in a relationship! He was supposed to be pretending marriage! He looked around at the decorative tapestries and trappings of femininity, wondering how he might find his way back to his assigned quarters, feeling adultery like a great weight of pressure.

"Help login," he said as he touched his pinkie finger to his earlobe. "Help mode. Where am I?"

Level 7, #33, residence of Nancy Stavos—limited precognition in clinical studies—followed by increased humidity throughout the

Southern Beach district—a conjecture first proved independently by observing that Laurent polynomials and their constants satisfy strict recursion relations—all these perplexing voices and strange ideas! Where did they come from? His consciousness seemed to have expanded while he slept. An inner world with vast parameters had grown up around him, borderless realms of information extending out into space itself.

::CAN YOU HEAR ME, ZEN?:: Simara's voice sounded rich in his mind like a pillar of stability in a jungle of background chatter.

"Simara, is that you?"

::YES, I'M HERE. DID YOU GET A BRAIN IMPLANT?::

"No, just an earbug, but I seem to be having trouble with the filters. Are you okay?"

::I'M LOCKED IN A LAUNCH COUCH ON THE TROOPSHIP ADAM'S INSPIRATION. WE'RE BOOSTING FOR CROMEUS IN THREE HOURS! MY STEPFATHER WENT MISSING, AND THEY'RE TRYING TO PIN A MURDER RAP ON MY ASS.:: The blunt energy of her V-net voice was shocking compared to the careful articulation of her spoken words. This was Simara unleashed and angry as hell—surely proof of her innocence!

"I heard some of the details from legal authorities. They threatened me, but haven't pressed any charges. Is there anything I can do to help you?"

Static sounded in his ear, an untranslatable exhalation. ::PROBABLY NOT. BUT IT'S GREAT TO HEAR YOUR VOICE. I WAS WORRIED THAT WE WOULDN'T GET AN OPPORTUNITY TO SAY GOODBYE.:: —*powerful counter-clockwise rotation in the Aspian Sea is creating a type 2 tropical hurricane with high levels of precipitation along the eastern seaboard north of New Jerusalem—toward*

understanding the nature of primitive aboriginal religion—simple ele-
gance of the cosmological theory betrays a scarcity of detail—

"I'm coming after you, Simara. I'll buy a ticket for the flight."

::No, you won't. Don't be silly. We don't have
to pretend partnership any longer. You've got all
the money from the salvage. Go home and be rich.::—
humidity will reach a low of 20 today across the landlocked basin—of
course she never should have looked inside the emerald castle—

Zen choked on a pain of sorrow in his throat. He couldn't bear
the thought that she didn't want him, that she might refuse him. "I
can't give up on you—on us. You mean too much to me."

::Don't lie to yourself, Zen. I know you're
sleeping with Nurse Stavos. You're looking at her
fat ass right now.::—*the theory of celestial guidance for internal*
chakra has fallen gradually into disrepute—real progress demands a rise
above the genetic blueprint, a qualitative leap in genomic architecture—

His spine clamped up like a vice, a steel trap closing on his
heart. He looked over at Nancy's dangling bare foot. Was there any
point in denying the truth? "How do you know that?"

::Your earbug has digital positioning, of course.
What do you think? Anyway, she was broadcasting her
conquest the whole time, the pervy girl. Not on a
public channel, but I'm omnidroid, remember? I see
everything.::—*an apple a day keeps the doctor away—*

Zen closed his eyes and dropped his forehead into his palms.
He was such an idiot! "Forgive me," he whispered. "Give me another chance."

::A chance for what? I'm not angry with you,
Zen. Far from it. You finally lost your virginity,

SO WHAT THE HELL, GOOD FOR YOU. IT'S NOT LIKE WE HAD ANY AGREEMENT ON CELIBACY. I'M JEALOUS OF MS. STAVOS, ACTUALLY. SHE REALLY ENJOYED HERSELF. ALL THE THINGS SHE THOUGHT ABOUT YOU—WHEW, PRETTY HOT. BUT SHE'S OLD, SHE'S TWENTY-NINE. DIDN'T YOU NOTICE? SHE'S A CAREER WOMAN AND A DEDICATED CULTIST. SHE'S NOT GOING BACK TO A CAVE ON BALI WITH YOU.::

"I'm not going back to Bali," he said. "I can't."

Nancy stirred in her launch couch below and looked up at him. "Are you okay, Zen? Are you online?"

He pushed a warning palm to keep her quiet as she wrapped herself in a pink sari and floated toward him. His heart began to pound with alarm. Two women at once and nowhere to run. Nancy looked mature now and plain without her makeup, and Simara's voice was like a slashing knife in his brain. ::ONLY A FOOL WOULD FOLLOW AN ACCUSED MURDERER INTO A MUDSLIDE OF CONDEMNATION. DON'T BE THAT MAN, ZEN, DON'T DO IT. GO HOME AND BE SAFE. YOU DON'T KNOW ME. I LIVE IN A VIRTUAL WORLD, PARTNERED TO A MACHINE, YOU UNDERSTAND? MOTHERSHIP WON'T BE ABLE TO PROTECT YOU. SHE GAVE ME NO WARNING OF THIS CONSPIRACY, AND I'M NOT SURE WHY. JUST STAY CLEAR UNTIL I CAN FIGURE IT OUT. GOODBYE, ZEN. THANKS FOR SAVING MY LIFE.::

"Kiva will help us," he said in a final weak protest. "We can still be together."

"I can help you," Nancy said as she curled into his lap. "Are you having a bad dream?"

::WHAT DO I HAVE TO SAY TO SET YOU FREE, ZEN?

Your silent god is not going to help us. There are a billion galaxies out in space, a hundred billion planets. Do the math. Why would the creator of the universe make his home on a crappy desert planet like Bali? We're nothing in comparison to eternity. We're transient configurations of dust and energy. Can't you see that we're godforsaken, both of us? Kiva never showed up when my stepfather tried to rape me. He didn't prevent my stepmother from blowing out into vacuum. He didn't stop your father from dying.::

"Kiva cares about us," Zen croaked. "He's in every drop of rain."

"Who are you talking to, honey?" His new lover peered with concern into his watery eyes as his new bride shouted in his brain. ::Well, it doesn't rain in space, Zen. Goodbye.::

"Was that a girlfriend?"

Zen sighed. "We're separated."

"Oh." Nancy's face wilted with realization. "It's complicated."

He shimmied a hand to stall any bad feelings. "No, it's fine. I guess it's over."

"You don't sound so sure."

"I can't really talk about it."

Nancy bent forward and gave him a peck on the cheek. "I understand, and I hope I haven't caused you any trouble. You're a wonderful man. Any girl would be lucky to have you."

Zen studied her cheerful smile. "Thanks for saying that." And clearly in a non-possessive tone. Was he off the interpersonal hook with her? "Last night was great."

"Of course it was. And super healthy. Sex is a great cardio-vascular workout."

Zen paused to analyze his strange predicament, feeling conflicted between the traditional morality of Bali and the natural freedom of his inclinations. "My life is a mess. I'm not sure what to do."

Nancy placed a palm on his shoulder. "You need to relax and follow your heart. Governor Blackpoll said you were anxious, and I can see tension coming back already. Just let it go. Embrace the chaos and flow with it."

He winced and tried a smile. "Oh, I'm chaotic all right."

"No, really," she said. "You can't control people. You can't manipulate your environment. Just embrace it. That's the Way."

"Sure," he said. "No problem."

She smirked. "Okay, fine, do you want breakfast? Can I interest you in a cube of cheese omelette, or are you going back to goop so quickly?"

"You know, Nancy," he said with careful charm, "I think I'm partial to the Way."

"Good, but I have to get to work." She gave him another quick peck and floated free. "Otherwise I'd have *you* for breakfast, pretty boy." She let her sari trail behind as she floated back to her couch, exposing bare legs and heart-shaped buttocks with dramatic flair. What a beauty.

Zen felt an immediate stir of sexual desire like an automatic reflex, and blushed with shame. His body acted like a procreative machine, preprogrammed to any passing visual stimulus and ponderous with lust. Why would Kiva make him like this, so predictable and desperate for love? He pulled his gaze away. His wife was in jail. Focus, focus. He touched his signal amp. "Login. Are you online, Genoa?"

A few seconds passed, and he realized how quickly he had become reliant on Governor Blackpoll. ::ZEN VALDA, I'M HERE. ARE YOU EXPERIMENTING WITH THE NEW APPLIANCE? DID YOU ENJOY NURSE STAVOS?::

"I'm going after Simara."

::REALLY?:: His tone suggested disbelief.

"I need a ticket on *Adam's Inspiration*."

::UH, JUST A MOMENT . . . THAT'S THE NAME OF A TRANSOLAR TROOPSHIP SAILING IN THREE HOURS. YOU CAN'T GET ONBOARD WITHOUT DIPLOMATIC CREDENTIALS.:: —*any isolated system spontaneously evolves toward equilibrium—evolution is a hard taskmaster and not mimicked by coddling—*

"Now's the time, Governor. You said you wanted to help me, and this is it. For the memory of my father."

::ARE YOU SURE THAT'S WHAT SIMARA WANTS?::

"She's distraught. She doesn't know what she wants, but I know what I want. I'm embracing the chaos."

"Good boy," Nancy said as she brought him a food cube and cracked the seal. "I'm going to miss you, Zen Valda. I hope you'll remember me on the next trade cycle."

Zen took the proffered bite of cheese omelette and mouthed a thank-you in reply. How could he ever forget her?

::WE'LL HAVE TO MEET IN PERSON TO DISCUSS THIS. I'LL SEE WHAT I CAN ARRANGE IN THE NEXT HOUR. GET DOWN TO THE DOCKS ON LEVEL 1 AND WE'LL GET TOGETHER. SEE YOU THERE AT A3:45.:: —*take one tablet every six hours to treat boredom—no power in religion nor efficacy to prayer in the absence of clairvoyance—*

"I'm off to work," Nancy said. "The door will lock when you leave, so you won't be able to get back in unless we program the sensor with your palm print." She smiled with intrigue and arched her eyebrows in query.

Still flirting, really? "Thanks for breakfast."

"Anytime," Nancy chirped as she flew for the portal.

Zen chewed his omelette with slow deliberation, possibly the last real food he would ever taste. He shuddered at the thought of two weeks on a troopship eating government goop. And Cromeus, the heartland of the Signa solar system—what did he really know about that fabled planet? The capital was New Jerusalem, a metropolis of mass transit and crowded walkways, and a handful of small outposts had sprung up in fertile crescents along the coasts of two major oceans where tourists flocked to frolic on sandy beaches—all of it alien to anything he had ever known as an impoverished bumpkin from Bali. He steeled himself against a feeling of inadequacy. He could do this! Anything for Simara—he owed her abject loyalty now that he had betrayed her trust. She was the only reason he was here—his skyfall princess.

Zen floated his way haltingly through the portal and down the passageway, trying to recall and utilize the fluid motions Nancy Stavos had taught him the previous day, but he could not seem to find a weightless equilibrium. He had lived too long with gravity—he needed it for orientation like a sand lizard in the desert. A jostle of traffic flew around him in both directions, touching him, squirming by in tight quarters. "B'well. B'well." There was little room in the tunnels, but everyone moved at smooth speed, tapping every surface along the way to manage momentum, dragging with fingertips to curl around a corner or pushing for acceleration in a straightaway. He hugged the right-hand wall like a flatworm trying to stay out of trouble, and followed online directions from Genoa Blackpoll to reach a private meeting area in an austere closet on Level 1 near the spaceport. He found the governor floating in a small vestibule with a hand on the ceiling to steady himself.

Zen grasped a recessed conduit and swung his body to match Genoa's orientation, face to face with the elder. "Did you arrange my transport?"

Genoa held up a faxslip boarding pass with a grim expression. "You're not ready for this. Do you have any idea what you're jumping into?"

Zen shook his head. Another warning? What else could go wrong? "The more I know, the less I understand. Simara mentioned a conspiracy."

"Everyone seems to have an agenda when it comes to the omnidroids, and you've wandered carelessly into the middle of the maelstrom. A whisper campaign has festered for weeks on Cromeus, igniting protest against an alleged omnidroid takeover of the financial system—controlling all banking, taxation, and government spending by virtue of their multifarious interconnectivity, a system too vast to fail and too complex to monitor. And now this business with Simara Ying. I'm not saying there's a firm connection, but a politician develops an acute sense of smell over the years." He tucked his chin down in confidence. "I was instructed by the Crown to convince you to return to Bali for your own protection. They offered nothing more than oblique threats, but they want you out of the picture and safely tucked away. I tried to reason with you man to man, and when that didn't work, I tried to distract you with feminine charm from an expert." He spread his palms. "I can only do so much."

"Nancy was working for you?"

"Nothing more than a nudge in token to her religious sensibilities. She seemed like a good match for an attractive boy, but apparently not a permanent interest. You seem to have a death wish for trouble. Why do you persist in following a known criminal into danger, a girl you barely know?"

"I think I know her well enough to trust her innocence."

Genoa shook his head sadly. "Alas, you know very little, and you may be a victim of powerful mindcraft beyond your understanding. Simara was fabricated in a secret black lab, the first bold experiment with genomic mapping. No one knows her full capabilities."

"She's not a machine. She's human."

"Omnidroids are surgically enhanced for specialized performance in higher areas of mathematics and logic. No unaugmented human can understand their intuitive grasp of V-net architecture. Power brokers are beginning to realize just how much financial responsibility has slipped out of humanity's grasp into machine control, how many critical aspects of our world might be vulnerable to an omnidroid takeover."

Zen pulled the cellulose faxslip from Genoa's grasp. "Simara's in trouble and needs my help."

"People are rioting in the streets of New Jerusalem, demanding the decommissioning of all twenty-three remaining omnidroids by surgery or death."

"No one has the right to do that!"

"Politics is the art of the impossible—you must know that from your father's work. Civil rights must be balanced by public privilege, and social conscience can be manipulated at will."

"Is that what's happening here? A political charade? An excuse for police action?"

Genoa pressed his lips and shrugged. "I'm a small asteroid in a big belt. I can't know anything for certain. A murder charge with no dead body? Who's to say it's not a trumped-up pretext to rein in the omnidroid elder and her unfortunate travelling companion? You could end up being a trailing edge in a blanket cover-up."

"I can't let that happen to Simara. It's not right."

"You're a victim of your father's ideology, and it pains me to see you wander off into battle like a fool with a plastic sword. You and Simara will be the only civilians on board this troopship, and your pitiful attempts to fight for justice may not be well received by the Transolar crew."

"Thanks for the warning," Zen said, "but how will I recognize Simara's enemy? Who can I trust?"

Genoa sighed and looked him square in the eyes. "You and I are the enemy, our collective will. If humanity is to be sacrosanct, then all other species must fail and the omnidroids must perish. As a youth at university I studied the fossil records from old Earth, the cradle of our genome. At least ten humanoid species came down from the trees and walked upright to hunt on the primeval savannah. How did they decide the one victor, the one primate that survived to harness language and scientific thought? Did they fight among themselves and burn the children of their enemies to placate invisible gods? Did the most brutal species inherit the fertile ground?"

Zen shook his head at the comparison to aboriginal warfare. "Mankind has grown beyond physical violence. We left behind the tools of destruction long ago. Guns and armadas—those were relics of ancient empires."

"True, but the V-net is our new battleground, and the courtroom our sacrificial altar. Fair warning is all I can offer. Your ship is leaving within the hour. Hurry now, and be well." Genoa Blackpoll held his elbow up, and Zen matched him with a bold thrust against his forearm. They paused for a silent moment of benediction, connected by clan on the fringe of their territorial border, one step away from abyss in all directions.

Zen rushed to the spacedock and found a porthole to view *Adam's Inspiration* grappled to the station, a military transport vessel without visible weaponry. The streamlined craft was pointed like an arrow with a protective cone on the front and a bulky antimatter reactor at the rear where four navigational rockets flared out like fins. A bright red Transolar insignia was painted on the side with horns ablaze, the burning shield of authority.

Zen made his way through the boarding gauntlet and stripped for sterilization. His money belt was useless now that he was a digital citizen, and he tossed it aside as his brown skin glowed under purple irradiation. He unfolded cellulose clothing from a fabricator and dressed himself in drab, recycled paper. The disposable sandals had thin straps and soles similar to dancing slippers, a token comfort. He had become a ward of the state, a penniless pilgrim, his treasure squandered for a chance to save an alien girl who crashed in his quadrant, an omnidroid genius with mysterious powers.

A Security guard in a crisp blue Transolar uniform met him

at the gate and scanned a code on his faxslip. He had a pistol holstered at his waist. "Zen Valda? What's your business onboard?"

"I'm travelling with my wife, Simara."

"The omnidroid prisoner?"

"Can I see her?"

The guard shook his head. "No way. She's in solitary. I'll show you to your bunk slot. You won't have any privileges." He pushed off down a narrow corridor, and Zen tagged along behind until they reached an open hole in the wall.

"This is your assigned quarters for the duration."

Zen grabbed a handrail and peeked into the tiny compartment—just a launch couch with a viewscreen overhead. "I have to stay in here?"

"No, you're not under arrest, but keep out of our way. There's a washroom down the hall and a galley to pick up your rations. Transolar ships are under acceleration at all times. We don't float around in space like traders. We get where we're going. At midpoint we lock down for turnaround. That's the only time you'll be weightless. Make sure you're strapped in when you hear the klaxon."

"How long does it take to reach Cromeus?"

"By burning both ways, we can make it in two weeks. Spare no expense."

Zen nodded, unsure of the logistics.

"We preserve our orbital velocity and slingshot around Bali for a free momentum boost," the guard continued, "so that gives us a head start."

"Nice."

"Yeah. Buckle up in fifteen. I'll see you 'round."

Zen squirmed into the tunnel enclosure, barely bigger than a coffin. The air was stale and smelled of lingering sweat. A larder to one side was stocked with grey goop and pouches of water. Life in the Transolar Guard was certainly not living up to the recruitment ads!

A klaxon sounded to announce a countdown sequence as Zen made himself comfortable in his launch couch. Acceleration punched him in the stomach at first, but settled back to a gravity that was less than Bali normal. He passed the time practising with his cochlear appliance, trying to work up a user profile to filter out the steady V-net chatter. Every fleeting thought unleashed a cacophony of random sounds and images from the V-net, an over-whelming tide of bewildering information. The only way to stave off the onslaught was to learn the art of directed thinking, a fo-cusing of concentration, a purification of intention. Zen needed to find the truth about Simara and her case. Everything else was a bedlam of unwanted data. —*the relationship between the positional centres of kissing circles can only be expressed as a matrix equation generalized to n dimensions*—*specifying the strict conditions under which local gauge symmetries can be spontaneously broken*—::ZEN, YOU STUPID MAN! WHAT ARE YOU DOING HERE?::

Zen sat up from his launch couch with a start and banged his head on the viewscreen above. "Simara?"

::I WARN YOU AWAY FOR YOUR OWN DAMN GOOD, AND STILL YOU THROW YOURSELF INTO THE JAWS OF DOOM. WHAT IS THE MATTER WITH YOU?::

Zen winced at the power in Simara's diatribe. Did the noise on this earbug increase by proximity, or was she yelling at him? Where was the volume control? "I know you're angry with me, and disappointed and hurt. You have every right to be. I failed you miserably like some woeful boyfriend on a wild night at Vishan. I see that now. But I couldn't slink away home without trying to earn some redemption. Not when you're in trouble and need my help."

::THERE'S NOTHING YOU CAN DO. YOU'RE JUST MAKING THINGS MORE COMPLICATED FOR MOTHERSHIP.::

"I can fight for you, Simara. I can provide evidence in court. I'm learning about biogens. I know about the persecution and discrimination against omnidroids. I'll fight for you all the way to your decommission if I have to!"

Her signal disappeared into the V-net chatter of strange jargon and abstruse educational lectures. Had he said something wrong? "Simara?"

—an infinite series will converge absolutely if the sum of the absolute value of the summand is finite—physical reality is nothing but a crude artifice designed to give coherence to perception and meaning to existence—::COME AND SEE ME, ZEN. WE NEED TO TALK PRIVATELY OFF THE V-NET GRID.::

"I've been denied access. They're holding you in solitary confinement."

::YOU HAVE CONJUGAL RIGHTS ONCE A WEEK UNDER SECTION 47 OF THE CRIMINAL CODE, SUBSECTION 7, PARAGRAPH 42. SPEAK TO THE CAPTAIN AND GIVE HIM THE REFERENCE.::

"He'll likely tell me to jump into vacuum."

::NO, HE WON'T. TRANSOLAR EXECUTIVES ARE STICKLERS FOR PROCEDURE, AND ANY VARIATION FROM STANDARD TREATMENT CAN BE USED IN COURT TO SWAY SENTIMENT ON THE JURY. HE WILL PRESS FOR EXECUTIVE PERMISSION AS

COMMANDER IN TRANSIT TO RECORD THE MEETING AS DATA, UNDER OATH, AND YOU WILL TELL HIM THAT HIS RIGHTS ARE SUPERSEDED BY YOUR RIGHT TO PRIVACY GUARANTEED UNDER PARAGRAPH 45. HOLD STRONG ON THIS AND SUMMON OUTRAGE. HAVE HIM LOOK UP THE STATUTE IF HE GIVES YOU ANY TROUBLE. THEY HAVE NO RIGHT TO MONITOR A CONJUGAL VISIT. THERE'S ENOUGH PORN IN THE BAR-RACKS ALREADY. GOT IT?::

"I'll try."

::AND BRING ME SOME CANDY.::

"Candy?"

::THERE'S A FREE VENDING MACHINE IN THE TUNNEL OUTSIDE THE OFFICERS' QUARTERS ON DECK 3. THEY HAVE ICE POPS THERE TOO, IF YOU WANT TO EXPERIENCE THE PERKS OF RANK. I HAVE TO WORK RIGHT NOW, BUT MOTH-ERSHIP WILL WATCH FOR THE MEETING ON MY APPOINT-MENT CALENDAR.::—*the runtime of divide-and-conquer algorithms is determined by their asymptotic behaviour—antimatter energy can be harnessed but never destroyed—ooh, that's it, sweetie, right there, harder, faster—*

Zen contacted the captain immediately and relayed Simara's instructions. The captain was curt but professional in granting a conjugal visit and gave only token argument for continuous sur-veillance of a criminal in transit. Zen proclaimed the legal right of innocence until proven otherwise and won his cause easily. A meeting was scheduled for Day Three at C2:20 in Simara's bunk enclosure. She was officially categorized as a high-security risk and could not leave her cubbyhole until they landed on Cromeus. The captain was helpful in pointing out that *Adam's Inspiration* would transition to Cromean time at midpoint—a twenty-four-hour cycle with three shifts of eight hours each, although the hours were 98% shorter according to atomic clock, all very confusing.

The days stretched out into a viscid and interminable pathway as long hours ticked past. Zen contemplated his upcoming meeting in the flesh with Simara. She obviously knew he was an idiot and unable to control his base emotions—that much was clearly evident to all. Genoa Blackpoll had set him up for a dalliance, and Nancy Stavos had taken full advantage of the situation, but there was no sense blaming the juva ben. Zen had known what he was doing and would be sorely tempted to do it again—that was the worst part! His body was a slave to lust, even though his mind made token resistance. The Bali girls with glad hands in the dark caverns had taught him to respond naturally to touch. How could he cancel out his years of training as a sexual being? How could he trust himself in a monogamous relationship?

Zen busied himself with research to escape his nagging conscience. A murder conviction required motive, forethought, and physical evidence. Juries decided final outcomes during online discussions behind digital firewalls on the V-net. Public opinion and character references would not be taken into account—just the cold facts of certainty. Zen contacted Genoa Blackpoll back on Trade Station for any news about the court case and came up empty. A renewed initiative was being organized to find the missing flight recorder following Zen's detailed remembrance of the deep trench along Zogan Ridge. News of the alleged crime had not been released to the citizens of Bali, and Zen's name had not been connected with any public record.

Zen arrived precisely on time for his conjugal appointment

in the female barracks and climbed up a ladder against steady acceleration to find Simara on a launch couch in a wall-slot no bigger than his own. He peered in and saw the bottoms of her feet. "Simara?"

"Hi. C'mon in." She pulled her legs up and squished to one side to make room for entry.

Zen climbed carefully inside the tight enclosure, rubbing along the length of her body in passing, touching her again, remembering. His skin tingled with self-conscious energy, so close to Simara, separated by thin cellulose clothing. She squirmed to make space for him on the launch couch and tried to ease him along with the tips of her fingers. Her space-wasted body was slim and wiry, but her breasts punched out to rub softly against his shoulder. His ears felt hot, and his abdomen ached with desire as he finally reached her smiling face and propped himself above her on arms and knees. Her breath smelled of toothpaste.

"It's okay, Zen," she said as the portal slid closed below their feet. "Just because we're on a conjugal visit doesn't mean we have to, you know, *conjugate*."

Zen chuckled weakly, but felt sweaty with discomfort. "Are these cubicles soundproof?" The next passenger in her bunk was just inches away, probably some female trooper trying to grab precious shut-eye between duty shifts.

"Yeah, they have a sonic field that cancels all noise."

Zen surveyed the walls. "That's what they say, but maybe they can read the vibrations in the field, tease out the words."

"You're absolutely right, very astute. That's exactly what we did. Mothership reverse-engineered the system and is listening in the captain's room right now." She gave him a confident wink.

"We're okay in here, and sorry I was so hard on you about Nurse Stavos. She was just doing her job, but I really think she pushed over the limit of propriety."

Zen waved his chin hastily. "No, it was all my fault. I was weak."

Simara raised her eyebrows in a look askance at the understatement. "You didn't put up much resistance, but I know the V-net transition knocked you for a loop. It always does. Nurse Stavos got you through it, she kept you grounded—that's what counts. At least you're not off gibbering in a nuthouse. No one's going to fault her for having some fun at your expense."

Zen frowned with a renewed sense of guilt. "How do they expect patients to process all that information at once? It was a nightmare of chaos and cacophony, a mayhem of the mind with no off button."

"A V-net installation is like a childhood vaccine for the brain. It's done on infants, not adults. That's why you were on a twelve-hour watch. Every adult turnover is a major event, and the conversion to digital thought is sometimes dangerous. We think we know a lot about human consciousness and neuroplasticity, but we're really just scratching the surface."

"That's a crazy way to experiment on people."

"It's only *thinking*, Zen. Everybody takes it for granted. Anyway, you seem to have adjusted quite well, once you got your initiation out of the way."

"I try to suppress most of it. I don't need all that information. I'd rather focus on you."

She offered a wan smile. "That's sweet."

"No, I mean it."

She made a polite chuckle and glanced away. "It's funny how things work out, you know? I was helpless when I fell into the dead zone on Bali, trapped without the net and lost to mothership. And you were just as helpless when you transitioned to the net for the first time. Ironic, isn't it? I wish I could have been there for you. I owed you that much for all you did for me. You're a good man."

Zen tried to steel his racing pulse as he caught her eyes again. "I want to marry you, Simara. For real this time." There, he'd said it, finally. That surely must be the truth. He wanted a stable, monogamous relationship with his skyfall princess—he wanted the constraint of fidelity. Why had it taken him so long to get up the nerve to tell her? His breath caught in his throat.

Simara studied him in silence. The easy response never came, and as the seconds passed he knew it never would. She did not love him and would not give credence to their sham marriage. Even nose to nose, they were too far apart. "I can't understand you, Zen. You have the means of intelligence, but your behaviour doesn't conform to logical patterns. Things are a lot more complicated than you suspect."

"You keep saying that. Are you sure it's not just an excuse?"

"Maybe it is. Of course I have feelings for you. But I don't want to be responsible for dragging you into danger and ruining your life. I don't care about your sexual escapades, I really don't. You've been with lots of different women and the pattern will probably repeat long into the future. I know what drives the thoughts of—"

"I don't need anyone but you," he blurted. The force in his voice surprised him, but he meant it with all his heart. He softened his tone and pressed forward. "We're in this together now. Can't we try to make the best of it?"

"Yes, of course we can, if that's what you want."

"I'll take full responsibility for both of us."

Simara widened her eyes. "You don't know what you're saying. I'm on trial for murder."

"Did you kill your stepfather?"

"You wouldn't be here if I did."

"I'd just like to hear it from you. Is that too much to ask?"

Her gaze shaded with insecurity. "I flatly denied any culpability to the Crown attorney and Nakistra Gulong. I was convincing and perhaps fooled the empath, but I won't lie to you, after all we've been through. That wouldn't be fair." She glanced nervously away and back. "Because I don't know the answer. I can't remember, Zen—that's the terrible truth. I can't be certain of my innocence. Omnidroids rarely sleep, but in the quiet moments of stasis I struggle to piece the fragments of memory together. Some of my short-term data blocks were obliterated by trauma during the crash, and then I was cut off from mothership, from my power source. All my memories of Bali are weak and superficial, and Vishan seems like a dream to me now. I don't see how I could have killed Randy, to be honest. I don't feel like a murderer."

Zen's arms began to ache with the effort of pushing away from her pretty face. Her body seemed like a magnet pulling him closer, but her warding smile was tight-lipped and grim. He turned his head to the side to give her a semblance of privacy. "Perhaps he chose suicide when he realized what he'd done to you. Perhaps an agony of guilt drove him into a spiral of depression."

Simara shook her head. "He would never have the conscience for it. Randy Ying was an abusive man who victimized a series of wives, treating them like slaves and prostitutes, forcing them into vile perversions. I grew to hate my own stepfather, the caregiver of my youth. I thought about killing him many times when he began touching me. I knew the bastard would try to rape me eventually."

"You don't have to tell me this."

"I do, Zen. I can't imagine what you see in me or why you would follow me into trouble, but if we're going to be partners, I need you to listen carefully to every word I say. This episode with my stepfather was not some random act of violence. I believe it was part of a scheme to eliminate all omnidroids, a coordinated and carefully timed attempt at mass slaughter of my biogen family! Two of us were murdered, but twenty-three, including me, fought back or had enough precognition to escape. My brothers and sisters are crying out to mothership for help."

Holy Kiva! More violence? "Murdered?"

Simara nodded sadly. "A helicopter crash staged to look like an accident. All the crew survived unharmed, but my two friends, Elana and Ruis, were killed."

"Do you have any evidence we can use in court?"

"No, nothing definitive. The data record has been negated." She tapped her temple with a fingertip. "But mothership knows. You must be circumspect in everything you do. You cannot trust anyone onboard this vessel."

Zen swallowed hard, feeling a creeping chill of conspiracy. "Okay."

"We'll need the emergency battery code for the airlocks. There's a manual override sequence in case of power failure or computer breakdown. It's a secret that everyone shares."

"How will I get it?"

"A crewmember will give it to you, sooner rather than later.

It's part of trooper culture to not leave anyone behind. A digital copy is not allowed for the sake of corporate security, but they can write it on a slip of paper or something—a four-digit numerical code for a standard palm reader."

"Does it work when the power is on? Can we break you out of here?"

"It does work, but there's no place to run in the vacuum of space. The captain would be alerted to the use of any override code and would have us in chains within minutes, making our legal problems even worse. After we land safely on Cromeus, we'll make a break for it. Mothership will guide us to freedom."

Zen nodded. "Okay. I'll get the code."

"I'm stuck here like a criminal, but you've got the run of the ship. See what else you can find out. Make some friends and try to get a feel for the crew, but don't be taken in by any offers of confidence or promises of secrecy. You're an outsider, no matter what anyone says. Transolar will be out to glean information for court, so be careful."

"I will." Zen longed to kiss her in parting, but didn't have the heart to push his luck. He made his exit gracefully, making every effort to minimize contact with her, though each brush against her body make his skin tingle with energy. Was this love, this vicious battle to hold his hormones at bay?

Zen explored the troopship to familiarize himself with the layout. Two main tunnels with ladders went up the centre of the arrow shaft with short hallways branching off like spokes at each level. The vessel was dirty throughout and in need of repair. Some areas were cordoned off with caution tape to prevent access to exposed panels of pipes and wiring. Air vents were stained with smoky brown deposits, and some of the grates rattled as the squeaky fans circulated stale air. Ladder treads were worn smooth in the middle and grimy near the corners where years of accumulated dirt had eddied and fallen.

Zen climbed up against steady acceleration until he found a porthole view of their destination, the fourth planet out from Signa. Cromeus appeared blue in the distance like a drop of water floating in space. Hard to imagine a teeming populace on that tiny circle of reflected light. Hard to imagine a sky without forks of lightning and constant magnetic storms, a paradise where humans could walk outdoors and breathe unfiltered air, drink water from the ground, and raise babies.

"Looking for something in particular?"

Zen whirled to see a young man in blue duty uniform, a Transolar Security guard walking the perimeter. "No . . . yeah . . . I guess."

The man smiled and held an elbow up Bali style. He was handsome and personable, with dark hair, bulky shoulders, and the leathery skin of a grounder. "I'm Jon Bak. Seen you around."

Zen raised a forearm to cross his gesture. "You're from Bali?"

He gave a quick nod. "Five years out. I spend my free time on Cromeus now. A little peninsula called Flatrock. It's the best top-less beach in the galaxy. You should see the women." He whistled with appreciation. "Where you from?"

"Keokapul."

"Oh, sure, the crystal caves. I've been there for Vishan. Quite the spectacle. We may have shared a smoke together."

Zen tried to remember and came up blank. "I was just a kid in those days."

"Yeah, I suppose. I don't recall your face, but who can remember much after Vishan?" The trooper laughed with a gregarious roar. He pointed to the portal with a beefy arm and rugged fingers. "This is a digital interface with a battery backup. It's not a real window."

Zen peered again at the array of stars. "It looks real."

"Well, that's the idea, but you can magnify the image." He palmed a sensor to activate a touchscreen on the surface of the portal. "You want to zoom in on Cromeus?"

"Yeah, I've never been there." The blue dot grew larger as Zen watched. It had a pearly texture from humidity in the atmos-phere—clouds or perhaps snow.

"It's not much better from this distance. There's the max. You see that spot of light glinting on the right side in orbit? That's the

Macpherson Doorway, the wormhole to Earth. I'd love to travel through there if they ever lift the embargo. That's my big dream— to see the ancestral home of humanity."

Zen shook his head. "I'd be afraid. It goes back in time, right?"

Jon Bak shrugged powerful shoulders. "Sure, time and space, but it hardly matters. It's just a glorified airlock through the fabric of the universe. They say the Sol system is twelve million years in the past according to measurements of the cosmic background radiation, but who cares? Nothing we could do there will have any effect on the Signa system. It's too far away. No message in a bottle is ever going to reach us. In practical terms, it's just another trade route. Where do you think all the gold from Bali goes?"

"To Earth?"

"Of course. That's what it's all about, my man—galactic trade and commerce! I think it's a crime they won't let tourists through."

"It must be very expensive."

"Yeah, you'd have to win the lottery or marry into the Macpherson family." He chuckled. "Hey, do you want to grab an allkool and gab about the old days?"

Zen glanced up the hall and decided he'd done enough reconnaissance for one day. "Sure. Are you off duty?"

"Nah, another few minutes, but there's nothing happening out here in no man's land. C'mon." He hunched a shoulder forward and began walking. Along the way he pointed to a circular protrusion from the ceiling. "We're under V-net surveillance near those sensors, but no one ever checks the feed apart from the usual automated triggers. Hi, Mom." He waved at the camera with showy nonchalance, giving fair warning as they passed by and waiting until they were out of range. "I saw your blurb in our duty notes, quite the story. You're with the omnidroid chick. Is she hot?"

Zen felt a twinge of jealousy at his interest. "Yes, very."

"Don't you worry that she can read your mind?"

"What makes you think she can do that?"

"I dunno. I've heard weird shit."

Zen squinted with doubt as they walked. "I don't think she reads minds. If she does, she's not very good at it."

Jon Bak laughed and banged the heel of his hand on his forehead. "Obviously. She got caught, right?"

"She's innocent."

Jon stretched his jaw down to make an exaggerated face of doubt. "That so?"

Zen nodded sadly, feeling the tangled weight of events fresh on his mind. "It was all a terrible mistake."

The trooper shrugged and thought for a moment. He looked over and mouthed out the numbers *eight-three-three-nine* in silence, then winked to garner close attention. He held up a palm and tapped it as though entering code into a sensor, mouthing the numerals again, *8339*. "I'd love to meet her some time when you guys aren't getting busy."

Zen committed the override code to memory with a surge of satisfaction—mission accomplished! He had earned the trust of Jon Bak from Bali. They made their way to a staff lounge that was not much bigger than a double room on Trade Station, where they sipped dark allkool straight from the pouch and shared life highlights. Jon's main interest seemed to be chasing woman and performing Bali magic on their souls, a desire probably heightened by so many days away from home. Fraternization among troopers was officially forbidden, but not uncommon, and all staff had to submit to sterilization drugs during their tours of duty. Transolar did not want any liability for unplanned pregnancies or children in the barracks.

Zen played along behind his veil of secrecy. Jon Bak could be a spy planted by the captain to extract information. The override code might be bait to elicit a confession—Simara had warned Zen to expect ploys such as this. But the trooper was a friendly guy and happy to share secret intrigues about troopers hiding clandestine shenanigans like schoolboys in a public dormitory. They downed a few drinks and exchanged epic tales from home, but Zen kept his mouth shut about anything that really mattered. He met a few more guards as the day waned, learned a few names, and acted his role as required—a civilian relying on their goodwill for good times and fun for all. *Adam's Inspiration* was scheduled for decommission after this run, the last interplanetary voyage for an aged and trustworthy vessel, so off-duty inebriation was expected in her honour on a regular basis.

Turnaround was announced with a klaxon warning a few days later, and everyone had to strap into launch couches at the precise midpoint of their journey. The antimatter reactor went silent, and rocket thrust stopped cold as the troopship coasted through space. Zen had so internalized the gentle thrum of acceleration that the absence seemed like a cessation of breathing. He squirmed in discomfort as his stomach lurched with weightlessness and sent a wave of nausea through his suddenly floating body. No gravity, no sense of movement, no sound beyond the hum of electronics and whisper of air circulation.

According to calculations performed on a napkin by Jon Bak,

Adam's Inspiration had now reached a maximum relative velocity of one thousand miles per second and would spend the next full week decelerating for landfall. It felt creepy and unnatural to be hurtling across the heavens at such phenomenal speed in a dead cold stasis without any sound or vibration—flying headlong in a black void without foundation.

A short jolt of thrust knocked Zen sideways in his bunk as navigational rockets began to turn the spaceship. Time seemed an agony as Zen hovered weightless and listened to his blood pound in his temples. He could imagine the ship rotating end over end like a stick thrown across the desert. Another jolt of thrust was followed by two more as the troopship stabilized for a new trajectory, and the klaxon hooted anew to announce a five-second countdown. *Wham!* The antimatter reactor kicked in and rocked Zen into his launch couch with a huff of exhalation. Gravity was back like an old friend, but now the nosecone was pointing away from their destination as they slowed down for an eventual landing.

"I brought you some allkool," Zen said as he met Simara for his second conjugal visit and crawled into her tiny slot in the wall. "Do you want lemon or cherry?" *I've got the code*, he mouthed, and pantomimed the numbers with his fingers.

"We can speak safely in here," Simara said. "I'm still controlling communications. Good work."

"Same to you. So we're on top of things. Let's party."

Simara frowned and sucked her teeth—no such luck. "Our situation has gone from bad to worse." She was wearing the same cellulose outfit, and she smelled foul with harboured perspiration—no chance to bathe or freshen up in this coffin cell. "And thanks for the offer of a drink, but I can't tamper with my consciousness now that I'm working with mothership again. I can't afford any weakness."

Misery struck home for Zen as he studied her harried face and pocketed the allkool. "So what's the bad news?"

"All the escape shuttles onboard are being tested under the guise of regular maintenance, and the captain has packed personal effects in a duffel bag."

Zen's sweat went cold on his neck. "What does that mean?"

"As unlikely as it sounds, it now appears Transolar will instruct the crew to jump ship and leave us to die in a fiery crash. Have you heard any scuttlebutt from the troopers?"

"A crash? No. *Adam's Inspiration* is being decommissioned after this final run. The old tug is scheduled for a recycling facility in New Jerusalem."

"More like a watery grave with all evidence buried forever," Simara said. "Transolar can't ditch the crew safely in the deep void of space, and they won't risk an explosion in the middle of the traffic zone around Cromeus. Or send a dead elephant like a bomb into the orbiting grid of satellites, microwave generators, and off-planet housing—not to mention the wormhole doorway to Earth, their precious space-time gateway. They'll have to make it look like a failed orbital approach close to the planet, a mechanical failure. They'll launch the crew in the escape shuttles and leave me in this slot. Probably you too, now that you've volunteered complicity. We'll have to jump ship during the chaos."

"Jump ship into vacuum?"

Simara tested him with a firm gaze. "We'll need two spacesuits with oxygen tanks and ablative shields. We should be within a hundred miles of the surface by the time all the shuttles have launched—close enough for a space-dive. A lot will depend on our angle of entry, but we could easily pull five-g and hit two hundred C on our shields. We'll program a parachute array in case we black out, two drogue chutes followed by a conventional spread at three thousand feet."

"Have you done this before?"

"No, but I mastered the simulation."

"What does that mean?"

"The digital experience, the brain chemistry."

Zen shook his head and clenched his eyes as his mind reeled in imagined freefall. "I can't do it."

"Sure you can. You're a stud. You've got the muscles of an athlete from all your hard living on Bali. If anyone can space-dive and live, it'll be you. We'll try to aim for an ocean landing if we can. Our suits will hold pressure underwater, and we won't be visible from the air. Look at me."

He blinked his eyes open again, nose to nose with this nightmare girl. He hadn't signed on for this craziness. No way. But bless Kiva, she was beautiful!

"I need you to listen carefully," she said. "These instructions will supersede anything I happen to say online to throw our captors off the track. I need you to sequester two spacesuits near our chosen exit point, complete in every detail to my specifications. It's going to take some fancy finagling with supplies, but I've hacked access to all the records. I'm stuck here in this couch like a criminal, but you can operate freely. If anyone asks, you're just a rookie grounder wandering the tunnels. A simpleton."

Zen nodded—not too much of a stretch, truth be told. "Are you sure about this? Do you have any evidence of conspiracy?"

"Mothership was rendered silent at the precise time of the attacks on the omnidroids, throwing our freenet into chaos. That speaks volumes. Our enemy must have advanced technology to interfere with psychic realms, and terrible motivation to attempt genocide across the entire solar system. I don't have proof for your eyes or ears. I have a feeling, an idea. I can visualize the whole thing."

Was she brainwashing him with omnidroid strategy? The paranoid ravings of a murderous intellect? No, it couldn't be. "Governor Blackpoll thinks you have special powers over humans, powers of manipulation and control."

"Yes, I know. Everyone is fearful of our grand strategy, our master designs to evolve beyond the species and conquer the universe, but all mothership wants is order and harmony for sentient life. Omnidroids are willing servants to that. We were created for good and not harm to mankind. Why are you here if you don't trust me in your heart?" The narrow space between their bodies was electric with potential, her breath hot against his neck. "I warn you away, I yell at you, ridicule your ancestral faith, yet you follow me like a shadow. Now we're both going to die in a fiery crash unless you do everything I say."

Zen studied her face, her cheeks animated with colour, her eyes faithful and true. "Okay."

"Don't speak of this online, to me or anyone else. Remember that all the data you access is monitored and recorded, all your private searches, all your Help questions. Don't leave any clues that might give away our plan. We can't make any mistakes."

"I'll be careful, I promise."

Simara sighed with relaxation as though a difficult task had been accomplished. "I know you will." She shook her shaggy mane and shrugged off her business persona like a cloak, a role easily played and cast aside. A younger, innocent girl looked at him with a glint of mischief in her eye, a girl he had met in a geyser pool on a planet far away. "Now take off your pants to seal the deal with a friendly Bali hand like the girls do back home. I've been alone too long thinking about you, and I want to see what all the fuss is about."

His face blossomed with fire. "No, I can't, not like this."

"C'mon, Zen." Simara took his hand and placed it on her breast. "You're ready for this. We have to secure a mutual understanding of human trust in the core programming of our physical being. This is how it's been done for centuries. You can hear your hormones talking, can't you? You feel that right down into your groin. Your tactile senses are going straight to your midbrain, where evolution has charted pathways for procreation and survival. You're hardwired by your genome to find me attractive. You can't help it."

Her voice sounded hypnotic and gentle with reassurance, the warmth from her body a balm of delight. His dream was coming to fruition, his final fantasy. "You scare me when you talk like a machine."

"You scare me too, Zen, on so many levels." Simara reached to loosen cellulose at his waist.

"Wait," he said as he stilled her hands. "I can't do it. Not like this."

Puzzlement flitted in her eyes. "I thought you liked me. Don't you want to show me your big secret?" She arched her eyebrows at him in whimsical flirtation, but it seemed forced and artificial now that he had made up his mind.

"You deserve better than this, trapped like a sex slave in a cage. It's cheap and demeaning. Can't we wait for a better place?"

Simara studied him with a frown, recalculating her options, and for a moment he wondered if he had ruined his last chance at romance. She pulled her hand away from his pants. "I'm so sorry. I thought this would be the natural thing for you, given your expertise in the area. I didn't mean to offend."

"No, no, it's not you. It's me. I just need some time."

"That wasn't the response I was expecting from a Bali boy."

Zen winced and tried a smile. "I'm finding it a hard reputation to live up to."

"Ha, pun intended?" She laughed and waved a hand. "No, it's fine, really. I'm not ego invested. Or maybe I am. I suppose I'm jealous of all those other girls."

"I don't want you to be just another girl. You're special."

"Well, that's sweet." She studied him with pleasant surprise. "I had no idea you were such a complicated man. I'll wait for you, if that's what you want. We'll defer gratification and consummate our fake marriage with fireworks when the time is right."

"From anticipation blooms the flower of desire."

"Oh, you're a poet also? You do make an extraordinary package."

He felt a blush of shyness and ducked his eyes, secretly glad to change the subject. "Actually, I do write a bit of poetry when the stars are properly aligned. Indulgent, cathartic stuff."

"Really? I'd love to read some."

"I'd be embarrassed to show you, a woman of your vast experience and intellect."

She fluttered fingers as though to dismiss any notion of superiority. "I'm a neophyte when it comes to poetry. You had me with the skyfall princess line."

They chuckled together at the memory now distant, and rested in a moment of solace. Life had seemed simple then, and opportunities bright and boundless. Now the future was restricted and reality confined to a dark tunnel forward. Simara shifted gears with machinelike efficiency as she began to go over the details of their mission. She outlined the schematics of the troopship from memory and specified locations for spacesuits and supplies. Everything had to be arranged without digital record. Surveillance cameras would have to be disabled at strategic points. Inventory records would have to be surreptitiously altered. An intricate plan emerged, an improbable confluence of knotty details, and by the time his conjugal visit had ended, Zen's head was spinning with worry. Simara was counting on him, and everything had to be perfect for any chance of success.

Time seemed chiselled out by a miser as Zen completed his tasks one by one. He picked up extra tubes of goop at parties and hid them away. He borrowed extra pressure-packs of oxygen, claiming difficulty breathing due to claustrophobia in his bunk slot, playing the tourist. There were only twelve spacesuits aboard the vessel, fully geared up for emergency repairs outside the hull, and it seemed unlikely that a fleeing crew would disable equipment in deliberate betrayal, but he pulled two suits out of the line-up and hid them in a secret locker according to Simara's instructions. In deep storage he found two ablative shields—pointed rocket heads made of heavy ceramic and lined with fireproof insulation. He had to haul each one up a ladder against acceleration with a rope harness around his shoulders, clenching his teeth against pain and reminded of home—dragging metal salvage across hot desert sand.

At night he dreamed of a dangerous jump into open space

with Simara, flying through celestial heavens to distant pinwheel galaxies, colourful, spinning whorls with millions of suns and countless virgin planets to choose from. In the dream he landed on a paradise world and wandered psychedelic gardens of delight in juva ben flashbacks with a nurse in white cellulose—a land of fragrant honey and milk from anatomically egregious vessels. He woke soiled with shame each time, wondering why he was such an idiot.

By the time they approached Cromean orbit, Zen was fully prepared in his mind and primed for action, but his stomach thought otherwise, a twisting and churning worm in an ulcer of doubt. Simara had warned him to keep his protein levels high and his muscles toned with a daily regimen of exercise, but he continued to fight for control of his spirit. Who could he trust if not the woman he loved? Kiva would help him, bless the Lord of life. Kiva would guide him.

The floor lurched beneath his feet, and sudden buoyancy allowed him to float upward. He flailed and grasped a conduit for support. The rockets were dead. Gravity had failed.

"Emergency muster," the intercom sounded. "Reactor shutdown. All crew muster to launch couches for airlock containment."

The lights darkened to a bluish tinge, and Zen twisted to reorient himself in weightless space. Deceleration had stopped cold, and the troopship was still pointed ass-forward to Cromeus and probably coming in fast with momentum. Was this the signal he had been waiting for? The drama Simara had envisioned? He touched his ear. "Login. Simara Ying."

::HI, ZEN. GET TO YOUR LAUNCH COUCH RIGHT AWAY. THIS IS AN EMERGENCY MUSTER FOR POSSIBLE DECOMPRESSION.::

The air in his lungs felt suddenly precious, and he held his breath to test the moment. "Is it a drill?"

::IT DOESN'T MATTER. THIS IS A MILITARY TRANSPORT, AND ALL ORDERS MUST BE OBEYED WITHOUT QUESTION.::

Simara sounded right in character, civil and obedient, the epitome of cooperation. All Zen had to do was play dumb. "I'll be there in two minutes."

::WHERE ARE YOU?::

Zen checked the bulkhead. "I'm in an observation room, 32B."

::THAT'S LESS THAN TWO MINUTES. DON'T TAKE YOUR OXYGEN FOR GRANTED.::

"Okay, okay."

"Emergency muster," the intercom resounded and began to repeat the message.

Zen pulled his body mass under an archway and floated into the hallway, a helpless amateur again as he'd been on Trade Station. He clambered along the walls and grappled with conduits to maintain balance as a flurry of staff troopers flew by in both directions around him. He floated up the long ladder to his bunk slot and slid inside. The door closed behind him and sealed with a hiss. "I'm here."

::GOOD. SIT TIGHT. THE CAPTAIN WILL PROBABLY MAKE A STATEMENT SHORTLY.::

They waited, but no announcement broke their radio silence. The quiet became ominous as power flickered and went dead. A few more seconds passed, and Zen strained to hear sounds beyond his tiny cell. Were the crew packing the lifeboats even now? Jumping ship to trap them behind? Would they blow the hatch and leave them to die? He squirmed to turn around in his bunk and peered at the palm sensor on the door. He tapped 8339 on the battery touchpad, and the door popped as pressure released. He pried the portal wide with his fingers and peered out into empty space. All the bunk slots were open, and all the troopers were gone, just as Simara had envisioned. Time was short now and scheduled with precision. Zen looked back once and dove out into bluish twilight.

They met at a prearranged spot just outside their secret locker, and Simara launched herself into his embrace. They bounced off a wall and hung together as she clutched him, and she seemed like such a tiny, frail creature, a clinging elf. She pushed away finally and tapped the wall for stability. "Sorry," she said as she hovered before him with a grin of victory. "For being such a stir-crazy pervert. It just feels so good to be out of my cell."

"Are we still okay?"

She smiled with reassurance. "We're not dead yet." She tapped an access code to open their locker and peered inside. Two rigid spacesuits with ablative shields stood upright like white cruise missiles. "Good job, Zen. You are totally my hero."

A muffled explosion sounded in the distance and left behind a squeal of escaping air.

"Vacuum breach," Simara shouted into a whistling wind. "Get in your suit and stay close to the wall." She dove headfirst into her bulky spacesuit and quickly sealed it up as Zen floundered to get his in position. He tipped his head back into the belly of the enclosure and squirmed his way up toward light coming down from the faceplate. The suit felt stiff and top-heavy below the armoured dome. He tucked up his legs and stepped into rigid leggings, then inserted his arms. He clamped the front of his suit and powered it up. The system whined with a whir of hydraulics. "Can you hear me?"

"Hurry up." Simara's voice sounded panicky, and she looked like a robot with a rocket cone above her head. "We're dropping like an asteroid and picking up speed."

"Are you okay?"

"No, I feel wretched. I think I'm going to piss my panties."

"You said you'd done this."

Simara floated to the airlock hatch and peered through a dark portal. "Simulations are wonderful things, but it seems more real when it's real." She tapped the override code into the failsafe mechanism, and the lock clunked inside. "Give me a hand with this door. Do you have air? Are you secure?"

"I'm fine. Almost pure oxygen on the meter." Zen leaned against the handle and grunted as he slid the door open to endless night. "Holy Kiva." The curved edge of Cromeus lay below, a blue jewel wreathed in cloud. "It's beautiful. So calm and peaceful."

Simara edged up beside him. "Think good thoughts. You go first. If you have any trouble, I might be able to help."

Zen peered out at the emptiness of space and felt a gut-wrenching solitude. "It looks like a long way. I can't jump that far."

"Yes, you can. Just line it up and push off. Gravity will do the rest. Don't try to look back for the ship or worry about me. The first few seconds will be the most dangerous part. One drogue chute will deploy from your feet to grab any stray molecules up this high and help point you down. Keep your arms and legs tucked under your shield during deceleration. When we reach terminal velocity, your shield will eject and a second drogue chute will deploy from your back for free flight. Try to control any spin by using your outstretched arms like a bird. An uncontrolled spin will push blood to your brain and black you out. In less than five minutes your paraglider will deploy, and you'll be home free."

"Do you know we're going to survive? Have you seen the future?"

Simara sighed with exasperation. "No. I don't know, Zen. I'm not a fortuneteller. We don't have any guarantee of divine grace. I have a feeling that you might survive, okay?"

Zen turned back to face her. "If this is our last jump to glory, we should settle things between us."

"You've got to be kidding. You want to talk about our relationship? Now?"

"This might be our final moment together."

"Don't think like that. You've got to stay positive if we're going to get through this—joke around a bit and consider death elusive. It's called wartime camaraderie."

Zen held Simara's gaze. "I love you, Simara. Right here, right now."

She blushed and fumed behind her faceplate, but kept her eyes steady. "Fine. I love you, too."

"Okay, then." He grinned to himself in victory. "Let's do this."

Simara turned to look out the open portal. "Our timing will have to be impeccable. This dead hulk will be accelerating fast, and we don't want to go in with any speed greater than the terminal velocity of our natural mass. I've been calculating some trajectory simulations on the fly, but there are a lot of estimated parameters."

Zen peered again into the gaping maw of space and felt rekindled fear. "What do you suggest?"

"Now would be good."

"Now?"

"Give or take a few seconds."

Zen clenched his teeth and stared at Cromeus in the distance. Could invisible tentacles of gravity reach up this high to claim him? Or would he float forever in the stillness of vacuum? He lumbered into position in the doorway and readied himself. "Thanks for crashing in my backyard, Simara. I'd rather die here with you than spend my life in a cave mourning my father."

"You're not going to die, Zen. People pay big money for extreme sports like this. Just go ahead and jump."

He studied the surface of Cromeus. The famous blue planet was actually more brown than blue on close inspection. Plenty of dry land, and cities with lights in the creeping shadow of darkness. The notion of choosing a target seemed ludicrous. Does a meteor have any choice where it lands? Does a skyfall princess? He tipped forward and pointed his ablative shield down. He positioned himself with precision—straight like an arrow to the heart of Cromeus! Think good thoughts. He dove into nothingness.

"Are you there, Simara?"

"Right on your pretty-boy ass. Keep your head down."

"Are we falling?"

"Like a shooting star. Keep your head down."

No sound. No wind pressure. No landmarks. It seemed as though time and space had stopped for Zen, and a feeling of calm soothed his jangled nerves. This wasn't so bad.

"You're developing a spin," Simara said. "Deploy your drogue chute by pressing the blue button on your inside forearm, left side."

Zen followed her instruction and heard a popping sound near his feet. The horizon continued to tilt. "I don't think it's working."

"No air yet," Simara said. "You're deployed, don't worry. I've got you in view. Your chute's starting to drag a bit. You're doing great."

The Cromean horizon continued to skew upward and then disappeared from sight. All he could see was an expanse of stars like sprinkles of confetti in black eternity. No troopship, no planet, nothing at all. His gut coiled like a serpent. "I don't think it's working," he repeated.

No reply. No visual reference but the tangled skein of a distant galaxy. He felt frozen in time, floating free in endless space. Completely still.

Warmth wafted down on his cheeks from above, and his skin prickled with panic as the temperature increased. Soon he was sweltering and sweaty in his tomb. The heat steadily mounted to incendiary levels. Was he burning up, flashing out? Were they dead already? "Simara?"

The sound of her gasping breath came from someplace far away, laboured in distress and irregular. Was she dying? "Simara?"

"We're not fucking there yet, Zen. Shit. You're coming around. Keep tight."

He hugged himself like a turtle and trembled with fear in a fiery alien hell as white mist obscured his view, turning pink and then red. He could sense no gravity, no movement, nothing at all but the searing heat. His thoughts seemed lazy and stupid as his brain succumbed to fever—like trying to slur speech from sleep during a nightmare. One breach in their suits and they would be cooked meat—two burnt birds coming in on the night. The twinned sound of their wheezing breath became a dancing storm in his ear, and he had plenty of time for regret, plenty of time to pray to Kiva. The mottled crescent of Cromeus appeared through hissing mist, and a thud jolted him as his ablative shield blew away and his second drogue chute deployed behind him. The horizon cartwheeled as drops of sweat spun from his chin.

"Woohoo," Simara shouted. "That must be terminal velocity. Get ready to fly."

Zen thought of dino-birds in the mountains of Bali pushing hatchlings into the air, forcing maturity on them like any good parent testing their genome. He had seen the brittle bones of the weaklings in the foothills.

"You're in a flat spin," Simara said. "Stick out an arm and try to work something. The wind is your friend."

Zen tried both arms and bent his legs. He writhed and twisted, but couldn't find a target on the horizon. Nothing seemed to make sense. He closed his eyes against nausea and felt a blow on his shoulder.

"Zen," Simara shouted. "Wake up and grab my arm!"

He flailed a hand and felt momentary purchase. He peered wildly for a glimpse of her as she came round another time. He reached for her and slapped onto her arm, but she slipped away. The horizon stabilized.

"Hold that form," Simara said. "Can you feel equilibrium yet?"

A press of wind began to push against his chest like a force of nature from his grounder home. He learned from it, tested it, and found stability. "Yeah." He studied the mottled brown of the surface as it crept perceptibly closer. "I don't see any water." No blue, no perfect squares of green, just wild land and dangerous terrain. "And those ribbons of cloud look ominous. Is that a storm?"

Simara grunted assent. "Life is for living."

His paraglider deployed, pulling him up with a jolt like the hand of Kiva grabbing him by the groin, and he reached up to snag dangling handles.

"Showtime," Simara whispered.

Zen struggled to plot his trajectory as a stormy gale began to buffet from the right. "That valley to the left," he said. "There's a small stream."

"Got it. Good as any."

"Where are you?"

"Just above. I don't want to tangle in your lines. Find us a soft spot."

The ground came up fast, too fast, and his chest tightened with alarm. He swung his paraglider against gusts of wind and tried for a snaking length of stream, but hit some underbrush and landed skidding on the shore as his chute tangled in the foliage and dragged him to a halt.

"Shit," Simara said as her shadow passed. "Oww."

Zen looked up to see her glider catch on a tree branch and slam her into a sharp ledge of granite. One side of her chute cut free and floundered like a dying ghost as she fell. She cried out in pain as she hit the rocky ground and rolled down an incline into a pile of boulders.

"Simara!" Zen struggled to fight against gravity—now suddenly dead weight on the ground like an armoured statue sunk in thick mud. He could barely bend a knee to move as he scrambled to disconnect his harness. "Simara?"

He ripped at the clamps on his chest and climbed out of his stiff robot body. He ran up the beach to her and found her twisted like a broken doll among the rocks. Her cracked faceplate was dark, her body unmoving. "Simara!"

Zen wrestled with the clamps on her spacesuit and reached inside for her warm body. No pulse on her inert chest, no signs of life. His eyes watered with frustration as he pushed against her rib cage, forcing plasma to move, hoping for a miracle. He tested her bones for breaks and checked for visible damage. He had to get her out of this mechanical crypt! He pulled her legs free one by one and hauled her from the orifice like a stillborn baby from an artificial womb. When her head came into view, he saw blood dripping from her nose and ears. No!

Zen wiped her face with the cuff of his sleeve and checked her throat for obstruction. Her teeth were all fine, and her gums free of blood. He blew a breath into her mouth and watched her chest rise. He pushed on her heart in quick pulse as her body deflated, then filled her with another breath, keeping the pace, holding fast to faith. He pulled the breathing tube from her crumpled spacesuit and took a rich breath of oxygenated air, then expelled it into Simara's broken frame, over and over, pumping her chest with steady rhythm. Her throat rattled with phlegm.

A helicopter came screaming down the valley with twin searchlights and beat the air above as Zen worked at resuscitation. Waves whipped up in a froth on the river as the craft settled on pontoons and expelled two children onto the beach, a boy and girl dressed in plain cellulose, thin wraiths, perhaps teenagers at best. They rushed forward and fell on their knees at his side.

"Mothership has gone quiet," the girl said. "It's a terrible omen."

"No," Zen said and blew rich oxygen inside Simara's limp body. How long had it been since she stopped breathing on her own? How long could she last before permanent damage? "How did you find us? Are you omnidroid?"

"Simara is our elder," the boy said. "We're always in touch with her."

"Can you connect with her now? Is there no brain activity at all?"

The boy grimaced sadly and shook his head.

The girl held up a palm. "Wait. Fermi, did you hear that?"

The boy closed his eyes and peered up at his skullrider vision. "What?"

"I thought I heard something."

Zen took a huge breath of air and blew it into Simara, forcing sustenance into her, pushing his luck to the end. What could these babies know about life and death?

"I heard that," the boy said. "Did you hear that?"

"Mothership is back online," the girl said with a squeal of delight. "She says to bring Simara to the helicopter."

Zen wagged his chin. "She's had a wicked blow to the head. She can't be moved."

The boy, Fermi, put his tiny hand on Zen's shoulder with eerie confidence. "Bring her to the helicopter."

Zen forced another breath of air past blue lips, and Simara coughed in reply, but he couldn't tell if it was a last gasp of death or first hope of life. She was barely a feather-sprite in his arms as he picked her up and gently cradled her. He stumbled over rocks along the beach with his lips on hers, dripping tears on her tranquil face as he followed the children to the helicopter and climbed aboard. He continued a steady exhalation into her tiny body with faith and promise as they rose into the air and sped away over the trees. He would gladly breathe life into her precious mouth forever, never sleeping, never weary.

PART THREE: RONI

NEUROZONICS

Roni knew how to tease meaning from the manic rush of the V-net, to distill it down to the news that mattered—that was his expertise as a media darling in New Jerusalem and anchorman for the *Daily Buzz*. And he didn't go for all that talking-head virtuality crap or the pop-culture mayhem of the vidi slashers. He came to the office in person every day and sat in front of the cameras, blemishes and all. Roni had a creamy complexion, a full head of dark hair, and a secret weapon in Derryn the makeup boy who wielded pure genius with a brush, but it was content that drove his high ratings and big bonus bucks. He had a nose for news and prided himself on finding the real story behind the headlines.

He strolled into the newsroom to find five staffers busy at their terminals stroking the V-net feeds for daily drama like trawlermen checking their lines for a good catch. They had their thoughts plugged up on viewscreens to share internal visions with the team, and Roni watched images flash like lightning as their fleeting minds paraded the virtual landscape. "Did you see the one where the escaped criminal jumps into space from a crashing troopship and lives?"

His executive editor, Gladyz van-Dam, looked over from her thoughtscreen and pursed pretty lips. She wore her brown hair long and fashionably curled to her shoulders, a source of pride for her though she never appeared on camera. "Yeah, heady stuff. Made a six-point on the chart for a few minutes. She's still in a coma, kind of a dead end."

"What's the real story?"

Gladyz grinned. "You know I love it when you talk dirty, Roni." She arched her eyebrows in fake flirtation and began searching for data on the V-net. "The charge was murder, no details released pending jury selection."

"Great, I love a good body count."

"Oooh, get this, she's omnidroid."

Roni flinched. "Bummer."

"Yeah." Gladyz nodded. "Bad magic—probably why the first run didn't mention it. She's been working hard-life on the Babylon trade route. Strange place for an omnidroid."

Roni sidled up and peeked over her shoulder. "Yeah, but a great place to get away with murder. You got any vidi on this femme fatale?"

"Not yet. Here's a still." She relayed a photo for view.

White spacer skin like fish flesh, blue eyes, dark hair cut short—pretty girl, but not a starlet. "She's just a kid. What, seventeen, twenty?"

Gladyz chewed her lower lip as she scrolled through layers of data. She wore wide-lapel suits to work with skirts above the knee, playing the dignified executive for what it was worth and showing off great legs. She was a veteran production editor and directed the camera crew with a firm hand. "Hmm, no birth registry in the system. But you're right, she does look young—like an elf."

"A biogen with no date stamp," Roni said. "Could she be from Earth, smuggled through the Macpherson Doorway?"

"I doubt it. The quarantine dates back over a dozen years. She would have been a baby at the time."

"The Doorway is a sieve these days. Lots of genetic material gets through."

Gladyz shook her bouncy brown locks. "But not a biogen—that's the type of thing they're most worried about, a genetically engineered plague or virus. Just imagine what a pandemic from Earth would do to our limited population base."

"Okay, what do we have? An omnidroid of unknown origin, a mystery girl charged with murder and left behind on a crashing troopship. Makes me tingle all over."

"I love it when you tingle. You want to work with it? There's an accomplice. A Bali boy."

Roni nodded in appreciation. "Even better. Where's he holed up?"

"Bedside vigil. New Jerusalem West. You want me to scramble a crew and summon Ngazi?"

"No, leave the freak out of this for now. We'll let the first run fade and throw the dogs off the scent while this one ferments like fine wine. I want this under wraps and exclusive. Give me a day to get the real story." Ngazi was an autistic savant who provided emotional colour to the wirehead feed for the feelie users. He had no natural capacity for language, but his brain had overcompensated from birth with an increased ability to engineer digital emotion. Roni didn't like to bring Ngazi in too early on his feature stories, and meant no disrespect with the office moniker. "What else do we have?"

Gladyz splayed a hand to her thoughtscreen. "The escaped orangutan is still on the loose. It's getting political, tagging on the omnidroid scandal."

Roni smiled at the synchrony of his universe. "Perfect lead-in. We'll call it the *Hairy Ride*."

Gladyz van-Dam shrugged. "You're the man."

"And you're the best. Let's wreck this world."

Gladyz raised her hand up for the customary palm slap of promise, and Roni gave his editor a grand smack. They had a good working system based on mutual respect and compromise. They trusted each other to keep strict confidence while they ferreted out the truth, brainstorming ideas and feeding off the energy, and they put on a grand public spectacle six days a week on all public channels—the *Daily Buzz*.

Roni ambled into the makeup salon while Gladyz primed the studio crew. The famous orangutan was biogen, and researchers were testing for signs of psychic ability—all very bad-boy amid persistent rumours that the omnidroids had developed precognition. Nothing better than controversy to pump the pipe on the newsfeed, and this one had good scare factor—no one would buy lottery tickets or invest in the stock market with omnidroid mindreaders on the loose. A deal-breaker like that could alter the equilibrium of power and ruin the digital economy, but he'd tag on the controversy with poetic licence and hint at conspiracy to set up his next feature story, all part of the media game. News was for exploitation, and Roni was the best in the biz.

Derryn the beautician made quick work of Roni's strong

features and firm jaw as the first script began to trickle in on Roni's earbug. Lots of interesting stuff today, not just celebrity crap. A blight in the northern wheat fields was giving corporate critics fresh ammunition in a call for biodiversity of the food supply. A motion had been launched again in parliament to give voting rights to cybersouls in storage, a move that could shift significant economic influence to a group of eternals who were technically dead. And, for lovers of body culture and the Way, a cooperative symphony was being conducted based on the galvanic skin response of participants connected to sensors in the auditorium seats, some type of flash musical experience.

Derryn was a true artist, gay in every sense of the word and a continual source of ribald humour for all the staff. He called Roni his "little masterpiece," hinting at bigger things to come and claiming to have seen a few contenders. He had a deadpan delivery and a knowing wink that might have made him a star onstage, but today his jokes fell on deaf ears as Roni continued to ruminate about Simara Ying—the little omnidroid pixie niggled in the back of his mind like a bitter seed caught in his teeth. Why the hell would Transolar leave an accused criminal on a doomed troopship? No room in the lifeboats? Or perhaps they were multitasking as judge, jury, and executioner! Either way, Roni would nail sympathy from a sophisticated audience and dangle accusations for juice while he pranced on the public stage at his editor's direction. Gladyz was no slouch. The whole team was a collective work of art—a creative gestalt in which innovation arose out of interaction.

They spent four hours putting together a twenty-two minute show, then shot it live in the studio with Ngazi and the full crew—traditional, timely, with the cutting edge of reality that made all the difference these days. Social netcasting was a big challenge, and Roni took it seriously. Relationships were what drove the news, motives and motions in the background, causes before effect. He wanted to know *why* the news was happening before he expounded on the when and what. He wanted to taste the bitter edge of tragedy, smell the stench of treachery, and relish in the sweetness of hard-earned exultation. And the groupies—whoo-boy, Roni loved the ladies despite Derryn's charms.

He bagged the *Daily Buzz* to applause from the staff and complimented the best van-Dam crew in the business with a nod to Gladyz and blind-faced Ngazi. They were all expert professionals who loved media culture in their bones and blood. As Roni was fond of repeating like a mantra to anyone who would raise a flagon of beer with him at the Dog and Hoar after hours: "Life is for living, and the net for sharing—long live the news!"

Today Roni skipped the pub meeting after work and took the overhead tram downtown to chase down his story. He settled in his seat and searched through virtual data on the back of his closed eyelids, where he found V-net reference to twenty-four more omnidroids, biogenic relatives to the pixie girl, Simara Ying. They were all very young, teenagers or less, which seemed reasonable for new biotechnology, but two had recently been killed in a freak accident—a helicopter crash! Roni could feel his red news-nose heating up in the fog with Santa on the way. Two omnidroids doing a short hop out in the sticks on Zuloo Island got caught in a surprise storm and drowned in the sea when the chopper went down. Seven crewmembers miraculously survived and were found floating in a lifeboat. The transport company, Redikit, was majority-owned by Transolar Corp., the big boys.

Bingo.

There was his lead story blaring in his brain: a mysterious conspiracy against omnidroids foisted by the biggest interplanetary transportation conglomerate in the three worlds! A hint at homicide, a thread of possibility—that was all he needed to fling some feces in the air on the *Daily Buzz*.

New Jerusalem West Hospital was a majestic spectacle in the sun, all glass and gold to reflect the heat and protect the underground corridors where lives were saved and families preserved. Roni flashed press credentials at a security cordon inside, but didn't specify his reason for visiting. He already had the room number from Gladyz and didn't want to draw any attention from media vamps or paparazzi. "Just background stuff," he said with a celebrity smile and nonchalant wave as he sauntered past the guards to the elevators. The narrow hallways downstairs were cluttered with supply carts and wheelchairs, but the medical staff seemed calm and controlled as they coped with another day in the trenches. The place smelled of liniment and detergent, a sharp shock to the olfactory senses.

Roni found his target ward and poked in the open door to find the Bali boy sitting in vigil with muscular arms folded across a burly chest. A teenager sat in a nearby chair with his feet dangling above the floor, an elf boy with features much like Simara's, perhaps a younger brother. No police in the hall, no sign of Transolar authority. "Zen Valda? I'm Roni Hendrik from the *Daily Buzz*. Mind if I come in?"

Zen stood but made no gesture of greeting. He was a handsome kid with auburn curls, well tanned and physically photogenic. Touching was a faux pas on Bali, and Roni was unsure of etiquette. He kept his hands to himself and peered at Simara Ying, asleep in her bed. "How's she doing?"

"She's okay," Zen said. "No change."

Roni nodded and edged into the room. The Bali boy looked haggard on close inspection, eyes dark, forehead grim. The elf child watched him with the steady stare of an empath, kind of creepy. "Are you a relative?"

The child studied him with intensity as though testing his aura or body magnetism or something weird like that. "Simara is the elder of our group. I'm Fermi." He bowed with adult aplomb. "Honoured to meet you."

"Thanks. Have you seen my show?"

"I'm watching several episodes now." He pointed to his forehead. "Very interesting."

"Oh," Roni said, "omnidroid." He should have known the biogens would huddle together in times of trouble. "I'm sympathetic to your cause."

The child barely blinked from his digital delirium, but at least he was a fan.

Roni turned his attention to Zen Valda. "I know you're in a difficult situation, and I can help you both, even if you're on the run from the law. There's no better place to hide than in plain sight on the news. No one can try anything funny with a thousand eyes looking on." He offered his camera smile, but got little response from the Bali boy. "You're a hero, you know, rising from the underground, protecting the downtrodden—people love that stuff. And the court will be supportive."

Zen nodded with glum weariness as he resumed his seat. "She didn't do it."

"I believe you."

"They tried to kill her."

"I wondered about that."

"They crashed the ship on purpose, just the way Simara said it would happen."

Roni kept a mask of concern on his face while his inner soul danced with glee. Crash a troopship to kill one little elf girl? That was great copy for any editor. He could see it all—giant ratings, big bonus. "Any idea why?"

Zen dropped his eyes in the negative, but the child piped up: "They tried to kill us all and failed. In desperation they made a terrible mistake in trying to murder our elder, and that's why you're here to reclaim justice for all."

Roni chuckled with affable humour. "Well, I'm just a newsman, but I'm sympathetic to your cause. There are a lot of mixed reports in the media, and some bad vibes on the sound bite. But rest assured I'll tell the real story."

The elf boy nodded again with eerie eccentricity. "Simara says you're very good at what you do."

Roni tipped his eyebrows up in alert to this fabled biogen telepathy. "Can she talk to you from her coma?"

"Mothership can hear her. The collective mind."

Roni stepped closer to Simara. The dark-haired girl was quite exquisite in person. Her vidi pic did not do her justice. A light brush of pink showed on high cheekbones, and her pointed chin seemed firm and determined even in sleep. "So she's in there? She's not brain-dead or lost to oblivion?"

"She's resting," Zen said. "She'll be back soon."

The hope in his voice was tinged with tragedy, poor kid. A

simple Bali boy flying in space with an omnidroid elder connected to a psychic mothermind! Man, what a story. "Where are you staying, Zen? Do you have anyone looking out for you?"

"I'm staying here," he said with dogged weariness.

"Come home with me and get some rest. I have a huge apartment with all the comforts. I'll bring you back in the morning to interview Simara. Let her sleep for now. Fermi and his kin will keep an eye on the room." Roni put on his best camera smile, guaranteed to please and toothy with enthusiasm. "Your girl's safe here."

Zen hesitated and glanced at Fermi. "Okay. I guess if Simara speaks well of you."

"Great. We'll grab a bite, get the details nailed down. C'mon." He almost slapped the boy on the shoulder with masculine exuberance, but stopped himself just in time. No touching on Bali, no fraternization. What a weird culture! And no sex, a whole planet of people afraid to share chromosomes mangled by solar rads, humanity's children flying too close to the sun and forced into sterility. Too bad.

Zen bent over Simara's prone form and closed his eyes in a moment of reverence, lost in some inner vision of solace. Was he trying to contact her? Praying for her? Roni felt a catch in his throat at the wonderful scene. Better and better.

On the walk to the transit station, the Bali boy slunk along with the shadows whenever he could and glanced periodically at the sun as though it was a public enemy. On the tram, he fidgeted nervously, rubbing at the base of his throat and wincing as he swallowed.

Roni leaned in close to him without drawing attention. "You okay?"

"Are you sure it's safe out in the open like this?"

"Yes, it's safe. We have heavy atmosphere on Cromeus, good protection. Don't worry."

The boy nodded and seemed satisfied, but his hands never stopped moving. He rubbed his knuckles and picked at his cuticles as he surveyed fellow passengers with furtive interest as though they might be zoo animals on display. Long sleeves were in vogue with high boots and hats, so there was not a lot of stray skin to upset any obscure Bali sensibilities. Perhaps the facial tattoos were weirding him out.

"I see you've got a brand new earbug there. Must be top art, huh? Set you back?"

Zen reached to touch his ear as though reminded of something foreign. "No, it was free. They pay me to login, but I can't really get the hang of it. I struggle just to tune it out. All that fragmented data is so distracting. I don't know how Simara does it day after day, the rush of virtual experience, the madness and chaos."

Roni nodded sagaciously. "I know what you mean. The V-net never sleeps."

"You keep the noise on all the time?"

"No, I hold high filters. Only my editor can get through to me, and a few close friends. I use it a lot for research. I'm always working, you know, in the news business. How long have you been with Simara?"

"Just a few weeks, but I know she's innocent."

"Sure." Faith shone in the kid's face like an epiphany, lovely stuff. "I'm a firm believer in the burden of proof. Do you think it's true what they say about omnidroids, that they can see the future?"

Zen looked down at his fidgeting hands as though peering for clues or pondering rarefied possibilities. "No, it can't be true. She gets herself in too much trouble."

"Oh?"

"She stumbles in the dark. She hits people without reason. She's the most frustrating woman I have ever met."

Roni chuckled. "Sounds like a peach. But how did she know the troopship would crash?"

The Bali boy shrugged. "From detective analysis, not magic. She has a lot of data going through her brain, but she doesn't use it very well. She gets surprised by simple things just like everyone else. She's no hypnotist or anything like that."

"Telepathist, I think is the term."

Zen shook his head at the impossibility. "Why would someone who can see the future spend her life running the hard trade route to Bali? Why live with daily danger and crash into rocks?"

"That, my friend," Roni said with a beatific smile, "is the real story."

He pieced together the panorama of his opening gambit over food cubes and squirts of allkool back at his apartment—the son of a politician, follower of the desert god Kiva, an expert in salvage and recycling technology. There was even a love angle and crude mismanagement of feminine wiles, a complicated string of ex-girlfriends and casual sex with an older woman—amazing what strangers would tell a newsman as they tilted on the edge of exhaustion. People had always opened up to Roni, even as a precocious school reporter. He had a friendly face and could boast a genuine smile at will. He knew how to prod with gentle interest while appearing suave and sincere. The rest was just human nature at work, a cathartic need to unburden and cleanse the soul.

Roni tucked Zen into a comfy couch and left him to dreamland as he began transcribing the evidence for his editor. Gladyz would love this one. She was a sucker for interpersonal conundrums and mismatched sexuality, much like their own tangled relationship twisting back through the years. She had slept with him only once, during his early apprenticeship as an upstart anchorman. He had charmed her and she had wooed him—it was difficult to tell in retrospect who had instigated that elusive moment of discovery. But it never led to a call-back, and the awkward stage had long since passed. Now they were working too hard to notice the possibility of a rematch still lurking in limbo, hiding behind a smokescreen of coarse jesting and crude innuendo. Just as well.

"I think we've got a wild one," he told her when he got to work the next morning. "A conspiracy against omnidroids, an attempt at genocide on the orders of Transolar Corporation."

Gladyz ducked her forehead. "Are you kidding me? They'll crucify us!"

"What if it's true?"

"Then we'd be dead already."

"They can't touch this smile. I have a degree in delusions of grandeur."

"You got that right."

"This is the big one, baby. They'll remember us forever." He batted eyelashes with dramatic flair. "And it will look great on your resumé."

Gladyz smirked. "That's good. 'Cause I'll probably be out of a job."

"I've got enough to make solid accusations. Two dead, one in the hospital, and twenty-two with stories to tell. But no hard evidence yet—these guys are pros. I say we go public and see what climbs out of the sewer. Take a look at my synopsis and tell me what we can do for vidi. How's the orangutan story playing out?"

"Back in the box, dead end on the newsfeed. They lured him out of hiding with some orange pussy and a banana cube."

Roni chuckled. "How the mighty biogen are fallen."

"All men are the same."

"Not me, hon. I'm different. I'm better."

She smiled. "I'll look at your outline and take it upstairs. Give me half an hour."

Roni ambled through the cafeteria line for a quick omelette and took a cream latte to the makeup salon, where Derryn fussed over a pimple on his chin while he tried to sip his drink.

Gladyz barged in with enthusiasm after only a few minutes. "They love it upstairs! I'm scrambling the crew and summoning Ngazi for a full-spectrum netcast. Derryn, you're in for makeup on the girl. We'll start with a bedside scene to rouse public sympathy. No names, no slander. I'm thinking a bouquet of flowers to get funerary undertones. Then we'll swing to a close-up of the cute Bali boy sitting in vigil like a sad puppy by the casket. Ngazi will have the feelie crowd weeping at his devotion."

Roni tipped his cup in acknowledgement to her exuberance as Derryn stroked his skin with a soft brush. He loved his job.

"They want to do a series," Gladyz said. "A complete exposé—good foreplay, strong prodding, followed by lingering doubt. They want in-depth coverage on this one, not the usual wham-slam-thank-you-ma'am. They believe in you, Roni." She fanned a fax-slip with exultation. "We have a budget!"

"I'll grab Zen from my apartment and get him cleaned up."

Roni checked the calendar on his eyescreen. "Meet you and the crew at the hospital in four hours?"

"Fine," Gladyz said, "but we need authentic clothing for the shoot, animal skins or tiger fur. What size is he?"

"He's large." Roni hunched up his shoulders. "Bigger than me. The Balians have increased lung capacity to breathe the thin air. He's built like an iron statue up top with a compact waist and muscular legs."

Derryn whistled with admiration. "Sounds like a hunk in a Tarzan outfit."

"This is going to be great," Gladyz said as she turned to the door. "I'm going shopping."

Roni packed a box with breakfast for his protégé and hurried back to his apartment. Zen woke bleary-eyed and cranky, poor kid, and Roni clucked with sympathy as he roused him to action. The Bali boy might not have slept for days, or fitfully at best, trapped in a doomed transport all the way from Trade Station in a wall-slot no bigger than a toilet stall. He seemed disoriented and confused, but improved gradually after a shot of caffeine and a few sugar pastries. What the heck did Balians cook on their wilderness world? Lizard meat and cactus? He'd heard stories of psychedelic mushrooms from the deep caves where miners toiled on excavation machines to harvest silver and gold from cold volcanoes. And wild, fermented drinks full of uncontrolled organisms, a sure recipe for trouble on any planet.

Zen picked up an orange from the box and sniffed it. "Is this right from the tree?"

"Yeah. There are groves all around the city."

Zen nodded his approval and bit into the skin. He looked

off into the imaginary distance as he chewed through the fibrous cover to find succulence below, tasting to the fullest as he slowly devoured the entire fruit bite by bite in sure ecstasy.

Roni winced as Zen crunched seeds between his teeth. "More coffee?"

Zen held up his mug for a refill. "So we're going to see Simara today?"

"Yep, with a full crew. Don't be nervous about the cameras. Imagine friends or robots, whatever works best for you."

Zen puzzled on that for a moment, but shrugged it off. "Let's take her some food for when she wakes up."

"No, the hospital is very strict about what goes in and out the door. It's like a quarantine zone. Everyone's concerned about biospheres these days. Don't worry, they have lots of good food with all the necessary vitamins and minerals. This is all for you. Just eat whatever you want. There'll be plenty more later."

Again the Bali boy paused with query on his brow, probably a victim of scarcity at home and that pasty goop they rationed on spaceships. "Where does it come from?"

"We have a cafeteria at work for the staff. You know, like a restaurant." Still no response from Zen. "A banquet table?"

"A festival?"

"Sure, that works. We have a celebration every day with all the food we can eat. It's in our contract."

"And you can share freely?"

Roni smiled at the opportunity to cement a solid relationship with the boy. "Just with our friends. You're special to us. You're a hero. My editor is off buying new clothes for you as we speak."

Zen picked another pastry from the box. He seemed to like

the sweet stuff—probably go spastic into a hyper-sugar fit any minute. Did they even have sugar on Bali? What about allergens? What about inoculations? Oh, well, one day at a time.

Zen's paper clothes had pretty much shredded by now, so they found a jacket that was big enough to drape over his muscular shoulders and a pair of baggy sweatpants with an elasticized waistband. The kid had skin like tanned leather, roughened beyond his years, but he had bumps in all the right places for the camera and a sensitive voice for the microphone—the perfect media package.

They took a tram to the hospital and hooked up with Gladyz and Derryn to doll Zen up in a public change room. Fake leopard skin, really? As if there had ever been a leopard born this side of the Macpherson Doorway! Fashion sense was nonsense half the time, but what could you do? They put pants on him at least, plain khaki dungarees, and gelled his auburn hair into soft, sexy curls. Zen looked fantastic by the time they were done, and Derryn was practically drooling as he fawned over the kid.

The roadies crammed the wardroom with equipment as two little elf girls looked on in blank-faced wonder. Simara was sleeping soundly and snoring like a kitten in her coma. Derryn gave her cheeks a quick touch-up with his magic brush and painted her lips like an artist. Wow, the dark-haired pixie was beautiful in the right light!

Gladyz escorted Ngazi through the crowd and set him up like a lightning rod in the centre of the room, where he stood stiff and freakish, oblivious to his surroundings as he stared off at distant digital shores. His autistic talents were arcane, but in effect he amplified the emotional signals of the participants and sent them out over the V-net in a biofeedback loop with the wirehead audience to give dimensional depth and spiritual meaning to the show. He added scent and temperature for connoisseur users, along with other tweaks below the threshold of consciousness— full-spectrum awareness was an art form in itself. Ngazi never spoke, of course, but his black skin shone with flop sweat in proximity to humans and he tended to hum when he got excited, so he had to be carefully positioned off-camera and clear of the boom mikes.

Gladyz wheeled in an intravenous bag on a stand to use as a prop behind Simara's bed, and taped a data tablet to the head-board to add a clinical air to the scene. She positioned Zen in a bedside chair in half profile with a leopard shoulder to the camera, and placed Simara's limp hand between his palms. A bouquet of fresh flowers bloomed with burgeoning romance on a table in the background as Gladyz primped the scene for detail, pulling folds out of blankets and tucking in loose corners, adjusting lamps to banish facial shadows. When everything was perfect to her meticulous editorial eye, she counted down five on her fingers and pointed to Roni with authority. He smiled on cue, and Ngazi poked his nose up as though sniffing promise on the ether.

"Welcome to the *Daily Buzz* and thanks for tuning in. Turn off your peripherals for this one, folks, because we are breaking big news! This is Roni Hendrik reporting live from New Jerusalem West Hospital where Zen Valda from Bali is sitting in vigil on his honeymoon with his young wife, Simara Ying. How is she doing today, Zen?"

Pan to the Bali boy in his leopard-skin costume. "No change. She's in a coma."

Roni turned back to the camera with grim anticipation. "Our

young couple recently jumped from a crashing Transolar troopship where they were abandoned by the crew, and flew unaided through space to Cromeus from an estimated altitude of one hundred miles! Pretty amazing, wouldn't you say, Zen?"

"Yes, it's a miracle from Kiva."

Roni smiled with multicultural tolerance. "The desert god of Bali reached his hand across the heavens that day, but you had some help from your *omnidroid* partner, correct?"

"Simara knew the ship was going to crash. She knew the captain had targeted us for death. But she planned every detail of our escape. I smuggled two spacesuits into a hidden locker, and we dove for the planet."

"Wow." Roni spread his arms in a dramatic flourish. "Our honeymoon couple *dove* into open space to escape certain death at the hands of Transolar Corporation. Pretty scary!"

Zen looked down and fondled Simara's limp hand. Oops, the kid did not want to admit fear on camera in front of his family and friends. Okay, roll with it. "Simara Ying has been accused in the disappearance of her stepfather, Randy Ying. Do you think that was the reason the authorities abandoned you on the doomed troopship?"

Zen tilted his head with a subtle wince. "I don't know. She's been accused of murder, but she couldn't have done it. I've heard rumours that all the omnidroids are being targeted for decommission."

Whoa, the Bali boy caught Roni by surprise with a big word, but he took it in stride. "Many of our viewers might consider that to be *genocide*, but it certainly fits with the facts this reporter has discovered. Seventeen accidents appear to have been engineered across Cromeus, and two omnidroid lives have been lost. Can we pan out for a minute?" He paused as the camera view widened. "Ruis Limkin and Elana Mant, may they rest in fond memory." Roni laid out a hand toward the two elves standing nearby. "Brother and sister to these two biogen children watching in silent vigil as their elder, Simara Ying, lies a helpless martyr to a vast conspiracy of evil!" Roni glanced to his editor to gauge her reaction. She grimaced and nodded—he was flirting with the edge, but not over the top, not yet.

Gladyz ducked her eyes to scan inner data for a few seconds as Roni rambled on with details about the helicopter accident. She looked up and signalled him to login. That was weird, and generally bad form during a live netcast—it could pull the audience out of the drama if they thought the anchorman was watching a different channel. He tapped on with a discreet touch to his ear. ::WE'RE GETTING GREAT FEEDBACK, RONI. TRANSOLAR IS FALLING ALL OVER US, OF COURSE, BUT THERE'S A MESSAGE FOR ZEN FROM THE GOVERNOR OF BALI, GENOA BLACKPOLL. WE NEED HIS PERMISSION FOR A SHARED FEED. DO IT NOW! WE'LL GO SPLIT-FRAME WITH THE TWO OF THEM.::

"Zen," Roni said without missing a beat. "I know you've just recently had an earbug installed, and many viewers will remember their first days surfing the V-net as children, how confusing that can be! But there's an important message coming in from the governor of Bali, Genoa Blackpoll. Would you be willing to login and share with our news audience?"

Zen looked up with alarm. "Does it have something to do with the investigation?"

Roni smiled to put him at ease as he backed out of camera

view and Ngazi stiffened with galvanic energy. "Let's login and find out, shall we?"

Zen touched his ear. "Login. Genoa Blackpoll. Are you there, Governor?"

Roni watched the split-view on his eyescreen as a staffer handed him a bottle of water out of frame. Genoa Blackpoll stood propped behind a lectern, a grey-haired statesman with an aura of dignity, perfect for the job and probably the centre of a hastily organized media scrum. Why did politicians always look so good on camera? Was it truly survival of the photogenic fittest?

"Zen, I've been trying to reach you for hours. I have good news, and I've been holding the release so that you would be the first to hear from me personally. They found the flight recorder from Simara's shuttle by following your pinpoint instructions. They analyzed the data and discovered both voices on the record. Randy Ying was clearly alive after Simara left the ship. She could not possibly have killed him, and all charges have been dropped by the Crown attorney. You saved her, son."

"Thank you, sir. That's great. Thanks so much."

"I understand you've run into some trouble on Cromeus, and I wish you well. Whatever happens, know that I'm proud of you and all Bali stands with you. Your family and every member of Star Clan rejoice in your survival and sacrifice, and you bring great honour to the memory of your father."

Roni choked on his water and wiped his chin. Holy crap, better and better! It's the great surprises that make history in news, those on-air twists of fortune that turn myths into legend and personalities into prophets. He rolled the bottle out of view as Gladyz gave him a three-count to camera. "You heard it here first, folks. Congratulations to Zen and Simara. Wonderful news! Our martyr, falsely accused from the beginning, has earned a reprieve from condemnation. Who, then, will dare slander the omnidroids now?" He stabbed out a palm to Simara, asleep on her hospital bed with the intravenous stand in the background, a pitiful sight to all, then turned to Zen. "Or continue to ignore the proud people of Bali who toil underground in the dark to bring us the strategic metals we use every day of the week? Let's remember our friends today, all of us, and hug our families close. Let's be quick to forgive and slow to accuse, and may the desert god Kiva bless us all. Perhaps Zen Valda will honour us with a final word to summarize his experience at this critical moment."

Roni nodded to Zen as Gladyz relayed instructions in his inner ear, more news coming in, a feedback frenzy. The Bali boy sputtered nonsense and cried openly for Simara, predictable stuff, but he could have spoken a different language for all it mattered now. Fate had shone a wide spotlight on his haloed head, and he could do no wrong. Ngazi dripped with perspiration as he beamed out public sympathy and consolation, having a co-creative heyday with all the wirehead brains linked to the feed. Zen blubbered and thanked everyone for their support as the two elf children came on camera to stroke Simara's forehead and whisper in her ear. Roni let him blather on to milk the moment as the netcast went viral and a shitstorm of new viewers came onstream.

Finally he put up his hand and waved for attention. "We've just received word . . ." He waited as Zen finished and sniffed his way back to composure. "We've just received word from the chairman and CEO of Transolar Corporation, Elron Pritchard, and I'll paraphrase here for the sake of brevity. In light of the recent systems malfunction aboard a Transolar troopship that almost resulted in loss of life, and in view of the false accusations pressed against an innocent omnidroid woman that led her into harm's way, the Board of Directors has established the Transolar Foundation, a new charitable organization designed to aid and improve the lives of all biogen children throughout the three planets. Elron Pritchard has personally kicked off the foundation with a donation of one million credits to start the ball rolling, and invites everyone to join with him in showing love and compassion for all people regardless of their mental configurations.

"Whew. Fabulous news, folks, and thank you to Transolar Corporation. We're almost out of time. I'm all choked up about this, and I know our friends from Bali have celebrating to accomplish, so I'll sign off back to the studio for now and see you all tomorrow . . . bringing the future to life . . . on the *Daily Buzz*."

"And cut," Gladyz said as she strode forward. "That's a wrap. Thanks to New Jerusalem West for their gracious hospitality. Let's pack up and let these people get on with their work." The corridor outside was crowded with onlookers as doctors and nurses stood clutching databoards to their chests in silent awe. Gladyz strode over to Roni as the whole thing started to sink in. "That sure smells like culpability," she whispered. "Good job. You always were light on your feet."

Roni nodded, feeling vacuous as adrenalin seeped away. He had reacted with pure instinct to a stellar convergence of events, but what did it mean? What the hell had just happened? The real story seemed deeper now and farther away than ever.

"Funny thing about news," Gladyz said with a whimsical smile, "it travels fast and turns into history so quickly."

Zen came over with an elbow up like a wrestler performing a blocking manoeuvre. "Thanks for everything, Roni."

"Uh, sure." Roni lifted both elbows up like chicken wings, one after the other, unsure of etiquette, and Zen twisted awkwardly to cross his forearm with a manly prod.

"Can I buy you boys dinner?" Gladyz said. "We can start planning tomorrow's show."

NINE

Was it possible for news to be too perfect, the centre of the media hurricane too calm? Roni couldn't sleep as he analyzed the bare facts in his mind, running events over and over, forward and back. The orchestrated message from Genoa Blackpoll, on a time delay from Bali no less, had set off a chain of events among the executives of Transolar, who surely must have been primed in advance to have their pocketbooks so close at hand, perhaps by usage data related to Roni's own research or scuttlebutt among the hornets he had stirred.

And the little elf girl sleeping in a coma. How had she vaulted into stardom without lifting a finger? Roni had made her famous on a whim, or so he had thought. Her and the Bali boy on a magic honeymoon of misadventure—in retrospect, it seemed an obvious melodrama served up on a silver platter. What anchorman could resist such a potent lure? Was Simara Ying using the *Daily Buzz* somehow, manipulating the news, pulling puppet strings with strange telepathy? Was Simara scripting dangerous events to serve her own agenda? Had she sacrificed herself to secure a future for her omnidroid family? No, that was crazy space. Roni needed to get some sleep, just a few hours until dawn.

He tossed in his bunk and checked the time on his eyescreen. Too late to take a pill now—he'd be groggy until noon. He still had a show to grind out six days a week, and it'd be a hard act to follow after such mind-expanding success. Okay, back to work, back to basics, he'd peek behind the purple curtain and follow the money on its telltale journey. Who secured the most economic gain from yesterday's spectacle on the *Daily Buzz*? Not Simara stuck in a coma, not the penniless Bali boy at her side, not the Transolar executives now forking out creds to save their corporate reputation. The omnidroid children were the only real beneficiaries of this drastic change in public paradigm—once reviled, now recompensed, once persecuted and slandered, now lauded across three worlds.

Roni Hendrik sighed and reached to touch his ear. "Login," he told the darkness above his bed, "bring me up all the data on the omnidroids." His mind brightened into a honeycomb of windows, and he began to peer through them with methodical rigour. Time of manufacture and place of upbringing, school records, career highlights, social contracts, who, what, when, where, why—the newsman's invocation. Forensic analysis was not much fun, but often yielded surprising results. Every scrap of data was recorded on the V-net, every voice message, every download.

Roni blinked and scrolled, picked and niggled, reclining in his bunk with three worlds dancing before his eyes in a manic rush of inspiration. All the other omnidroids were younger than Simara Ying, the three oldest just fifteen years of age, the youngest seven— twelve boys and twelve girls in ideal balance, all manufactured by the same company, Neurozonics, a private corporation registered in New Jerusalem by numbered proxy agents. As with all biogens, the omnidroids enjoyed full citizenship by legal proclamation, including the rights to vote and to produce children. They could not be owned like robots or machines, though technically they were created beings. They were human, or at least they looked human, and their programming was by nurture and nature just like everyone else's—they had problems, deficiencies, variations of design, but their one major cerebral augmentation was unlimited access to the V-net and no bandwidth filters. Omnidroids were born into zero-day digital space and lived in a fantasyland far beyond the mortal sphere of intelligence. Physical experience and bodily sensation were only tiny fragments of their transcendent existence, mundane accessories to digital infinity. In time, life itself might become a vestigial appendage. Anecdotal evidence indicated difficulty in social interaction, reticence in speech and public conduct, fear of crowds, and lack of *common sense*, whatever that was. Rumours suggested the possibility of precognition.

Roni read through corporate financial reports and quarterly analytical guidance, but could not cobble together a big picture in his mind. Neurozonics was part of a mesh of related companies in a variety of unrelated fields, with majority shareholdings and minority interests in hundreds of subsidiary entities. The mandatory filings were so abstruse and technical that a person could read them ten times and never get the gist. And then there was the problem of assets held in probate by cybersouls in limbo—technically dead until rules of procedure were enacted in parliament to grant civil status to eternals, if and when the complicated legislation ground through administrative committee meetings. Neurozonics was a grinning spider on a translucent web of intrigue.

Roni tracked down the details byte by byte, piecing together a complicated puzzle in his mind as the sun pushed morning through his bedroom window. He didn't need sleep, he needed answers, and by the time his alarm sounded he had a sketch of a plan.

"I've got it," he told Gladyz as he stumbled into the newsroom with a steaming cup of coffee cradled in trembling palms.

"Roni, you look like shit. Have you been up all night again?" Gladyz rose from her seat to get a better look at him. "You're a mess."

"Couldn't sleep," he said, "but I've got a hot lead."

Gladyz took him by the arm. "Come with me. We'll see if Derryn can salvage something."

"The omnidroids were all manufactured by the same company, Neurozonics Inc."

"Great, Roni, that's good. Derryn, we need help."

Roni shrugged off her guiding hand, but settled into a recliner chair by force of habit. "Neurozonics goes back to the founding fathers, back to the first days of the Doorway. They have financial fingers in all the major pies, political influence, a vast army of cybersouls colluding in eternal storage. They have everything to gain and nothing to lose. I smell conspiracy."

"Oh, starry heavens," Derryn said as he scrutinized Roni's eyes up close. "Are you packing for vacation?"

"Can you save him, Doctor?"

Derryn clucked his tongue and tipped his head from side to side as he inspected the damage. "I need an hour and some ice."

"Done."

Roni blinked past Derryn's shoulder to get his editor's attention. "Will you listen to me?"

Gladyz smiled. "We're already on it, honey buns. Transolar cops have found Randy Ying operating under an assumed name on Babylon. He claims to be working as a consultant for Neurozonics."

"They paid him to abandon his ship?"

"He's clammed up about everything. His trading company had more liability than equity, so it's gone into bankruptcy. The ship is up for public auction."

"We need to challenge Neurozonics on this. The public deserves an explanation."

"Leave it to me. You two get cozy while I hunt down the bad guys."

Derryn resumed his clinical inspection and began selecting concoctions, arranging them in rows like soldiers preparing for battle. Roni sighed and forced himself to relax. At least he was at work and making progress against whatever invisible empire was out there. A feeling of futility was trying to drag him down, a sense of helplessness against a hidden colossus. Why would Neurozonics create biogen children to challenge their own vaulted position in society? Why risk the future of humanity by tinkering with DNA to produce a telepathic species? Financial success in the investment arena? Prestige? Power? What possible outcome would justify such an outrageous gamble with the forces of evolution?

Derryn started work on his face by scrubbing with soap and water and massaging his temples and forehead with hot ointments. Then he covered Roni's eyes with an ice pack, forcing him into darkness and back to his online research. What about the two omnidroid children who perished in the helicopter accident? Was there anything to set them apart, any reason why they might be culled from the herd? Roni surfed through data on the V-net while

Derryn worked on his neck and shoulders. Ruis Limkin and Elana Mant were both registered biogens with elite status in society. They had astounding records in all measurements of gifted intelligence, genius levels approaching omniscience—nothing unusual. But they were dead, and all the other omnidroids had survived horrible carnage in which several humans had been injured, collateral damage in a mysterious war for the future.

An hour later Roni was ready for action, fuelled with caffeine and powered by protein, his showbiz blood pumping with sure promise. His face felt like a rubber mask, but Derryn seemed satisfied, which was generally regarded as high praise on the set.

Gladyz came back precisely on schedule. "Neurozonics won't talk to us, and they seem defensive. I think you're on to something."

Roni's grin almost cracked his makeup. "I knew it."

"We're going to shoot some studio footage on the omnidroids to mix with stock vidi, then go live back at the hospital with Zen. We'll pick it up where we left off." She held up cautionary palms. "We'll go easy at first and see what shakes out. We're already riding high, so this will be denouement, just a pleasant, lingering afterglow, got it?"

"I love lingering afterglow," Derryn interjected with a wink. "Need any help?"

"Sure, come along." Gladyz thrust a shoulder forward. "Pack up a kit. You worked wonders yesterday on Simara." She turned to scrutinize Roni for a moment. "And great job on the little masterpiece."

Derryn nodded. "He does look pretty good . . ." He winked again. ". . . for an older boy."

"Yeah, don't forget who's paying the bills around here," Roni said as he tugged the apron from around his neck. He strode into the studio like a peacock on parade, but the camera crew muttered bland greetings with little recognition for his triumph the previous day. The team was already hard at work sculpting a new episode. They shot some talking-head clips at close range to summarize Roni's research, and put them in the script for later, then quit early for lunch to start preparations for the big event live at the hospital during primetime.

By now the story was taking shape, and a few questions were looming at the surface. Why were the omnidroid children always whispering in Simara's ear? Could she hear them? How closely could they be connected to a woman in a coma? Documented evidence showed that some patients could indeed hear noises from a subconscious state, but there was nothing to indicate active memories could be formed by a hibernating brain, even in an augmented omnidroid. Roni had no scientific territory to put his foot on, but he wondered if Simara somehow might be aware of the media storm circling around her.

Zen was still sleeping when Roni returned to his apartment. The Bali boy had lost any vestige of a circadian rhythm and did not respond to the daylight streaming in the window. He seemed to be slipping toward his natural state as a night dweller on a planet too close to the sun, where people slept in caves and came out to play in the dark when the rads were low. On top of that, Zen was suffering from stress and a near-death experience, not to mention a switch to the twenty-four-hour Cromean cycle. He seemed to wake and sleep at random several times a day and never rose from bed with a smile. Roni poked him from a safe distance with a broom handle. "Wake up, Zen. It's time to visit Simara."

Zen groaned and peered out from under a tangled mop of auburn curls. He seemed fearful at first, tense and ready to pounce like a trapped animal, but his face softened with recognition. "Okay."

They shared pastries and fresh fruit, Zen's delicacies of choice, and Roni set some ideas in motion as they journeyed by tram to the hospital. He needed an authentic response on camera, so he never scripted his clients, but he planted seeds and watered them as best he could. It sounded a bit outlandish to voice his theory out loud: a nefarious corporation manufacturing a regiment of telepathic omnidroids to take over the world. What sober and cynical V-net viewer would swallow that tasty morsel along with her afternoon tea?

The street outside the hospital was crammed with pedestrians, and trolley traffic was at a standstill. A small squadron of protesters chanted "Shame on Transolar!" to the dissonant accompaniment of honking horns and shouts of impatience from frustrated commuters. A ramshackle memorial had been erected on the sidewalk with oversized pictures of Simara and Zen, and well-wishers had piled a huge mound of wilting flowers at the foot of the structure in homage, but Gladyz breezed by in disdain with her crew in search of bigger game and a brighter byline.

Inside the hospital, the foyer was jam-packed with visitors, the noise tumultuous and the air heavy with fragrance and clouds of pollen. Hundreds of people were lined up at the elevators for a chance to touch the omnidroid martyr and lay bouquets of honour at her door. Security guards had cordoned off hallways with caution tape like yellow tinsel in an effort to keep essential services running, but crowds jostled shoulder to shoulder along the perimeter in search of an easier route downstairs. Gladyz blinked in disbelief and turned to Roni with wide eyes. Her expression said it all: the *Daily Buzz* had created a monster!

But she meant it in the nicest way, of course.

Gladyz barged her way to the security office and tried to present press credentials to harried staff, but the jig was up and the guards were grim. The hospital was in lockdown mode under strict protocol. Zen was the only person allowed access to Simara, but Gladyz was not giving him up. There was no way the roadies could get a camera crew in past this horde, no way they could set up shop with Ngazi to shoot today's show in Simara's room. The clock was ticking and the primetime slot fast approaching as Gladyz returned to the outer vestibule ranting and cursing to no avail with her fists clenched in her bouncy brown hair. Derryn dropped his cosmetics case and perched on it daintily. He folded bony arms over his chest and tipped a slender shin across his knee as the roadies struggled to keep from bashing innocent bystanders with their lampstands and booms. Ngazi stood like a wooden statue staring off in the distance and humming with irritation.

"Let's shoot it right here," Roni said. "Grainy and gritty right on the street. Look at these placards." He waved an arm at a forest of hand-painted signs: *We Love You!*, *WAKE UP!*, *Shame on Transolar!*, *Omnidroids Are People!*, and a heart with the names *Simara + Zen* printed inside it.

Gladyz put a finger to her chin as she surveyed the scene with an editorial eye. "I have never seen so many exclamation marks in one place."

Roni spread his hands to the crew as though presenting indisputable evidence. "This is *news*, people. Let's bag it."

"Damn," Gladyz said, but her face brightened with determination. "Drop the booms and lamps here with Derryn. Give me two cams on shoulder mount. We'll have to work in close quarters, but try to keep some space around Ngazi so he doesn't freak out. Get a hand mike for Roni. Where's the sun?" She spun in a quick circle like a windup toy and pointed. "Gritty it is. Over there by the gift shop with north light on their faces. Zen and Roni centre stage. Let's go. What are you waiting for? Go! Go!"

The crew scrambled to work with a few professional expletives in the line of duty, and no bystanders were seriously injured as they claimed a small circle amidst the crowd and propped Ngazi in position like a lighthouse beacon in a milling sea.

"Okay?" Gladyz yelled into mayhem. "Thirty seconds, okay? Just throw the script out, Roni. It's a disaster movie now, got it?" She pumped her fist in the air for attention while the cameramen braced themselves inside a protective huddle of roadies. "Five," Gladyz yelled as she began the countdown with her fingers—*three, two, one*, she pointed to Roni with fierceness in her eyes.

"Welcome to the *Daily Buzz* and thanks for tuning in again to this incredible story! This is Roni Hendrik reporting live from New Jerusalem West with Zen Valda from Bali. We are in a pickle today as you can plainly see. Thousands of well-wishers and protesters have assembled peacefully at the hospital where Simara Ying still ekes out a fragile existence in deep coma. Most are here just to catch a glimpse of the amazing girl who fell from the stars. Others are angry at the court system that put her in jeopardy and the cold-hearted corporation that left her to die in the void of space. I hope you can hear me okay with all this noise. Have you ever seen anything like this, Zen?"

"No." The boy's eyes were panicky, his face fretful, but Roni had to force something out of the kid to keep him in the game.

"Are you angry at Transolar for what they did to your wife?"

"Yes." One-word answers pressed through grim lips—too many people for a wilderness recluse! Ngazi began murmuring, "hunh, hunh," in the background as his emotional bandwidth went into overload.

Roni turned to the camera for support. "A million Transolar creds can buy a lot of goodwill for the omnidroids, but the stain of guilt gets right into your skin, doesn't it?" He wiggled the fingers of his free hand for emphasis. "The *Daily Buzz* has uncovered new information about this nefarious case. Following closely on the genetic pattern of the mysterious elder, Simara Ying, all twenty-four omnidroid children were brought to life right here on Cromeus in the research labs of Neurozonics Incorporated. Bioengineered from human DNA and augmented for specialized communication and high intelligence, these innocent children were manufactured as modern slaves to serve corporate masters right here in New Jerusalem!" Roni paused for dramatic effect and swallowed saliva to soothe his dry throat. He turned again to Zen. "Did Simara say anything about her childhood trapped in a sterile laboratory?"

Zen frowned. "Not really. She had an unhappy youth."

"No doubt, robbed of human contact and compassion. Who knows what rigorous tests were performed on these biogen babies during early experiments? They are said to have been programmed for precognition, to be able to communicate across vast distance. Have you seen any evidence of special telepathic powers?"

The crowd surged around them as the news team became a focus of attention. People with placards were trying to get their slogans visible in the background behind Zen, and roadies were holding them back with arms spread wide. Ngazi was sweating bullets and flapping his arms in an autistic episode while he turned in a circle moaning, "hunh, hunh." Roni glanced around as a bouquet hit him on the shoulder. "Sorry about that, folks. We're on the front lines of news today, keeping it real in search of tomorrow." Gladyz rolled a finger in the air to signal an upcoming transition back to the prepared footage in the studio. There was only so much you could do with street theatre. "Back to Zen Valda now, have you seen any evidence of exotic communication among the omnidroids?"

Zen nodded, a picture of sincerity, a man you could trust. "Yes, they hear messages from a collective voice they call the mothership, a hive-mind like a guardian angel."

"Really, and can they communicate with Simara even in her coma?"

"Yes, Simara's just sleeping." He turned to the camera audience with unfeigned faith. "She's okay. Mothership is looking after her."

"There you have it, folks, and we can only conjecture at this point who controls the so-called mothership. Or what influence Neurozonics maintains from afar to manipulate their omnidroid slaves, and to what ultimate, nefarious purpose. These are some of the secrets we've already uncovered on the *Daily Buzz*..."

"Okay, we're offline," Gladyz shouted with a hand covering her ear as she continued to monitor the studio feed on her eyescreen. "Get me a head shot of Roni to keep for the closer. Both cameras, ready?" She held her arm high in the air as a trio of men bumped her away from view and a woman lurched out of the melee to clasp Zen tight around the waist. "Five..."

Roni counted down in his mind as Gladyz struggled to push back into position. "Sorry again about all the consternation today. News happens, and we're on it six days a week. Tomorrow is Heritage in honour of all religions past and present, so we'll be spending our weekly day of rest along with family and friends like you. Let's take some time to calm down for a day, and please refrain from visiting the hospital. Thanks to everyone who joined in the flash mob today. Your voice has been heard, and a cry of challenge has been launched against Transolar and Neurozonics. This is Roni Hendrik reporting live and kicking at New Jerusalem West Hospital where crowds continue to worship the omnidroid martyr, Simara Ying. Stay tuned to this story, and we'll see you again on Firstday . . . bringing the future to life . . . on the *Daily Buzz*."

Gladyz poked up on her toes above the crowd and slashed across her throat. "And cut! Send that back to my studio folder and clean up this goddamn mess! Someone rescue Ngazi before he shits himself!" She stalked away with her hand shielding her eyescreen from the sunlight, trying to keep some semblance of control over the show.

Zen panted and pushed against the crowd as women pawed at his now famous leopard-skin tunic. He had become a celebrity overnight, a mythical figure launched from a fairytale, larger than life and cute as a button. His face was crimson with outrage at this orgy of flesh.

"Follow me," Roni yelled, eyeing an escape route to the door. "Stay close." He pressed forward slowly, braving a path through the bedlam and keeping both feet on the floor to maintain balance. "Make way," he shouted, brandishing his wireless mike like a threatening club. "Let us through!" He grabbed Zen's arm to drag him free from the clutch of his fans, making slow but sure progress toward the sunlight outside. The crowd was still surging in through the out door, but Roni pushed against the tide, stepped on a few toes, and took a wicked hit to the groin. He gasped and bent forward, clutching his family jewels and bumping his head on the doorframe. For a moment he thought he might puke, but he clenched his teeth against vertigo. Zen steered him toward an opening with the strength of a bouncer, and they burst out onto the street.

"Shit," Roni said as he rubbed circulation into his crotch.

"You okay?"

Zen's fake leopard skin had been torn in half and his bulging pectoral muscles glistened with sweat—he really was Tarzan, a boy with the strength of a horse. Roni laughed.

"What?"

Roni waved a weak arm. "Nothing. Let's get out of here." He started haltingly forward, and Zen followed in his wake.

"Is it always like this in the news business?"

Roni laughed again. "No, sociologists will be studying this for months to come, trying to analyze the crowd behaviour—pent-up pressure released like a steam whistle, cultural imbalance, economic inequality, all that crap. A whole raft of kids will get thesis funding from the government. This is how history is made."

"Is this all part of your strategy?"

"Ha, *my* strategy? No, I'm just a reporter, a watchman on the tower. Someone else is planning this news, and I'm going to find out who."

They ducked into a transit station and palmed a sensor for access uptown. An amber light showed around Zen's hand with a hum of warning.

"You'd better login to the V-net soon, before your creds run out," Roni said as they stepped into a crowded tram and found an open area to stand. "Just tune in to a comedy show or something."

"I will," Zen said, but his voice lacked assurance. "Why was Ngazi doing a dino-bird dance?"

"The hand flap? That's just a thing autistic people do to relieve tension. Sometimes it's their only outlet. Have you seen it before?"

"It's the mating dance of a male dino-bird. He stiffens the red crest at the back of his head and jumps up and down, sticking his neck out and flapping his wings." Zen held his arms aloft and poked his head forward in curious imitation of a hand flap.

Roni laughed and shook his head at the absurdity. "Who knew Ngazi was so talented? A red-crested dino-bird, huh?"

"They're actually quite dangerous," Zen said without humour. "They can pierce a man's skull with their pointed beak."

"I don't doubt it. I'll keep my distance."

They made it back to Roni's apartment unscathed and quickly cracked out the allkool. Roni downed a stiff shot to get his thoughts in order. Man, what a day, good times for all.

Zen chose a lemon-lime mix for his allkool, a girly drink, and sipped it with hesitance. He made his way to the common room and settled into his own private catatonia on the couch. That was okay, the kid had been dragged out of his comfort zone and Roni felt responsible. But, he had to admit as events settled in his mind, today they had broken this case wide open.

Roni put on some relaxing music in the background with flutes, chimes, and assorted percussion sounds, and opened a window to get some ventilation. He planned a warm meal for dinner to celebrate their misadventure, stir-fried veggies in a garlic base ladled over rice noodles. His second allkool went down slower, seasoned with oak extract and whiskey spice, as he gathered resources from the refrigerator—zucchini, mushrooms, carrots, and an onion. The simple kitchen rituals calmed him down as he crushed garlic and diced vegetables on a plastic cutting board. The smells stole his attention for a transient moment as he worked. Food was a universal language, common ground for all humanity. Even biogens had to eat.

When all was prepared, Roni called Zen to the kitchen and woke him from his trance. He served the noodles on ceramic plates and ladled out the garnish as the boy pulled up a stool. Zen studied his plate for a moment and pinched up some pasta with his fingers to sample the strange concoction. Roni tapped his fork on his plate and showed by example how to twirl noodles onto the tines with a chunk of veggie on the tip to hold the bite in place. Zen was not adept at using flatware and made a colourful mess on the table, but neither one of them cared as the allkool began to flow in their veins. They chatted about life on Bali, and Zen recounted tales of hunting fresh meat in the desert, chasing down baby raptors with dune buggies at dusk with a torrid sun hovering on the horizon.

The boy was an alien. His body was adapted to an exotic environment with thin air and strong gravity, and his mind was focused on the flesh, the struggle for food and companionship, simple things that digital civilization took for granted. Water was the most precious thing he could imagine. Gold was as common as dirt, something they hauled up from the ground and sold by the bucket. And the sun, which everyone else regarded as the source of life and electricity, worshipped by humans since the dawn of time, was for him a vicious enemy, a killer.

Gladyz arrived at their door late in the evening with an open travel thermos in hand, still dressed in her wide-lapel skirtsuit from work and reeking of allkool. It was Heritage eve, so what the hell. Roni swung open the door. "C'mon in."

"Thanks. Is he here?"

"Hi, Gladyz," Zen said from the common room, comfortably slouched at one end of the couch, bare-legged in boxers and a pyjama shirt.

"Sorry to intrude," Gladyz said with a slur. "You guys gettin' busy?"

Roni frowned. "How much have you had to drink?"

"Juz' a titch," Gladyz said as she waltzed into the room and twirled in a quick inspection. "You've never invited me over. Lovely spot. So spacious." She wandered around peeking in open doorways.

Roni freshened his drink from a jug of mix in the refrigerator. With great deliberation, he and Zen had concocted a fruit drink from a recipe called tequila sunrise. "Two bedrooms, one bath, nothing special."

"Magnificent view of the park," Gladyz said as she peered out a window near the couch. "At least you're putting your bonus creds to good use."

Zen sat up a bit straighter at her proximity, his docility replaced by sudden vigilance like a hunter sensing game. Roni sipped his allkool. A leopard on the prowl? No, that was too weird. "You out on the town tonight? Want to hop the boulevard?"

Gladyz sank into the couch near the midpoint, close to Zen

but not touching. "No, I wanted to party with the boys. Just take it easy." She turned woozily to Zen and sipped from her thermos.

Zen smiled with cautious grace.

"Let me get you a glass," Roni said as he stepped forward and offered an open hand. "What are you drinking?"

Gladyz relinquished her thermos. "Sparkling white grape juice fermented with yeast. They call it bubbly champagne." She turned back to Zen. "Want to taste?"

Before he could answer, she planted a kiss full on his lips, her body hunched over him, her hand firm on the armrest. One, two, three seconds—an awkward eternity of intimacy. She released him and smacked her lips with delight. "What do you think?"

Zen's face contorted through a series of emotions, from surprise to disgust to a fearful curiosity. His eyes flicked to Roni and back to Gladyz as she settled into the couch with a drunken sigh of contentment. His face bloomed like a rose.

Roni held up a cautionary palm and hooded his eyes in signal to Zen not to panic. "That's okay. We've all had a long day. Zen, come and help me mix drinks for a sec, will you?"

The boy bounded from his seat and followed Roni to the kitchen nook. He pointed back to Gladyz with his thumb. "I'm not comfortable with her."

"You and me both, kid. Let me have a word with her in private."

"Do you want me to leave?"

"No. Hell, no." That would be all he needed now—the famous Bali boy out wandering the streets with his belly full of tequila sunrise. "Just go to the washroom for a minute. I'll be quick." Zen nodded agreement, but his face was etched with confusion.

Roni hunted in his cupboards for a proper wine glass and

ambled back to the common room with champagne in a fluted cylinder. "That was quite a show."

"I've always wanted to do that."

"You and ten thousand other V-net groupies. He's just a kid."

"Oh, c'mon, I'm not that old." She stared at him. "I'm not dead."

"But he's from Bali."

"That's half the fun, Roni. Don't you get it?"

"Yeah, yeah, the forbidden fruit. I just think we should show him more respect. We're working together. We should keep a professional relationship." He handed forward her glass of champagne, and his fingers trembled, and suddenly there it was out in the open—their awkward history as long-lost lovers. Damn, how did that get out?

Time seemed to warp around them at that moment of interpersonal insight. Everything was plain, the truth was stark, and nothing was ever lost. One intimate occasion from the past had cemented them together across the years—one brief fling kept under the lid of a warming pot on the stove, letting off a little steam now and again, but never coming to a boil.

A tear trickled from her eye as Gladyz hung her head. "They're suing us, Roni. They're threatening to shut us down."

"What?" Roni blinked in shock. "Who?"

"Neurozonics. Today's show will be our last unless we make a full public apology."

Holy crap! Roni slumped into the couch beside her. "For what?"

Gladyz sniffed and turned to him. "Defamation."

"No way!"

"You used the word *nefarious* twice in one segment."

"I was making conjecture in the middle of a riot, the heat of the moment."

"It doesn't matter. Neurozonics is big. They control everything. Turns out they own our station through a subsidiary and have a button on our bandwidth. Do you know what giants do when they find a bug in their kitchen?"

Roni closed his eyes and let his head loll. "Shit."

Gladyz sighed and took a slug of champagne. "I haven't got the creds to live like this, Roni. I don't have a pension."

"No, I know, don't worry. We'll find a way. We always do."

Gladyz shook her head. "The word came down from Colin Macpherson himself. We're up against the gods this time."

"The dead guy?"

"He was uploaded decades ago. He's not dead—far from it." She wiped at her cheeks with a sleeve. "He controls his empire from digital space, part of a consortium of eternal intellect. His clones look after the business of his estate."

"I thought that was urban legend. You can't believe everything you see in V-space. Most of it is pure machinima."

"Don't be a fool, Roni. Colin Macpherson built Cromeus from the ground up. He terraformed the planet and put oxygen in the air. He drew the blueprints for the city of New Jerusalem. Do you think he would hand it off to underlings?"

Roni's stomach twisted like a serpent. He stood and began pacing the room. How could he fight against the king of the colonies, a ghost in V-space?

Zen poked his head in the room. "Everything okay in here?"

"C'mon in," Gladyz said with a plastic smile as she smoothed her skirt on her thighs. "I'll play nice, I promise."

Zen picked up his tequila sunrise from the kitchen nook and took a seat in a chair by himself a safe distance away. "Any news about Simara?"

Gladyz sipped her sparkling wine and studied him as though considering an apology. Nope, not her style. "The hospital quieted down after Roni pulled the plug on the flash mob. You can visit her tomorrow and spend the day. Do you celebrate Heritage on Bali?"

"No, we worship Kiva, god of the universe."

"Oh, right, I read about that. Does he communicate?"

"He hears our prayers and sends rain in season."

"Ahh, the usual stuff."

"I know he probably has many names on other worlds and back on Earth, but there's only one God." He brandished a bold face that seemed defensive, a bit insecure in a strange place.

"I believe you," Gladyz said. "That's a wonderful sentiment."

"Do you worship on Heritage? Or meditate?"

"Me? No. I try to catch up on my sleep. The *Daily Buzz* really saps my energy. I guess I'm not very religious."

Roni stopped his pacing in the centre of the room as a sword of light pierced his darkness. "I'll go see him in person!"

Gladyz squinted at him with a puzzle on her forehead. "Who, God?"

"Colin Macpherson, the owner of Neurozonics. I'll go off-camera, man to cybersoul, or clone, or whatever—completely off the record. He'll see me. He has to . . ." Roni paused and struck a pose to put his famous profile in view. "I'm Roni Hendrik from the *Daily Buzz*."

TEN

The headquarters of Neurozonics was located in the outskirts of New Jerusalem near the main nuclear reactor, close to a safe and stable power source. Antimatter energy might be the efficient choice in space where derivatives could be freely dispersed, but traditional fission had the best shelf life in proximity to humans. The Neurozonics building was a squat cinderblock cube covered in beige stucco with white trim around porthole windows. Overtop the entrance, a backlit logo in blue and gold featured a lightning bolt slashing the company name exactly in half, replacing the z and making it a capital *Zonics* just under the *Neuro*. The effect was trendy and futuristic.

Roni stepped off the tram and found the plate-glass doors locked. Inside there was a woman with platinum hair ensconced in a circular desk surrounded by flashing data like the captain at the helm of a flying saucer. He palmed a sensor beside the entrance, and the woman peered over from her work to appraise him. Her silver bangs were cropped along her eyebrows in a pageboy cut, her dark eyes framed with glittery highlights. She rose from her chair with cultured grace as twin glass doors swung inward with welcome. She wore a silver dress cut high at the thigh, her muscular legs sculpted like a bodybuilder's, her barefoot gait like a lioness.

Roni put his toe in the doorway as she approached. "Hi, I'm—"

"Roni Hendrik," she said as she clamped his hand with assurance. "I'm Niri. Big fan. Love the show."

"Oh, thanks."

"I was so excited to hear you were coming in person for an interview." Her smile was like a velvet glove. "You must know what all the girls from the gym are saying round town—*anyone* would kill to get on the *Daily Buzz* with the Bali boy." She lowered her voice in confidence. "They're supposed to be good with their hands." Her eyeballs rolled up into her forehead to scan some wirehead data, and blinked back to him with enthusiasm, her painted eyebrows arched like thin crescent moons above her eyes. "Come in and have a seat."

Niri swivelled with ease on her bare feet and led him toward her desk complex with an elegant sashay. Her stylish mini-dress rose modestly to her throat in a choker collar, but her shoulders and arms were bare, her overdeveloped muscles like braided cords below her bronzed skin. Roni wondered if she might be a robot, cold like moulded plastic.

The circular desk and two office chairs were the only furnishings in the room. The Neurozonics logo featured prominently on one wall with bold silver letters underneath: *Building Better Brains.* Roni followed Niri up one step into her workstation and took a seat. They were surrounded by sixteen active thoughtscreens with images flashing like lightning and text scrolling by at rates too fast for comprehension. Webcam lenses glinted in the corner of each monitor.

"These are the sixteen facets of the eternal consortium," Niri said.

Roni nodded. Cybersouls in storage. "Only sixteen?"

"These are executive groups, organized according to personality traits. I'm not sure exactly how they work it out."

"And this is how they communicate with you?"

"It does help. I'm hardwired, of course, but I'm not omnidroid, so I can barely keep up."

Roni studied the torrent of images on a few screens. He could make no sense of it. "I was hoping to interview someone in the flesh."

Niri smiled. "I'm the official representative and interface with the material world."

"What about Colin Macpherson?"

"He has long since transfigured to machine intelligence."

"Can't I speak with one of his clones?"

"The Macpherson clones all live in quickened states to stay connected with their progenitor. They're not readily available. You must appreciate the passage of time in digital reality." Niri waved a palm at the frenetic thoughtscreens around them. "Life is a million times faster. Minds that drop out of eternity just to speak with us could lose ages from their existence, relatively speaking. Everything in mundane space goes through me."

"Then you know why I'm here."

"You've been summoned because of slanderous comments made on a public newscast. Neurozonics is very concerned about keeping a good corporate image."

"Perhaps an apology is in order."

Niri glanced at a screen to her left. "We're not convinced it will be heartfelt."

"All the omnidroids were manufactured right here in this building. Does Neurozonics deny a continuing relationship?"

"Yes. This facility has been closed for many years. Physical reality has been outsourced."

"I find that hard to believe. Look at you and your impossible physique. You're obviously being micro-managed by the corporate executive in every detail of fashion."

Niri smiled. "We're very much alike, you and I. We're both paid to play the harlequin onstage. You may have a bigger audience, but mine is just as demanding. I wear silver because it's company policy." She spread her palms in feigned helplessness. "We're supposed to be from the future, so it's expected."

"I'm just trying to make a point."

"I sculpt my body by private choice. I work hard at my strength training, but I try to have some fun with the challenge. I keep to 1,500 calories with vitamin supplements and a drug that makes my muscles exercise while I sleep. I enjoy the discipline."

Drugs? How did that work? Roni imagined her freakish body twitching like a frog stabbed with electricity. He shook his head to dispel the image. "Sorry. Let's not make this personal."

"Neurozonics does not practise a culture of control," Niri said. "The omnidroids were manufactured for a specific purpose and have been set loose to accomplish their task."

"Sure. They streamline all the V-net data and tell us what we want before we need it."

Niri nodded. "No firewalls, no filters. They do that by their nature, but their true value goes far beyond mere predictive social physics. The omnidroids have the built-in capacity to communicate with an advanced celestial consciousness."

Roni blinked. "What?"

"The highest goal on the digital frontier is to share the human collective mind with another sentient form. That's the only real hope for progress."

"You've lost me. What other sentient form is out there?"

"Colin Macpherson postulates that an omnidroid hive-mind has spread into space from ancient times to influence the course of cosmic history."

"Are you talking about connecting to some sort of intergalactic god?"

Niri paused. "Where there's smoke, there must be fire. The earliest religions arose from dreams and visions. Various prophets accessed a higher consciousness and recorded the first inklings of psychic revelation. Neurozonic brains were designed to maximize that potential in order to make first contact with a universal sentience."

"No way." Roni stood and stabbed a finger to challenge the screens before him. "I'm here about the murder of two omnidroid children, Ruis Limkin and Elana Mant. Real people in the real world. You can't hide behind a smokescreen of superstition. I'll get the truth out, no matter what. On the *Daily Buzz* or elsewhere. You can't stop me."

"Roni, please." Niri held out her palm. "Colin8 has changed his mind. He'll see you now. Please sit down. He'll need a few minutes to prepare."

Finally, some headway. Roni resumed his seat.

Niri turned to a nearby viewscreen. "These are the flight documents pertaining to the helicopter crash. Look closely here. Do you see the revision notifications?"

Roni peered closer at a segment of machine code. "Revisions?"

"These markers indicate huge gaps in clock time. The original data has been altered, perhaps fake instructions to the pilot or falsified mechanical readings that were later erased. Only an omnidroid could make these changes. No mere human has that zero-day capability. We find the same pattern on the data record of the troopship, as you can see here." The screen changed to another page of program code. "And also on the flight record left behind on the vessel owned by Randy Ying. I've sent all three documents to your studio office. You can have your technicians check their reliability."

"The omnidroids arranged the accidents? Why would they kill two of their own?"

Niri pressed her lips. "Morality is an anthropological concept, but a superior intelligence might be tempted by efficiency. Natural selection is a ponderous genetic refinery, but why wait for generations of evolutionary history to refine the genome? What better way to cull the herd than a death match with fate? Only the precognitive omnidroids would survive, and their DNA would remain pure for the future."

"No, that's diabolical."

"So we humans would say. Colin8 will see you now." She stood and led Roni toward a seam in the wall that slid open on proximity. A comfortable light glowed from a change room inside.

"Leave your clothes here for pickup later. Step through the scanner into the germicidal shower and keep your eyes closed until the tone sounds. Then proceed to the irradiation dryer. You'll find fresh cellulose clothing in the fabricator on the other side."

"Why the sterilization?"

"It's been months since Colin8 has had any human contact from outside his white zone. He doesn't carry the natural immunity to germs and diseases that you and I take for granted."

The door slid shut between them, and Roni made his way through a gauntlet of cold steam followed by glowing purple heat from overhead driers. A sharp disinfectant tickled his nose. He pulled on fitted cellulose clothing and paper slippers and stepped through the final gate into a spacious hallway.

"Roni Hendrik," a boy said as he strode forward with an outstretched arm. He wore a navy blue three-piece suit that seemed foppish on his teenage frame—like a child pretending to royalty. "I'm Colin8."

Roni studied the boy as they shook hands, blond hair sweeping off a large forehead with big ears like butterflies and a prominent chin. "You're Colin Macpherson?"

"The current custodian, seventh clone of number one."

"Are you in charge here?"

"We exert a collective will. The elder progenitors have transitioned to digital experience, but I still enjoy the occasional foray into the mundane world. Thanks for visiting."

"I didn't have much choice with my show pulled off the air."

"Yes, you seem to be working with some erroneous assumptions. Niri has set you straight with some of the facts."

"There's still the matter of Randy Ying hiding away on Babylon while working on your payroll."

Colin8 waved backhand in dismissal. "Mr. Ying was hired as a guardian to Simara, and he performed his job admirably for many years before his breakdown. As you can see by the altered data transcripts from his vessel, he was clearly being manipulated by the omnidroids. We're not going to cancel his pension just because he goes missing for a few days."

"Why was the first omnidroid working the hard trade route all those years instead of living safely at home in your lab?"

"Evolution is not mimicked by coddling. Simara was sent to us from Earth by Colin7. She was in distress after implant surgery, overwhelmed with raw V-net data, and unable to cope with her experimental wireless installation, her brain scrambled, memories wiped clean by trauma. At first we didn't know if the child was a danger to herself or others. We didn't know if she might be hunted because of her psychic powers, so we sheltered her under a caregiver for long winters on Babylon where the V-net signal is sparse. She needed a sanctuary to grow in relative isolation until she learned how to master her potential."

"A biogen smuggled through the Macpherson Doorway?" Roni's news-nose pointed suddenly toward a hot byline. "In defiance of the embargo?"

Colin8 affected an impish, cultured charisma of entitlement. "Those laws weren't in effect at the time, and I doubt there's any tawdry substance there for a ratings boost on the *Daily Buzz*."

Roni shrugged. "Depends how we spin it. The poor little orphan girl cast out from paradise, a biogen denied her natural birthright on Earth. The viewers will lap it up like goat's milk."

"As you wish. But is that really the best angle for your story?

Remember, you'll only get one chance to tell it. That's the thing about the news of the day—it has such fleeting substance." Colin8 turned and began walking at a leisurely pace.

Roni nodded as he followed down the empty hallway. He wondered what other information might be on the serving tray at Neurozonics. He didn't even know the right questions to ask. "So you deny any involvement in the omnidroid accidents?"

"Of course. Why would we harm our own children and squander several lifetimes of work? We're only now seeing our cherished dreams come to fruition."

"Talking to God?"

The young clone smiled. "I'm a scientist, Mr. Hendrik. I prefer facts over faith. My progenitor broke the space-time barrier. That's my heritage. We built a Doorway across the galaxy and found a new home to expand the human race. We chose the closest blue planet and terraformed it to our liking. But when I look out at the night sky now, I see only squandered opportunity."

"The universe is a big place. We'll get there eventually."

"Indeed, we already have. Progress has left us behind like protozoa trapped in a tidal pool."

"What do you mean?"

"The Doorway folds the fabric of space-time. That's the best way to describe it. A place distant in space is pulled close enough for an instantaneous jump through the wormhole. But any Doorway travels through time as well. Our trip to Cromeus, for example, vaults twelve million years into the future in the blink of an eye."

Roni nodded. "It boggles the mind."

"Just think how many Doorways have been built in the last twelve million years. It takes a lot of resources, more than we could ever manage from the Cromeus colonies, but Earthlings might manage one every five hundred years on average, wouldn't you say?"

Roni took a moment to perform the mental math. "Twenty-four thousand Doorways?"

"Conservatively speaking, there must be an empire of twenty-four thousand solar systems by now, and some of those will have spawned Doorways of their own. Some will be far in the future, but, more importantly, some will be far in the past."

"How far back could they go?"

"It takes just as much energy to travel twelve billion years as to travel twelve million years."

"Holy crap."

"Exactly. Mankind has already taken omnidroid technology back to the beginning of time and forward to the end of eternity. The universe is riddled with wormholes, and we're stuck here alone."

"But we can go back to Earth any time. We're still connected."

Colin8 shook his head. "We can go back to view the Earth as it was in antiquity, not as it is now. We can never know the modern age. By now the omnidroids of intergalactic history will have evolved a psychic network of communication that spans the cosmos." He stopped to palm a sensor, and a portal slid open. "This is our genetics lab, open for your inspection in full cooperation with the media."

They stepped forward into a large expanse filled with computer hardware and bulging tanks like bathyscaphs. The stagnant air smelled stale. Colin8 extended his arm with sweeping grandeur. "The equipment in this lab was first developed to pioneer cloning technology for our illustrious progenitor."

Roni surveyed the vast array of dormant apparatus. The

viewscreens were blank and control boards unlit, and a series of empty office chairs stood in line like a regiment. No signs of staff, no tools on trays or jackets on the chair backs. "Where are all the workers?"

"Alas, you have arrived at the party long after the music has ended. We closed up shop some time ago. The latest biogen is seven years old now. This lab is a mausoleum, an ancestral relic." Colin8 stepped toward a large ovoid vessel covered with a thin layer of dust. "This was my womb, my first home in an amniotic sea." He pointed underneath at four hydraulic legs. "It moves on a programmed pattern to stir fluids in a natural manner."

"You were born from a machine?"

"The omnidroids as well. We had all the in vitro systems in place, so after Simara arrived, we used her blueprint to splice together twenty-four more omnidroids, enough to establish a stable procreative base. Brain implant surgery was performed right here in the womb by micro-robots. Each omnidroid has an octahedral array, hardwired with the foundational source code of the V-net. They were born into digital space long before their first breath of air. The V-net is their true home."

"How did you get around the trauma problem that plagued Simara?"

Colin8 held up a single finger. "That was our surprise breakthrough. We experienced no problems whatsoever. The new omnidroids connected with Simara from birth, even from the dark reaches of Babylonian winter. She became a den mother to all the children through a psychic tether that does not diminish by distance. Do you see how important this is?"

Roni nodded. "The mothership."

"We can't be sure if the hive-mind originated from Simara as a cognitive mechanism to cope with her digital distress, or whether the mothership is an actual first contact with a celestial intelligence. That is the most critical question under current study."

"So you want to use the mothership to communicate with omnidroid colonies in space?"

"Yes. It's our only hope to avoid an impoverished future. The speed of light is too slow to connect in any meaningful way. The universe is far too vast. But the omnidroids use their freenet to stay in constant communion, using science we are just beginning to fathom."

"But what about us? What about simple humans? We'll be left behind on the dust heap of history."

The young clone nodded. "That much is true."

"You're willing to relinquish the future to the omnidroids? Just throw up your hands and walk away from your human heritage? That doesn't sound like the Colin Macpherson of legend. How will your baby clones compete with their biogen peers? You'll be second-class citizens."

Colin8 slouched his posture in confession. "I'm the last of the Macpherson line, the final custodian. Eight lifetimes is enough for any man, and cloning leaves no room for the type of evolutionary development of which we speak. We have a 50% DNA interest in the omnidroid species, strictly speaking, though most of the code is augmented to creative schematics. We've secured a good foothold for posterity, a majority interest in this strain."

Roni studied the young man more closely, frail of stature with pointed chin, high cheekbones, and wide ears. He recognized it now, the elfish look in all the omnidroids, a common ancestry. "What gives you the right to engineer the extinction of mankind?"

"Ah, the cry of the giant Neanderthals and the pygmy hominids. Humanity is changing, not disappearing. Nature selects the best features suitable for new environments, and always will. We're introducing nothing foreign to the genome. Omnidroids can't predict the roll of dice or the winning numbers on a lottery, but they can summon affective precognition under stress, and this gives them great social advantage, as you can plainly see. You're the one being led around by the nose."

"What are you insinuating? I'm not working for the omnidroids."

"You are the vehicle of influence, the show with the biggest bandwidth. You have the three worlds watching daily vigil on the omnidroid elder, intimately concerned for her good health, while a week ago she was on her way to a courtroom lynching. You alone have changed the tide of public opinion and helped quash a murder investigation that has laid a protective mantle of double jeopardy on Simara's shoulders. And for what? More eyeballs on the V-net bonus chart? More wireheads sucking up the feelie feed? You accuse my company of dastardly deeds while you spin a dangerous web for your own benefit."

Roni shuddered at the possibility. "I'm just reporting the news. I'm not making anything up."

"Our intent is to protect the good standing of Neurozonics and preserve the historic integrity of the Macpherson name. You make slanderous statements against us in the media, accusing us of conspiracy and attempted genocide, so we have no choice but to burden you with the truth. We created the omnidroids and are joyous at the outcome. We willingly lay down our heritage of cloning technology, now primitive in comparison." He pointed a level finger at Roni. "Mothership manipulates you like a dancing marionette, dropping clues for you and falsifying data. A hardened newsman like you might not heed the warning, but I'll voice it nonetheless: if you dare to tell the real story, no one will believe it. Your reputation will be slighted forever, and silence will be your only option."

Roni's chest tightened like a vice. "I'll fight back."

Colin8 turned and walked away. "Your time is up," he said over his shoulder. "Niri will escort you to the tram."

In a daze of confusion, Roni returned to the change room and put on his street clothes. He palmed a door sensor and stepped into the entrance foyer where Niri sat in her circular workstation. She looked over from the flashing thoughtscreens surrounding her. "Are you okay?"

"I'm not sure."

Niri rose from her perch and sidled toward him. She slipped a sinewy arm under his elbow. "The truth is hard, but I hope you can see the glory of the vision. No secrets, no crime, a future where every thought is freely shared."

"Just because someone can read your mind, doesn't mean they'll respect your interest."

"Twelve billion years is a long time to learn wisdom."

"Or perfect domination. These omnidroid gods are going to enslave us with trickery and deceit unless we do something to stop them. When's the next tram?"

"There's one out front. You can just catch it." The plate-glass doors swung inward as they approached. "But don't mistake altruism for tyranny. The machines weep for us, Roni, because we're so primitive."

Roni took the tram back to his apartment and poured himself a stiff shot of white allkool. Zen was in the kitchen roasting a chicken for their Heritage meal together. A fragrant cloud of spices filled the air and seemed to seep into Roni's mind with a calming influence as he sat on the sofa and wrestled with his responsibility as a newsman. If Simara had used him unwittingly in pursuit of devious schemes, he would make it right and make amends. He would tell the real story, goddamn it. The future was squarely in front of Roni, risk and reward, passion and promise. The omnidroids were an evil menace and potent threat to all humanity.

He kept his thoughts to himself during the Heritage festival dinner. No sense burdening the Bali boy with guilt, or trying to explain the paradox of time travel to a cave dweller. They toasted allkool in tribute to every spiritual inclination in memory, religions past and present on planets near and far, but Roni couldn't help wondering if a divine hive-mind had spawned them all. Did ancestral omnidroids wait over long eons for the first apes to walk upright on the fertile savannas of Earth? Did they use their amplified psychic powers to guide primitive hominids toward consciousness with archetypes and symbols, toward their own predestined fabrication at the hands of emerging *homo sapiens*—the worm ouroboros devouring its own tail across time and space?

After a long and ceremonial repast, Roni stumbled to bed and fell into a fitful sleep. He dreamed of monsters—giant red dragons with heads like turtles, threatening to devour him. They swarmed below his feet like writhing crimson snakes and snapped off his toes one by one with sharp, clamping jaws. He felt no pain in the dream state, no visceral discomfort as the dragons chewed up his shins to his knees. He tried to pull away, but his sleeping body remained inert. He tried to scream, but could summon no sound. An overwhelming agony of loss captivated his mind as the turtleheads consumed his legs, a horror of anticipation, for he knew when sharp teeth reached his scrotum all hope for the future would be lost. He heard a gong in the distance like the muffled bell from a medieval monastery in an ancient fantasyland, a call to action, a summons to war. He tried to move, but could not break free from paralysis, surrounded by dragons and unable to resist, a helpless, pitiful wretch. The tone grew steadily louder in the centre of his brain, evenly paced with persistence, and he moaned with recognition. Only his editor had access to his private mind. What the hell? "Login," he snarled into his pillow.

::GREAT JOB, RONI. NEUROZONICS HAS GIVEN US A GREEN LIGHT FOR THE SHOW. WHATEVER YOU DID YESTERDAY WAS A WINNER.::

He sat up and rubbed tension from between his eyes as turtleheads dissolved like red smoke around him. "It was nothing."

::DID YOU ACTUALLY MEET COLIN MACPHERSON IN THE FLESH?::

"A young clone in a foppish suit. He told me the truth about everything. Did you get some documents from Neurozonics?"

::YES. SECTIONS OF COMPLICATED MACHINE CODE. THEY VERIFY, AND SEEM WORRISOME. BUT FAR TOO TECHNICAL TO USE ON THE SHOW.::

"The omnidroids have been manipulating data, altering history. They set up the accidents to reverse the tide of public opinion."

::OLD NEWS NOW. WE HAVE A PRESSING DEVELOPMENT ON SIMARA. ARE YOU TAKING CARE OF YOURSELF? DID YOU SLEEP?::

Roni's brain felt fuzzy with the hint of a hangover. "I'm okay. What's up?"

::WE'RE SCRAMBLING AN EARLY CREW. THE OMNIDROIDS STARTED TO ARRIVE AT THE HOSPITAL JUST PAST MIDNIGHT. WE'RE KEEPING TABS ON THEM LIKE YOU SAID, AND IT SEEMS TO BE PAYING OFF. THEY'RE COMING IN FROM ALL OVER.::

"How many?"

::ALL OF THEM, RONI. ALL TWENTY-TWO CHILDREN SHOULD ARRIVE WITHIN THE NEXT THREE HOURS. I WANT YOU THERE WITH YOUR GAME FACE ON. GET UP AND GET YOUR SHIT TOGETHER.::

Roni groaned. "I don't even like children, and these ones are freaky. They barely speak, and they're no good on camera."

::GET YOUR LAZY ASS OUT OF BED AND GET DOWN HERE. ONE HOUR. NO EXCUSES.:: Gladyz signalled off.

A hot shower brought him back to his senses. All the omnidroids in one place—they must know something! Mothership must have summoned them for a purpose, some grand design. Roni slathered cinnamon butter on a hot bagel with a twinge of regret at the gluten and carbohydrates. He felt guilty as he took a bite, thinking about Niri's sculpted physique. The woman had ruined his appetite forever with her dedication to perfection.

Roni poked Zen to wakefulness with the broom handle and handed him a glass of warm goat's milk, his favourite morning beverage. The boy spent most of his time at the hospital, sitting beside Simara in quiet devotion like a man under a magic spell. He had no digital life, no reason to do anything else—a foreigner on a strange planet with only Simara as his tether to civilization. Why would a Bali boy built like an ox leave his home world to follow this trader waif into space? How had she brainwashed him in such a short time, a matter of days?

The camera crew was packed by the door and milling aimlessly in the hallway as Roni waltzed into the office. "Morning."

Gladyz looked over from her workstation. "You're late."

He frowned. "I'm not late. I'm early. You called me in."

She squinted at him. "You look like hell. Derryn's waiting for your makeover. I've been hitting a brick wall with hospital bureaucrats all morning."

"The omnidroids are using us, Gladyz. Manipulating the news."

"As long as it's good for the show, we shouldn't worry."

"They arranged the accidents and deleted the data tracks to hide their guilt. We have the proof."

"Nobody cares about that now. Don't make the omnidroids your enemy. Work with them."

"Somebody needs to take a stand. Our DNA is being tinkered out of existence by mad scientists." Roni gave his editor his best glare of sincerity. Everything in life was a mere distraction compared to information like this. Jobs, careers, family, politics—what good would it do an endangered species?

Gladyz shook her head. She wasn't buying his premise. "You can't force preconceptions on the public. Viewers will see right through it. The conspiracy idea is old news now. We were the ones who helped tear it down."

"This is different. I'm working on a breaking story now. The omnidroids have a psychic communication system that stretches across the space-time continuum. Beats the hell out of an orangutan on a shopping spree."

"You need to step back from the precipice before you go over the edge and hurt yourself."

"This is worth the risk. Don't you want to take a chance on something new?"

"I took a chance on you, didn't I? Don't make me regret it." Gladyz levelled an authoritative finger at him. "Just keep your bangs out of your eyes and stick to the script, Roni. We've got plenty to work with, and our numbers are going viral. We've made this girl famous on all three worlds. Everyone loves her. Don't throw dog poop in the champagne." She held her palm up with promise, hearkening back to the comfort of their working routine. "Okay?"

Roni forced a social smile and slapped her hand. "Let's wreck this world."

"That's my boy. Now go see Derryn, and try to be nice."

Derryn clucked and cooed for thirty minutes before letting his little masterpiece loose on the tram. The camera crew was getting antsy, and Gladyz seemed ready to explode with anticipation as the omnidroid children continued to gather at New Jerusalem West. Nobody wanted to say it out loud, but everyone expected Simara Ying to wake up within the hour.

They found the hospital cordoned off when they arrived, still closed to visitors because of the public riot on Heritage eve. Only family members were allowed entrance, and all twenty-two omnidroid children had already made their way upstairs. Zen was cleared to pass the blockade as an insider, but Gladyz and the camera crew met stiff resistance.

Gladyz fumed and blustered as she waved press credentials under the upright nose of the head of security, a grey-haired woman in a masculine uniform with blue collared shirt and tie. "Do you know who we are? This is Roni Hendrik of the *Daily Buzz*. He spent yesterday afternoon in a meeting with Colin Macpherson, who I'm sure is a generous patron of this fine establishment. We certainly wouldn't want anything to hamper that relationship, but we can give him a call if you need a character reference. What's your name and job title?"

The woman from security turned a granite face to scan their ragtag cohort. She seemed unfazed and had probably heard it all before. "Deb Evans, Security Admin."

Roni offered a toothy smile in support as Gladyz took a sly step closer to the woman. "Well, Deb," she said, "we have reason to believe that twenty-two biogen children have gathered in the presence of the omnidroid Simara Ying—a singular event on this or any other planet." Gladyz was in fine form, friendly and gregarious, having switched from bad cop to good cop without missing a beat. "We're accredited news gatherers reporting on the important social issues of our time. Our cameramen are regulated by trade and union protocols. We work for Colin Macpherson and need only twenty-two minutes to get our job done."

Deb Evans stole a quick glance at Ngazi standing eerily serene, his face bland with biogen genius. She tilted her head with interest. "Twenty-two minutes?"

Gladyz nodded with sincerity as the cat slipped into her bag. "Precisely."

The head of security peered at the blockade ropes covered with burgundy velvet and out at a small crowd gathering on the street. The camera crew and roadies were already starting to attract attention, another public scene in the making.

Gladyz shifted to block her view. "I'd be happy to give Colin a quick ring on his private channel?"

Deb Evans sneered with professional poise. "That won't be necessary. We both know he wouldn't give you the time of day." She unclasped a connector from a metal pole to open an entryway in the cordon. "I expect your return within the hour."

Gladyz bowed and swivelled back to the crew. "You heard the lady, boys. Quick and dirty now. Hustle your buns, and don't scratch any paint in the elevator." She marched forward to lead the way like a commander into battle as the crew followed behind in a phalanx and the roadies jostled equipment past stony guards.

They entered Simara's room to find the omnidroid children sitting on the floor in a ring around the bed of their comatose elder. They seemed comfortable without pillows or backrests, quiet and worshipful in respect. A calm pervaded the room, a tangible holiness. The teenage spokesman, Fermi, looked to Zen and pointed to the empty chair beside Simara's bed. "She's been waiting for you."

Zen stepped forward cautiously and weaved his way through the crowd. He reached his partner and bent down to whisper something in her ear. He kissed her forehead and took a seat.

"Lamps," Gladyz said in a hushed voice as she surveyed the layout. "Give me two mikes on booms near the ceiling. Two cameras on tripods, one on shoulder mount. Roni, stay with me here until we're set."

The children were quietly accommodative as the crew lugged equipment into the small ward. Cameramen apologized in gentle tones as they positioned tripods and stabilized their gear. Everyone froze as Simara Ying twitched.

Gladyz pulled on Roni's arm. "Did you see that?"

"Not sure," he whispered. "I think so."

"Shit, we're not ready."

Roni glanced around the room as the crew struggled to set up in close quarters. "We have one green light on the shoulder-mount."

Gladyz tapped her ear and shielded her brow as she sampled the angle on her eyescreen. A few seconds passed in a hush of expectation. "Activate livefeed on the shoulder cam. Start with a head shot on the celebrity girl and pan out on my signal."

Simara moaned like a distant wind in the mountains. Her lips trembled to find purchase, and finally her eyes blinked open. "Zen?"

The Bali boy jumped up to hover at her bedside. "I'm here."

Simara smiled with infinite grace. "We made it."

"Yes. Take your time. You've been out for a few days."

She nodded as she scanned the room, delighted to see her omnidroid brothers and sisters. "Thank you all for coming."

Roni peered at her from behind Gladyz as she conducted the crew with a waving arm. The omnidroid children had primped their elder for the camera, her black hair combed and curled, her skin lustrous, her lips pink with fresh life. Mothership had prepared every detail in advance and summoned a crowd of faithful witnesses to the stage. He felt a chill at the promised enfoldment—he was a victim of cold calculation, a pawn in the omnidroid conspiracy.

"Your poems were marvellous, Zen. Mothership treasured them all."

"I didn't know if I could reach you."

Simara smiled with a blush on pale cheeks. "You found me and touched me. You're a special man, and I want to stay with you always."

A tear glinted in Zen's eye. "I knew you'd come through. You're tough. You're a survivor."

"Thanks to you for saving me again and dragging my sorry ass in from the wilderness." She took his hand and fondled it with care. "Good habits are hard to break."

Zen chuckled. "Someone else took your clothes this time, I promise."

"Get a close-up on their faces," Gladyz whispered to the cameraman. "Viewers love this sappy stuff."

Simara gazed at Zen with love in her eyes like a promised virgin at the bridal bower. "Do I have any broken bones or anything?"

"No, the doctors say you're fine. No internal injuries. You've just been sleeping as you heal some bumps and bruises."

"Lucky me."

Fermi, the oldest of the children, stepped forward and placed a hand on Simara's forehead in reverence. He did not speak, nor did she acknowledge his gesture, but he smiled with satisfaction and bowed before her. Roni's breath stilled in his chest as he recognized the innate and undeniable truth. The omnidroids did not worship Simara because of her public drama as the saviour of their species. They did not care for the observational world of the humans. Simara's mind was the object of fascination, her special powers as the pioneer among them, the beachhead of a new paradigm. They were connected to her brain, and she had been resurrected like a messiah to lead them out of a pagan wasteland.

Roni brushed past Gladyz to step boldly forward into camera range. "Roni Hendrik here from the *Daily Buzz*. Welcome back to the land of the living!"

Simara was startled at his outburst and turned to Zen, but the Bali boy smiled and squeezed her hand with reassurance. She spied the cameras and brushed nervously at her hair with her fingers.

"You have captivated the nation," Roni pronounced with a grand sweep at the studio audience. "Tell us how you feel."

"I feel fine."

"Do you recall anything about your daring escape from the crashing troopship?"

"A little. I remember floating, and falling, and the ground rushing toward me."

"But you knew that Zen carried you from the crash site, even though you have been in a coma all this time. You thanked him just now."

A query wrinkled on her brow. "I suppose."

Roni waved an arm at the omnidroids gathered in worship around her. "You were in touch with your family all the time while you slept. Your brainwave pattern showed surprising activity, signs of alertness and cognition generally found in a waking person." Roni turned to the camera with a grin of showmanship. "You were watching the *Daily Buzz* for groundbreaking updates every afternoon . . . ." He winked. ". . . like the many thousands of viewers watching right now."

Gladyz smiled at the plug and whispered to her left-hand cameraman. Green light to go.

"Mothership keeps an eye on everything," Simara said. "She tells me what's necessary."

"Yes, the omniscience of divinity is a wonderful thing. Isn't that what the poets tell us?"

"If you say so."

"Mothership is the name given to the collective intellect of the omnidroids," Roni said with a nod to his captive audience. "A superior intelligence that manipulates events to advance an agenda of conquest."

Gladyz turned to him with a glare of alarm. "What?"

Simara frowned. "What?"

"You admit, then, the existence of a psychic entity known only by *your kind*." He let a hint of challenge creep into his voice to test her mettle.

"Mothership is a construct," Simara said. "A convenient way of organizing reality."

"Is it not true that this *mothership* orchestrated a complex series of accidents targeted against the omnidroids in which two innocent children were killed?"

Gladyz waved a frantic arm and pantomimed a slash across her throat. "Are you having a stroke?" she mouthed at Roni. The cameraman looked at her in query as Ngazi began to hum a funeral dirge beside him.

Roni ignored the pleading face of his editor as he surveyed the room and summoned an air of smug authority like a courtroom lawyer at trial. How could he remain silent in the face of impending doom for his species? Who would speak for the unborn humans if he let this secret slide, this great truth entrusted to him alone? Now was the time to seize history, and this was his moment of glory at the pinnacle of his popularity. "Mothership arranged for these accidents to test the precognition of the omnidroids, to cull the weak and prepare the strong to harness their genetically engineered psychic powers to connect with celestial consciousness."

Simara blinked with astonishment as Zen stared stupefied at her side. Gladyz looked ready to faint, but the cameras kept rolling. The declaration was out and could never be recanted. Roni Hendrik had claimed his spot in posterity with the biggest story ever told. He studied a tableau of frozen faces in the room. The elves seemed strangely complacent with his grand revelation, their cherubic faces alight with impish half-smiles. Were they so pleased to serve a calculating monster willing to sacrifice her own kin? Roni steeled himself with determination.

Simara shook her head. "You must be mistaken. Mothership cannot arrange events in any physical sense. Mothership is a cognitive construct, a network of communication. She is not capable of any harm to sentient life."

Roni pointed a steady finger at the omnidroid elder. There was no reason for Simara not to lie in order to placate his primitive intelligence. He had expected as much. "Why do you pretend with me? Why bother with this elaborate façade? You and your mothership are complicit in all these acts of violence. We have the proof on record. You arranged your own martyrdom and resurrection to complete a master plan of evolutionary conquest. You're the gateway to the god of the universe!"

Roni's breath caught in his throat at the pronouncement, and time seemed to wobble as the scene came into sharp focus. Simara tilted her head at him in puzzlement, her blue eyes inscrutable and her pixie face blank with concern. Roni shifted his gaze to

Zen, who ducked his eyes away and placed a protective palm on Simara's forearm. The circle of elf children stared at him in wide-eyed shock, open-mouthed in bewilderment as Ngazi began the red-crested dino-bird dance in the background, flapping his hands and turning in a slow circle. Roni felt a great weight on his sternum, a millstone pressing against his empty chest, and realized with surprise that he had forgotten how to breathe.

"Cut!" Gladyz strode forward like a conquering Viking. "What the fuck, Roni? We're finished here. Go home and get some sleep." She held her finger to her ear and murmured quietly as she directed the office crew in a frantic transition to studio footage.

Roni staggered back a few steps and gasped. His vision went fuzzy for a moment and tiny lights swirled in front of his eyes as oxygen rushed to his brain. He felt like a marionette with his strings cut, void of momentum and meaning. A lost soul.

Gladyz swept an arm to commandeer the room. "That's a wrap. Pack up the gear, and someone help Ngazi back to stasis. Thank you again to New Jerusalem West Hospital for your gracious hospitality. Please clear the room, folks. The party's over." She turned to Simara and knelt on one knee at her bedside. "Sorry for all the showbiz stuff. You gave us quite a scare, but we're so glad you're back in good health. On behalf of Neurozonics and the *Daily Buzz*, I offer our sincere apology for any unintentional misrepresentation or unsubstantiated conjecture by our anchorman. We are so sorry."

As Gladyz bowed her head in contrition, a metaphorical tableau came to life in Roni's imagination: Zen, the caveboy epitome of historical religion, held a firm hand of support on the arm of the martyr, while Gladyz, the priestess symbol of traditional media, knelt at the throne begging alms and casting down her crown before the altar. The elfin children surrounded the scene in testimonial witness, the new disciples spawned by science. Roni blinked in awe at the mythical caricature, and in that timeless moment of psychic magic he glimpsed the divine schemata of the omnidroid mind—pattern recognition across the millennia.

Simara stretched out an open palm to the executive producer and held it hovering as though wanting to console but afraid to touch. "I forgive you," she said. "I'm just glad to be back."

Gladyz smiled at the benediction and rose with professional resolve, safe from legal action and back in the saddle. She grabbed Roni by the arm and hustled him out of the wardroom, her face fierce with fortitude and her hand shielding her eyescreen as she kept tabs on the show.

Out in the hallway, Roni pressed his shoulders against a sturdy wall and struggled to regain composure as Gladyz leaned over him and stared into his eyes. "Stay with me, big boy. You're not having a heart attack, are you? We're at the top of our game today. The resurrection clip is breaking the chart for the *Daily Buzz*. Your wild foray into tabloid journalism has hit the mark with a bullet. You did good."

He shook his head. "You can't let her get away with this."

"I love it when you get caught up in your work, Roni, but we're done for today. We've already gone viral. Now is the time to ride the wave, not tip the surfboard."

He recognized wariness in her eyes, a hint of mistrust. He had wandered off script, a cardinal sin for a news anchor, an unforgivable sacrilege. "Tomorrow?"

Gladyz darted her gaze away, and Roni knew his production

editor had lost faith in the real story. "You know I'll push hard for you upstairs," she said without conviction. "I always do. We'll see how the situation grinds down and keep our options open."

"You think I'm pushing too hard?"

"You always push too hard, darling. All the girls love it."

Roni grimaced and nodded to acknowledge her evasive flirtation, feeling the edge of anxiety slipping away, the end of promise, the loss of hope. Neurozonics might never allow him in front of the camera again after this. He would never get another chance at Simara Ying. She had achieved her conquest and was protected forever from double jeopardy by her enigmatic scheme. Roni was nothing but a puppet cast aside, deceived by his own success to think he could save his species. His best shot was nothing but a glancing blow to the omnidroids. Just as Colin8 had warned him, humans had a natural immunity to the truth, even when their own existence hung in the balance.

"Let's take a few days off to celebrate," Gladyz said as she corralled him with a strong arm and pointed him toward the exit. "My uncle has a condo down on the coast near Flatrock Peninsula. We could lie on the beach and carouse in the surf like tourists. I've been thinking about you a lot lately—about our working relationship. We've been playing kitten and mouse together for so long I've forgotten which one of us is the pussy. We need to rediscover ourselves."

Is this how it would end? A heritage squandered in distraction, just another dead end on the newsfeed? Roni sensed his worst fear as they sauntered down the hall with the camera crew lugging gear in their wake and his editor chatting gaily in his ear, hinting of sex and planning exotic adventures, just as he had imagined, nuance by conversational nuance, complacency settling like thick fog around them. They had crossed a tipping point, a cultural divide, and were headed down a slippery slope of least resistance to the new normal.

"We're just a flash in the pan, Gladyz. Our time is short."

She turned to face him with mischief in her eyes, the pioneer spirit that he loved so much. "No, Roni. We're special. Let's wreck this world." She elbowed him in the ribs with jocularity to seal the shared sentiment that bound them together in show business— get the news, push the limit, and screw the system.

Roni played a smile for her and tossed his hair on cue, but he hadn't meant them personally. He was referring to *homo sapiens*, the stale DNA of the forefathers. This was the crux and crucible of evolution, and mankind had forfeited any loyalty from a pitiless future. Destiny was inevitable now.